A Tail for All Seasons

Volume 1

A Tail for All Seasons

Volume 1
A collection of Manx stories

editor **Linda Mann**

Priory Press

Published by Priory Press Ltd
The Priory, Abbots Way, Abbotswood,
Ballasalla, Isle of Man IM9 3EQ
www.priory-press.co.uk

ISBN-10 0-9551510-3-1
ISBN-13 978-0-9551510-3-3

Although this book is set in and around the Isle of Man some
of the characters and locations are purely fictional and any
similarity to anyone living or dead is simply coincidence and
the product of the various authors' extraordinarily vivid imagi-
nations.

Edited and typeset by
Frances Hackeson Freelance Publishing Services,
Brinscall, Lancs
Printed in Great Britain by
Cromwell Press, Trowbridge, Wiltshire

contents

preface

Many years ago I had a bright idea and bounced it around a few unlucky bookshops – unfortunately it was met with such unbounded enthusiasm that I thought I'd better get on with it.

The idea was that of a book of short stories set around a year on the Isle of Man; each tale was to feature a month on the Island and would have a little twist at the end. However the trick would be to find twelve stories which not only gave a feeling of the Island but would also compliment each other.

Features in the local press and on Manx Radio produced over forty manuscripts which were then whittled down to a shortlist of twenty and then the final twelve – and here they are. Some are by published authors, others by complete un-knowns but each stands alone as a jolly good story.

I hope you like them as much as I did when reading them for the first time and that you will go away when the last page has been consumed knowing a little more about the myths and mountains of this enchanted Isle.

Linda Mann

foreword

Firstly, thank you for reading the preface to *A Tail for all Seasons*. If you're reading this in a bookshop, take it to the nice person at the counter and buy it – you will earn the respect and gratitude of the authors and the publisher. I thought it would be hard to read the stories and then judge other people's work; it was very hard but very enjoyable, then the publisher caught me in a weak moment saying "Could you just write a few words as a Preface?" Easy, thought I; wrong was I!! Committing words to the page for others to read and hopefully enjoy and just talking on the radio and letting your words go out over the ether are very different.

Help was at hand – that nice person at Mann Towers gave me details of the eleven authors of the short stories, so I was able to put flesh on the bones of the talent: just analyse these authors, I thought, and I will get an idea of the traits needed to become a scribbler. For a start it's half and half between locals and stopovers, and then 50% male, 50% female – we're on our way, I can be an author!!!

Hobbies include gardening (don't mind that, generally from a deckchair but weeding is gardening), painting is another hobby (two undercoats and a top coat I can do, not quite the same as landscapes but we are getting nearer), cookery is another interest in the authors (my cheese on toast is admired … by me anyway, but it's cooking) … I can be an author.

When alcohol was mentioned as a hobby I was there … wrong again, I'll leave it to these winning authors in the first volume of short stories based on the Isle of Man. The short story is the 100m sprint of the literary world and these eleven authors have all broken the 10 secs record and are gold medallists of the word. Looking forward already to Volume two of *A Tail for all Seasons*.

Bob Harrison
Afternoon Extra
Manx Radio

acknowledgements

With many thanks to Bob Harrison of Manx Radio who took time out from slaving over the airways and living in a goldfish bowl on a cliff, to go through the shortlisted manuscripts and then to read them all again for the Foreword.

To Frances Hackeson who worked her usual impeccable magic on the chosen twelve and helped polish them to perfection.

To Rosemary Derbyshire who read all of the stories and amended any Manx that needed it with notes sufficiently succinct that even the most learned writer heeded them.

To Victoria Harrop who swapped a towpath for a Manx stone circle and waited all day for the right wind to turn the pages of a large book.

And to all the writers who had to put up with Mrs Publisher and her editorial hat!

Linda Mann

✳ January ✳

Angie Greenhalgh has lived in Africa, Germany, the Far East and mainland UK until settling on the Isle of Man with her husband and two sons. She graduated from London University with a B.Sc. in Economics and Geography and in 1973 was awarded a scholarship to study for her MA in Canada where she worked afterwards as an economic development planner, spending time with the Ojibway people and the Innuit.

Angie is a keen gardener and was instrumental in the creation and planting of a tract of woodland, dedicated to St Brighid, known today as Bride's Wood. She is also the author of various published works in the UK and abroad and her book *Forgotten Magic of an Enchanted Isle* is available from the Shearwater Press and all good local bookshops.

Laa'l Breeshey

Angie Greenhalgh

January 31st 1990
Santon, Isle of Man

"It's a filthy night to be going out. Just listen to that wind!" muttered my husband, watching me pack a wicker basket with pots of silver and blue paint, paintbrushes, a battery-operated radio cassette player and the large bundle of rushes that I'd hand-picked, in silence, that afternoon.

He pointed at the nine silver candlesticks and their candles from the dining room that I'd finally placed on top.

"They're a bit too good, aren't they? Why can't you use a torch?"

"It wouldn't be right!" I retorted, anxiously glancing at the clock ... It was already seven thirty.

"How do you know that?" he asked, clearly irritated that I was going out. "Times change ... technology moves on."

"Some things never change," I sighed. "It's the intent that matters. Simplicity is what counts."

He followed me to the back door. "I think you're totally insane to do it tonight ... going out in this gale."

"It has to be tonight. It will be too late if I leave it till next year … It has to be done before we move in!"

I shivered as the wind shrieked into the house through the half-opened door.

My husband grasped the handle to steady it, his tone now softer with concern. "I don't know what you're talking about and quite frankly, I don't want to know. But please be careful driving. Do you want me to come with you?"

"I have to do this on my own. I mean, traditionally, it's the woman of the house who does it. I'll be back as soon as it's done. It'll be fine."

July 1988
Malew, Isle of Man

"What about this? A building plot with two and a half acres and outline planning permission. It's been on the market for a very long time," muttered the estate agent, handing us the details unenthusiastically. "It's in the south of the Island, just north of Ballasalla. In the countryside, but feels as if it's in the middle of nowhere. And access isn't too good. Very rustic. I'd advise wellies if you go to see it … quite a walk … and can be a bit muddy."

The following day, brimming with optimism, my husband and I were on our way to the "middle of nowhere".

At first the lane was wide enough to allow our car to slide slowly along the muddy ruts but after we'd passed the last house the way ahead was impassable. The massive unkempt hedge banks on either side had slumped in on the last vestiges of the lane and rampant gorse, bramble and blackthorn formed a determined barrier.

"Hmm … 'access isn't too good' – an agent's understatement!" observed my husband with a wry grin.

Abandoning the car, we spent the next half hour trying to battle our way through unyielding vegetation. Thorns the size of one-inch nails tore at our clothing, and underfoot, thick squelching black bog sucked at our boots.

"'Very rustic' and 'can be a bit muddy'!" I giggled. "But how will we know where the 'middle of nowhere' actually is?"

"The drawings show the remains of the old farmhouse, which was built alongside the old road, somewhere along here on the left," he replied.

"You mean a Tholtan!" I exclaimed. "That's what the Manx call the old deserted farmsteads."

I'd often paused to wonder about the generations who'd lived in such places, farming and fishing the herring. Their 'Spuds and Herring' economy, like the crofters of the west of Scotland and Ireland, meant a hard, simple existence. However, they were more in harmony with nature and the ancient rhythms of land and sea than most of us today.

Now the ruins of their forsaken homes dot the Manx countryside. A disorganized graveyard for an existence long since departed.

"I hope they found what they were looking for ..."

"What the hell are you talking about?" He was getting short-tempered as he grappled with another tendril of thorns.

"The people who abandoned their homes and land in search of a better life."

But now it's us, I reflected. Now it's us. Funny how things have gone full circle. We'd quit the madness of urban life in England in search of a better life in the Isle of Man. We'd wanted to bring up our young family in a safe, beautiful, peaceful environment. An environment where common courtesy and manners still prevailed and where graffiti was only a foreign word. Now we were the ones searching for a new home in this place that the last inhabitants must have been so sad to leave.

"Ah, what's this?" He'd halted beside a straggling old ash tree and was peering through the dense undergrowth. "I think that's the remains of the chimney and a gable wall."

I struggled to join him. The vague outline of stonework was a dark shadow against the luxuriant cascade of red fuchsia flowers which were probably the unruly descendants of the original garden's hedge.

We clambered into what had once been a small cottage. A few rotted timbers, now green with moss, half a chair and a rusted pot poked through tall nettles that had taken possession of the interior. Previously, it would have been just a clay floor, perhaps strewn with rushes.

A gnarled elder bush spread its branches protectively, like an ancient guardian, where once a thatched roof would have been. I'd been told that every Tholtan had its own elder tree, traditionally planted near the house to protect the place from evil. Known in Manx Gaelic as the 'Tramman', it was bad luck to cut them down.

The large lintel that slewed sideways across the gable was all that remained of the 'Chiollagh', the big open fireplace and the most important feature of the house, within which gorse sticks and peat cut from the bogs in summer would be burnt. The primary importance of the hearth was to provide a home fire for cooking but it was also where the family would huddle for warmth during the long winter nights, reading the Bible and recounting stories about the fairies, known colloquially as 'Mooinjer Veggey', 'Themselves' or 'The Little People'.

"Well, it's because of this heap of rubble, that whoever owns the land now, managed to get planning permission for a new dwelling." He squinted at the plans he was holding.

"Come on … let's try and see what the land is like. The planning approval shows that the new house has to be built in the centre of the plot and where we're standing at the moment is in the extreme south-east corner."

Two flat fields formed an almost perfect square. An old haw-thorn hedge topped the grassy banks of the perimeter bound-ary. Gorse, rush and bramble had reclaimed any useful grassland and stunted common ash and willow or 'Sallies' oc-cupied the remainder. With years of neglect it had reverted to rough land or 'Garey' as it is called in the Manx.

Together we surveyed the virtually uninterrupted views of the southern coastline and to the west, the skyline ridge with the summit of Cronk-ny-Arrey Laa, an ancient 'Hill of the Day Watch', where in the past wardens would keep watch for sea-borne invaders.

How wonderful, I thought, to be able to see the glorious sunsets from here ... sun for nearly all the day – windy – but, "Where you get a view on the Island then you'll pay for it with the wind!" one of my new friends, Manx-born, had told me. Her house was in the shelter – and shadows of a valley glen.

"Well? What do you think of it?" he asked.

"I like it very much. Perhaps we can make something out of it and bring a place that was once a home back to life, even though the new house will be on virgin ground. We can drain, plant and landscape."

"Once we've managed to put in a better access" he laughed. "Oh well, a place 'in the middle of nowhere' it is then!"

"No," I said softly, "it's not in the middle of nowhere. From now on it will always be the place in the middle of the fields."

"I'll put in an offer to buy it tomorrow" he said emphati-cally, and he turned and began to walk back to the car.

I savoured the momentary solitude while I remained in the centre of the site, alone and insignificant under an immense sky, caught in that peculiar light unique to being in the middle of the Irish Sea. The silence was pierced by the haunting cry of the curlew on the wind.

This is special, I thought. And in that moment I made a promise, not only to myself, but to the place itself, that if we were lucky enough to buy it, then we must respect the land and the values of those who had gone before; the history and lore of the Isle of Man, our chosen land. We were only new-comers, but like everyone, we are all just passing through.

Two days later our offer was accepted.

And so began a chapter in my life that would change me and the way I perceived the world, forever.

January 31st 1990
Malew, Isle of Man

The car, captive in the grip of the gale, was buffeted along roads littered with writhing branches and swirling leaves freshly snatched from overhanging trees and hedgerows. I had to drive cautiously and worried that the journey was taking too long, that I'd be late.

Eventually I reached the plot and parked in front of the almost completed building. I switched off the engine. The light from the new moon was weak and intermittent between the huge banks of dark clouds that raced overhead. The house was a black silhouette against the night sky. Almost threaten-ing. An alien construction upon the land.

Unreasoned panic surged within me. Suddenly I was reluc-tant to leave the security of the locked car. A primal fear of the dark? Or was it something else that was frightening me? What had seemed like a good idea in daylight had somehow altered into something different. I wanted to leave.

What would it matter if I changed my mind now? It was after all only my idea. Nobody was forcing me to do this. No-body apart from my husband would know if I didn't complete what I'd set out to do.

The darkness outside the car intensified. And so did my fear.

I glanced down at my wristwatch. Eight twenty. It was now or never.

I grabbed the basket and ran toward the house. For a fragment of time there was the automatic light from inside the car, but then I was plunged into an even darker quality of blackness as it faded.

I stumbled against the front door and clawed wildly for the handle. As it opened, the wind pushed me through into the hallway into still deeper darkness. I struggled to shut the door.

There was no electrical supply yet, so I had to rely on memory and my sense of feel to find the way through the empty shell of the house, now sinister and unfamiliar in the dark. Clutching the basket, I gingerly groped across to the double doorway leading into the lounge. The gale roared around the house. Inside, loose timbers creaked and rattled. I scuttled across the lounge and into the cathedral-ceilinged room that would eventually be a study.

A large window had been positioned in the western gable to take advantage of the views of the sunsets. Thick sheets of plastic, temporarily secured across the unglazed frame, heaved and flapped like huge bellows.

Almost eight thirty. I'd have to work fast.

I put down the basket. I had the feeling that somebody was behind me. Or was it *something* watching me from the doorway through which I'd just come? I struggled with the mounting panic.

Take control. Stop being stupid – I tried to reason with myself. Then, fumbling with the basket, trying to find things: there was no script to follow, nobody to ask. I felt like a pilgrim on an unknown path, following intuition perhaps?

First, the music.

Trembling, I switched on the battery-operated cassette player. Tracks from Peter Gabriel's composition, 'Passion': North African drumming, bagpipes, high ululating voices – primitive, raw, powerful rhythms that I'd thought right for the occasion. I turned up the volume, the music gave some comfort from the wind and the other strange noises I didn't want to think too much about.

Next, the candles.

In a large circle on the bare floor, all nine of them: three times three, for her triple aspect as a goddess and the trinity of her church when a Christianized saint. Hard to light with the flickering flames sucked out by gusts of cold air.

Still the sensation of being watched ... But I daren't turn round and look. Terrified in case something is actually there, I'm trapped in here, can't get out. Whatever it is, it's blocking the only exit.

Stop it. Focus. Get a grip. Breathe slower ... breathe ... breathe ...

Eight thirty-five ... Quick – time's running out. What's next? Where are the paints? Quick, must go faster. Where's the blue paint? Right, grab the brush and now ... deep breaths ... must stop trembling.

The drumming is more insistent – and why is it suddenly louder? I haven't touched the volume control. Don't think about that too much, get on with the painting. That's it ... there we go ...

My spirit seems to soar with each sweep of the brush on the bare wooden floorboards: three big blue spirals, a faithful copy of the Triple Spiral symbol engraved on the stone at the end of the internal passageway at New Grange. According to legend the Irish prehistoric home of Dagda, the chief God, supposedly Brigid's father. New Grange, an ancient monument predating the Pyramids – was that her first constructed home?

The Triple Spiral. Now reproduced as the symbol for the Prehistoric Society of Great Britain, further reduced into the lucky clover, logo of Aer Lingus and closer to home, possibly reduced to the three spinning spurs on the three legs of Mann.

The final brush stroke in blue ... that's it, almost perfect.

Now, quick – the words ... paint them carefully. Paint them beautifully ... this is important ... this is reverence. A dedication.

"To you, Brighid. To things past but not forgotten, Laa'l Breeshey. Imbolc 1990."

I speak them slowly as I paint each word.

Yes, that's looking good. But ... are the candles, are the candles burning brighter? Why? It's not possible. Must be my imagination.

Eight forty. Only five minutes left. Quick – now for the silver, like icing on a cake. The paint slides over the floorboards, highlighting the blue. A silver ghost-image of the spirals and the words. Like a halo. Every line followed and flowing into everything – timeless.

Just in time – it's eight forty-five. Fifteen minutes before nine. Now to start ...

I turn the volume very low. The music becomes a distant whisper. I unfold the paper. My hand-written copy of the ancient Hebridean chant used for the purification and blessing of the entire structure of the house, passed from mother to daughter, by word of mouth, from time immemorial.

At first my voice is weak against the wind, but gathering conviction from the purpose of the words strengthens me. For this is the reason I am here, to seek blessing and protection for this house, this structure on virgin land. I hear my own voice ring loud above the wind as it fills the echoing space we have constructed.

"May Brigit give blessing
To the house that is here.
Brigit the fair and tender,
Her hue like the cotton grass.
Rich-tressed Maiden,
Of ringlets of gold;
Both crest and frame,
Both stone and beam;
Both clay and wattle;
Both summit and foundation;
Both window and timber;
Both foot and head;
Both man and woman;
Both wife and children;
Both young and old;
Both maiden and youth."

As I speak, I feel linked to all those women of the past who have done this, as if a bond of sisterhood unites us all, just by speaking these timeless words and sharing the simple desire to make mere houses into safe homes by requesting a blessing from Brighid on this certain night.

Then I stand in silence. The wind seems less threatening. The candles burn brighter still. The shadows have retreated.

I pick up the bundle of rushes and turn towards the dark doorway. Should I take a candle? No, just the rushes, says a voice inside me. Intuition? Or something else?

I steel myself to walk back into the darkness and carry the rushes to the threshold of the front door.

I open the door and stand at the threshold. It is three minutes to nine. Now to speak the ancient Manx words inviting Bridget to enter and lodge here for the night.

"Vreeshey, Vreeshey, tar gys my thie, tar dys y thie ayms noght.
Foshil jee yn dorrys da Brede, as lhig da Brede cheet stiagh."

(Bridget, Bridget, come to my house, come to my house to-night, open the door to Bridget and let Bridget come in.)

I strew the rushes on the floor, as had been the tradition, to provide a carpet or bed, "Briid's Bed", for Brigit.

The cold air shrieks through, forcing the thick plastic sheeting stretched across the windows to expand and contract like enormous lungs, like the first breaths of a newborn child coming to life.

Suddenly I remember the candles. The violent wind will surely blow them out and it has to be me, not the wind, who does that.

I run through the darkness, expecting to find the flames extinguished. But as I enter the study the painting of the Triple Spiral seems to be surrounded by a ring of fire.

Perhaps the candles just appear to be burning more strongly? But strangely the room now appears to be filled with light. Perhaps it's the result of the extra draught from the front door? Perhaps my eyes have adjusted to the darkness?

It is now just after nine o'clock. I pack everything back into the basket. Strangely, the candles seem reluctant to be blown out. So I resort to licking my fingers to snuff the wicks between dampened forefinger and thumb.

Somehow the sudden darkness is not as intimidating as before.

As I leave the house, I continue the tradition of wedging the front door so that it cannot close. To maintain the open threshold of welcome for Brigit, throughout the night.

July 5th 1992
Barbecue at Corlea, Ronague, Isle of Man

Time passes.

We'd moved into our new house named 'Middle of the

fields', or 'Mean y Vagher' in Manx. But after two very happy years living there, our family requirements changed and in March 1992 we moved and sold the house to George and Penny Brown who were coming from Cheshire to live on the Island. They too wanted a safe and peaceful environment in which to bring up their two young daughters.

Although I felt sadness at leaving, it was pleasing to know that the new owners had fallen in love with the home that we'd built.

But that was four months ago.

The sun is hot on my bare arms and shoulders. I lean back against the warm stones of the barn and balance my empty plate and glass on the adjacent wall. The party is in full swing. Lots of people, music and laughter.

The completion of a new farm shed has provided a good excuse for our neighbours to hold a barbecue – well, neighbours from when we had lived at Mean y Vagher.

The view from their farm of the south of the Island is amazing on a fine day and I gaze fondly at the roof of Mean y Vagher far below in the distance. Just a tiny dark grey patch amongst the bright green fields.

"Hello, I was hoping that you'd be here!" A friendly, female voice disturbs my reverie. I turn, raising a hand to shield my eyes from the strong sunlight.

It's Penny Brown, the new owner of Mean y Vagher.

"Hello," I reply. "How lovely to see you! Funny, I was just looking down at the house. How are you settling in?"

"Oh we love it and it really feels like home now. But we've had so many visitors since we arrived. Family and friends. You know, coming to see what we've bought!" She laughed. "In fact I was going to ring you last week – one of my guests wanted to meet you, but I didn't like to intrude."

"Oh you should have come to see me and brought her with

you," I replied, wondering why one of her friends would wish to meet me.

"Well ..." she hesitated. "I hardly know you and I don't know if you're into such things ... because ... well, Marilyn's a bit different from most people."

"In what way?"

She put down her plate beside mine and took a deep breath. "Well, I suppose ... I don't know where to start. Marilyn is a very old friend, I've known her a long time. She's actually very sensitive in ways most people aren't – you see, she's a Medium."

I said nothing but surprise must have been written all over my face.

"She has a tremendous gift. The police use her sometimes in murder and kidnapping investigations. Members of the English and Spanish royal families too. She knows things that nobody could know ordinarily. But her powers make her quite weak physically and she suffers from a lot of ill health. It was a tremendous effort for her to travel over to see me on the Island."

"So why should she want to see me?" I asked quietly.

"Well, I picked her up from the airport and as we drove through the gates and down the drive to Mean y Vagher, Marilyn gasped and said she'd never seen anything like it before. I assumed that she was talking about the external appearance of the house and I said something about the architecture, but she said no, it wasn't the look of the house she was talking about – it was the psychic veil that surrounded it."

"What did she mean?" I gasped.

"Well, I asked her the same question and she explained it as being something like the TV adverts for the 'Colgate Ring of Confidence' or the one for 'Ready Brek', where the children have a warm glowing halo around their bodies – that was what she was seeing, something like that on a spiritual plane, enveloping the whole house."

I reached for my glass, but it was empty.

"Anyway," continued Penny, "as she entered the house, Marilyn commented on the peaceful atmosphere inside, on the strength of the feeling of tranquillity and security. She said it was quite unique. And then George brought the girls home from school and nothing else was said until later."

Penny took a sip of her drink.

"And this is the strangest part of it … It was about a quarter to nine and we were watching TV after supper and suddenly Marilyn asks, 'Has anybody called Bridget ever lived in this house?'"

At the mention of Bridgit I feel a sudden chill. Despite the sun's warmth, goosepimples crawl across my skin. I shiver. I can barely breathe.

"Well, I tell her that I'm not sure about any Bridgets having lived at Mean y Vagher, but she then says that she feels Bridget's presence and that she has never felt anything so powerful or ancient before in her life. She wanted to know the history of the house and when I told her that you'd only just had it built, she asked about you. Not your husband. She said it was something to do with you. That you'd brought Brigit into the house."

Penny looked at me expectantly, closely watching my reactions.

I was totally shocked. Dumbfounded. How could this Marilyn know about Bridgit? I'd told nobody what I'd done. But then as the enormity of the implication began to sink in I felt as though my sense of reality was slipping. I was floundering on the edge of a precipice of the unknown. My twentieth-century perception of reality was crumbling into a perceptual abyss.

What I had done was purely symbolic. A gesture to customs of the past. To a tradition. Just seeking to bless a newly constructed house … I felt faint. The truth was, I'd never really believed in the existence of that which I'd addressed. Bridgit for me was just a name in a book. A goddess from ancient British/Irish mythology, Christianized into a saint.

"It isn't possible," I muttered.

"Are you all right?" Penny asked with some concern. "You've gone very white."

"I just cannot believe this." I could barely speak.

From across the lawn I could see our hosts making their way towards us carrying large bowls of strawberries and cream.

"What do you mean? Do you know what Marilyn was talking about?"

"Look Penny …" My voice faltered. How could I even begin to explain it to her? Or anybody else, for that matter?

The strawberries and cream were almost upon us. There would be no time to explain.

"It's a long story, Penny. I don't think this is the right place to tell it. Can we meet up for coffee or lunch? Then I'll tell you everything."

July 14th 1992
Coffee at Rafter's Restaurant, Douglas, Isle of Man

Penny was looking at me expectantly from across the small round table. I took a deep breath and began the explanation.

"It started when we first saw the plot. Before we even began building. I just felt that in the past people thought more about the building of their houses in remote rural areas. They spent more time working out the best orientation, knowing the land and local weather and how it would affect their site than we do today. The location of water etc. They had to be self-sufficient. They couldn't rely on modern services or central heating!

Now it's up to the planners in their remote urban offices, telling us what we can and can't do and where we can build!

"Anyway, before modern planning, they intuitively knew the difference between good ground, meaning healthy sites, and bad ground as being unhealthy. Today people talk about Feng Shui as though it's something special from the East but in the British Isles we had a long tradition of similar practices. From the practical to the obscure."

"Do you know that in the Island they would put test piles of stones where the house was to be built in case they were going to block a fairy path? If the stones were continually knocked down they would re-site the dwelling so as not to offend the Little People!"

"Sounds like an early form of planning refusal!" Penny laughed.

I smiled and stirred my coffee slowly. "Anyway, I went to the Manx Museum to find out more about the actual background of the site and soon was entranced by the fascinating history and folklore of the Island. And as the house grew out of the ground I felt that I wanted to protect the space, to prevent anything bad ever happening in it. So that it would always be a good, happy place to live in and be safe. I liked the idea of blessing it. I'm not a practising Christian so it seemed a bit hypocritical to ask a priest to come and perform this.

"It was whilst I was doing this research that I learned about Brighid. She has always been the most important goddess in the British Isles. The stem of her name Brig is Indo-European in origin and means high, bright or powerful one. She may originally have been a sun goddess, but she's generally regarded as a triple aspect goddess, meaning that she not only represents the three stages of womanhood but also has triple attributes.

"She is the goddess of healing, of smith-craft and poetry, all forms of useful and inspired wisdom. She is the goddess of fire, especially in the hearth of the home where, apart from cooking, the fire was used for divination, healing and protection. Also the goddess of fertility, of helping all creatures to give birth and come into milk.She is also associated with sovereignty and protection of her isles and the sea. The image of her as Britannia was maintained until recently on the old penny coins as the symbol of British sovereignty. As Brigantia she gave her name to tribal lands in the north of England.

"Throughout the British Isles and Ireland through the ages her name has been spelled in so many ways. From Briggidda, Brede, to Brighid. In the Isle of Man she's known as Breeshey, Brideey, Bridget and Bride. St Bridget's Day was called 'Laa'l Breeshey' meaning Bridget's feast day. In the past, St Brigit's Eve was the greatest occasion in the traditional domestic year. Although the festival of her birth or death was on February 1st, the Imbolc quarter-day and start of spring, in the Celtic calendar the nights were just as important as the days and so the eve of a feast day would be important, possibly more so than the day itself. Some sources suggest that the feast day also extended into February 2nd as well." I paused to take a sip of coffee. "Look, tell me if I'm boring you. I don't want this to turn into a lecture!"

"No, no. I don't know anything about this. I'm finding it really interesting. Do go on."

"Well, Brigit, in the early Irish mythology was regarded as a daughter of the Dagda, the Supreme God and sometime sister, of wait for it, our own Manannan Mac Lir. Manannan was an Irish Sea God reduced through history to become a magician king with a fort on South Barrule. The evangelising force

19

of the Christian church wanted to remove the pagan or country people's devotion to Brigit so they cleverly canonised her goddess characteristics and gradually she became regarded as a saint. In rural Ireland there are still far more customs that are maintained than anywhere else and the St Brigit's cross of plaited straw, a pre-Christian sun wheel, is traditionally hung in Irish kitchens for protection of the home up to this day.

"Christian historians tell us that St Brigit was a woman born in a druid's house at Tocharmaine in AD 453. 'The Life of Brigit' states that she was born neither within the house nor without. Her mother gave birth with one foot in and one foot outside – on the threshold!

"Her life was full of magic and miracle and the date of her death was purposefully aligned with Imbolc. So highly was she regarded that her role of goddess and saint became so entwined that she became known as 'The Mary of the Gael' and even sometime midwife at Christ's birth.

"On the Island there are numerous places now associated with the Christian cult of Brigit. There are seven ancient keills named after her, a parish church and the northern Parish of Bride itself. Also the nunnery outside Douglas was called St Brigit's. St Brighid is reputed to have founded it when she visited the Island over a thousand years ago. It may have replaced an earlier pre-Christian shrine dedicated to the goddess. But whether a human Brighid actually ever came to the Island is a matter for conjecture."

I pushed a sheaf of photocopies towards her. "I don't know how much you want to know but these are just a few excerpts from books on Ireland, the Outer Hebrides and the Isle of Man. You can read these at your leisure. They'll explain everything more fully."

Penny reached for them. "But how does all this concern Mean y Vagher?" she asked thoughtfully.

"Well, I decided to follow the ancient practice of asking Brighid for a blessing on the house. I did it on 31st January 1990, St Brigit's Eve. I just followed what I'd gleaned from my research."

And then I quickly told her what I'd done that night in Mean y Vagher.

"But, Penny," I continued, "I have to admit to you that I am still finding it hard to come to terms with what Marilyn told you. I just cannot believe that Brigit actually *is* ... I did it all symbolically. I didn't really believe in her except as the focus of a cult belief. But for her to actually *exist?* It confounds everything ... I mean this has totally overturned my conception of what is real. My logical and scientific pragmatism cannot come to terms with it. However, objectively, what is equally inexplicable is how could Marilyn know what I'd done? Okay, my painting is still there – just! The joiners planed a lot of it off when they were finishing the flooring. But now it's all covered with underlay and fitted carpets. Only my husband knew what I'd intended. Nobody else!"

I took a sip from my cup, but by now the coffee was quite cold. I'd talked too much!

"You probably think I'm mad, but my intentions were pure, honest and good. I could never have anticipated what Marilyn told you. It's just mind-bending."

Penny smiled.

"Don't worry. I loved the feeling of the house when I first visited it. I knew it was special. I like what you've done. I feel even safer now, knowing what you've told me. I'll read what you've given me and perhaps I'll ask Brighid to continue looking after the house next year."

From her mischievous tone I couldn't be sure if she was joking.

February 1st 1993
Santon, Isle of Man

I answer the phone.

"Hi. Sorry to bother you. It's Penny Brown." Her voice sounds strained. "Have you got a minute?"

"Yes. What's the matter?"

"Well, last night as you know was Laa'l Breeshey. I opened the front door and read out those words in Manx inviting Bridgid into the house. You remember? You gave me those photocopies? And I left the door ajar all night … which says something for living on the Isle of Man! I didn't say anything to George about what I was doing. You know how men scoff! But the strangest things have been happening since."

There was a pause before she began to speak again.

"This morning George took the girls to school as he usually does and after they'd gone I went to my bedroom. I was just doing my hair, sitting in front of the dressing-table when I heard singing and laughter. Like lots of people walking through the house. It seemed to be a procession of singing and dancing. It didn't make any sense. Had George suddenly come back with some people? Or had one of the girls left on the radio or TV? So I rushed through the house to see what was going on. But there was nobody there and nothing had been left on."

Before I could ask her if she was really sure that she'd heard the sounds, she continued breathlessly, "When George came back I was about to tell him what had occurred. But as soon as he came in he said that something strange had happened to him last night. He told me that he'd been woken in the middle of the night by giggling in the bedroom. He felt a child jump onto the bottom of our bed and then run off giggling down the corridor. He thought it was one of the girls, only they

22

wouldn't normally behave like that, so he got up, still half asleep and went to their bedrooms to see what was going on. But they were both sound asleep. It wasn't them!

"He looked around the house but couldn't find anything unusual. There was no other child anywhere. Do you think it has anything to do with what I did last night for Brighid?"

Again I felt that chilling sensation. Fear of the unknown? This was way out of the ordinary realms of existence. And I was responsible. What was going on? But more importantly, were the Browns and their little girls in any kind of danger?

"Are you still there?"

"Yes I am ... and Penny, I really don't know what to say. Do you feel threatened or does the house feel different?"

"No, in fact, it feels happy and there is an elusive perfume, like the distant smell of flowers. I don't feel nervous – I just wanted to tell you."

"Well I'm glad you have. I'll see if I can find out anything that may explain what you and George experienced."

We concluded the telephone conversation with the promise of a future meeting. All I knew was that Penny and I had dabbled, innocently enough with something we didn't understand. What had we invited into the house? Were the little girls at risk?

March 2nd 1993
Lunch at Rafters Restaurant, Douglas, Isle of Man

"Do you know, I haven't been here since our last meeting?" I said, noting with relief that across the table Penny looked well; quite relaxed with no visible sign of anxiety.

The waitress came and took our orders.

"Has anything else happened at Mean y Vagher since we last spoke?"

"No. Nothing. What are your thoughts about what I told you?"

"To be frank, Penny, I didn't know what to think. But I was worried enough to want to speak to somebody who might have experience in such things or would at least understand the traditions concerning Brighid. I eventually contacted Caroline Matthews in Oxford. She has written a lot of books on Celtic mysticism. She's quite an expert on British and Irish mythology and the Hermetic traditions of the British Isles. I just left a message on her answerphone giving a brief description of what we'd done at Mean y Vagher and wondered if she would think I was a crank. But she kindly phoned me back."

I paused momentarily as the waitress returned with our food.

"What did she say?" Penny asked breathlessly.

"Well, she was very matter-of-fact about the whole thing. I mean she just seemed to accept the existence of Brighid as though it was nothing new to her at all. But she spoke of her more as a goddess than a saint. She said that the fires originally burned to honour Brighid as fire goddess on the second of February, Feailley Vreeshey; St Bridget's Festival as 'Mary of the Gael' is still indirectly being continued on the same date in the Christian Church in the form of Candlemas Day.

"She said my use of candles, dedicated to Brigit, had been very important. And whilst she was talking I recollected that the candles I'd lit had burned with an inexplicable intensity. They'd seemed like a ring of fire. But only *after* the dedication.

"Because my heart and mind were open and my intentions pure, I was what she called a 'willing vassal'. She said that in simple terms I'd opened a doorway between different dimensions and created a type of portal for beings that modern Western minds just cannot comprehend. All spiritual services conducted within the Church are opened and closed by the priest in a way that keeps the spiritual realms confined to goodness. To use a metaphor, she said that just as a goblet can be filled with something good to drink, it can also be filled with poison and that similarly although good energies may now fill the space at Mean y Vagher conversely bad energies could also invade it. The question of controlling what is in that space is in either my hands or yours. We can ask for goodness or evil. As we've asked for Brighid she feels that it's her force of goodness that fills the house.

"She said that the convictions and belief systems of thousands of years had created a pattern that was self-perpetuating and the proof of continuation for so long, by thousands of people and in so many geographical locations was a sign that the annual invocation of Brighid had always been a good thing.

"But she worried me when she said that this door we've opened remains open. We haven't closed it or terminated the 'service'. If things change and you feel at all uneasy then we have to close it down immediately and politely but very firmly say that we, who once extended an invitation, now ask her to leave."

Penny was silent for a moment before she replied. "Well, I don't feel anything bad at all at Mean y Vagher. In fact just the opposite. I've spoken with Marilyn and she says that the house is full of light and goodness, in fact all the attributes Brighid is supposed to bring. But I'll bear in mind what you've just told me for the future."

She seemed unperturbed by what I'd told her. But I felt apprehensive. I was worried.

2007

Many years have passed since that meeting. We hardly ever spoke again about what we'd done. Happily, there was no need.

Penny and I remain good friends.

The Browns continued to live at Mean y Vagher and their two daughters grew into beautiful, highly accomplished young women whose academic and personal achievements are so out of the ordinary that they verge on the extraordinary.

Penny, with support from her husband, amongst many other various successes and accomplishments whilst living at Mean y Vagher, raised the profile of a little-known cancer charity into something that is now of significant size and international importance.

While I would not take anything away from their personal achievements, I sometimes wonder if Brighid's influence has helped?

And now for the twist in the tale, that makes you, the reader, gasp with incredulity and reflect upon the true meaning of this story about Brigid.

Well I'm sorry to disappoint you, but there isn't one ...

Unless you thought that this was just a fiction, only a figment of my imagination? Well if so, then there really is a twist, for this story is as *true* as this final full stop.

Author's note

I have changed the names of people and certain places to protect their true identities.

Obviously Brigit is Herself, although I seem to have *unconsciously* changed the spelling of Her name several times. And as the Goddess seems so firmly entrenched in this land in every other way, perhaps that's how She prefers it?

✝ february ✝

Colin Fleetney was born in Kent and lived there until the 1980s when he moved to the Island to become Vicar of Lezayre. Before being ordained Colin worked as a seagoing engineer and then as a hospital engineer in a large psychiatric hospital. After ordination he continued to work at the hospital as their chaplain and then became Team Vicar for five parishes outside Canterbury.

Now retired and living in Port Erin with his Manx wife Joan he contributes factual articles to magazines in the UK as well as writing short stories and building working steam engines in his garden shed.

The Bracelet

Colin J. Fleetney

On the Isle of Man, February 1909 did indeed live up to its reputation. The Sulby River, Santon Burn, the Neb and all the other gentle, homely streams had become torrents of seething peat-brown water. The narrow waterfalls that plunged hundreds of feet down the side of Mount Karrin to the Sulby River had developed great spouts that leapt clear of the rock face to be caught by the south-westerly gales and lifted, billowing as misty spray, high across the glen. Downstream from the reservoir, the people of Baldwin lived uneasily, the background to their lives being a continuous, sullen roaring as overflow water, like a thick white curtain, roared down the sloping stone face of the great dam at Injebreck into the River Glass. Although four years old, the dam was being subjected to its first serious test. That the massive wall should fail did not bear contemplation.

February was traditionally reckoned to keep the clergy busy in the burial grounds and this one was no exception. Among the many who died was General Sir Maitland Coleford-Colley. Sir Maitland's death should have been no surprise, as he was, after all, ninety. Yet as is our nature, people were surprised, for the old man had seemed to be indestructible. He had been very active; rode, took part in most social activities, was avuncular, hearty and saw himself as a ladies' man. It was the General's death that set in train the events recorded below.

★ ★ ★

"The servants are, as usual, off duty until five, but Charles will be back on the half past four at Lezayre." She was looking at her reflection in the full-length mirror as she spoke. He watched, fascinated, as her fingers flew over hooks, buttons and bows as layer after layer of clothing fell in a circle around her feet. Finally she turned, beamed that absolutely stunning smile, took his hand and led him to the bed.Gradually the colour was leached out of the countryside as the December afternoon drew on. He watched as the Lezayre Tops turned black against the grey of the clouds that lapped and spilled over their crest. Every few seconds the wind rattled the windows and boomed over the roof.

"Run over our plan again, my love," she said, leaning up on one elbow.

"James! You're not listening to me!"

"Oh, I'm sorry, dearest, I was listening to the wind. I fear it'll be a bad crossing tomorrow."

"A choppy sea'll not worry you, surely? Anyway, you must go and discuss our business with your friend as soon as possible. In order to plan our future we need an estimate of the value of our treasure. So, as I asked a moment ago, run over our plan again."

"As I said; it came to me after the funeral back in February. All that treasure is ours for the taking! There are four generals, and an admiral, all, like Sir Maitland, wearing full dress uniforms, complete with decorations, orders, medals, presentation swords and the like. Then there's a bishop, he's in full fig too, with a huge ruby set in his episcopal ring, while his crozier and mitre, encrusted with jewels, are lying on top of the glass lid, there for the taking. The others, various civilian members of the Coleford-Colley family going back to Queen Anne's reign, men as well as women, are all bedecked in jewellery too. Furthermore, dearest, no one will ever know. Sir Maitland was the last Coleford-Colley. His son died at sea some thirty years ago. The vault will never again be opened.

"So as I see it, dearest Annabel, our troubles are over. It will be the simplest thing in the world for me to enter the vault, remove the glass lids of the coffins and take everything that appears to be of value. I can then ship it out to my friend Walter Gropius, in Liverpool. As I have told you, Walter deals in anything and everything, no questions asked. He'll play fair with me – he owes me a debt or two – I can tell you! Yes, Walter'll get us a good price. I estimate that the whole lot's worth around eight thousand, but I'll find out for certain when I've told him all the details. With the majority of it invested, it'll be enough to keep us in comfort for the rest of our lives.

"And what about your part in the scheme, Annabel? Your reason for going across will be to visit your aunt? Where'd you say she lives?"

"Chester."

"When can you reasonably go?"

"Not until early January."

"Ideal! By then Walter will have disposed of the goods and I'll have the money. I will then book us, as husband and wife, of course, under an assumed name, first class on a Cunarder to New York, and we can disappear in the United States."

She thought for a moment, squeezed his arm companionably and said, "The train will soon be in; time for you to go, my dearest Inspector of Constabulary and Churchwarden."

She stood at the window and watched him walk down the

31

drive to the main road, tall, fit, strong, the long, dark blue, brass-buttoned overcoat swinging, the crown of his uniform cap glistening with sleet. She smiled, sighed and went down to prepare tea for her husband.

* * *

The Reverend Charles Tillotson was the youngest son of a youngest son and his father could only settle on him an allowance of two hundred a year to augment the Church's stipend. Annabel, who had married against her mother's wishes for love, still cared for her husband. She was, however, tired of constantly worrying about money, of constantly being careful over clothes and practising frugality behind the scenes in order that they might appear comfortable and maintain a good table when parishioners dined. Further, she was bored. Annabel wanted something more than boring impoverished gentility. Preferment, and with it promotion, was unlikely for Charles as he had no influential friends, and anyway the Church of England tended to promote men who were, to say the least, comfortably off. She considered herself still young at twenty- six and James Hurst had presented her with perhaps the only opportunity that would ever come her way.

* * *

With his swagger stick clutched under his left arm and his gloved hands clasped behind his back, Inspector James Hurst walked to Ramsey, head bent down against the wind and sleet. As he walked he reviewed the astounding, almost unbelievable good fortune that had come his way.The army being no profession for a man with hardly any private means, he had been on the point of resigning his commission when the Boer War had started. To avoid the possible accusation of cowardice he had stayed with his regiment, saw plenty of action and was slightly wounded at Magersfontein. At the end of the war he had resigned, with the rank of Captain, and taken the post of senior police officer for the north of the Isle of Man. This proved to be a comfortable enough job with a nice house in the parish of Lezayre, horse and stabling provided. As near as dammit one's own boss and quite well paid for what one was expected to do. Society had accepted him as his pedigree was sound enough, and he had been educated at King William's College. He had been invited to take the office of Church-warden at Lezayre and had, of course, accepted. So life went on, boring in the sheer inevitability of whist, bridge, concerts, dances and, in the summer, garden parties.

*   *   *

In February, due to the interregnum – the new vicar was due to be inducted in June – it fell to Hurst and his fellow churchwarden to arrange the socially very important Coleford-Colley funeral. His colleague assumed responsibility for the service; the bishop would, of course, officiate. Hurst, there-fore, turned his attention to the committal at the vault.

The Coleford-Colley vault was situated in the eastern ground of the big cemetery. The Old Eastern Ground, as it was always called by the villagers, had long been filled. In-deed the sextons believed that the interment of Sir Maitland's wife in the family vault back in 1893 – some sixteen years before – was not only the last burial in the Old Eastern Ground, but probably the last time anyone went in there.

On the Monday before the funeral, Hurst and the two sex-tons, Bill Mylroie and Juan Kewley, walked over to the Old Eastern Ground. After ripping the ivy and elder away, they were able to force the gates to the abandoned cemetery par-tially open. Then, each wielding a razor-sharp brushing hook, they slashed their way slowly through the saturated bushes overhanging the gravel drive. After half an hour's hard work, the senior sexton, Bill Mylroie, paused, drew breath and pointed, with a wave of his brushing hook, through the dense undergrowth of brown and sear briars, bracken, elder, nettles, ivy and rowans that had engulfed headstones and monuments, to a pair of elaborate wrought iron gates. "That's it. Hope you thought to bring the bloo– blessed key, Captain!"

The gateway was flanked by two six-foot tall cherubs standing on plinths, who, while looking mournfully across the gateway at each other with that dreadful wall-eyed gaze of statuary, had each inverted their Torch of Life to extinguish its flame at their feet. The ivy that swathed the cherubs had also woven itself through the gates. Another ten minutes hacking and tearing was required before they could force open one gate. Beyond the gates a flight of wide, shallow, stone steps led down some fourteen feet to a bleak space in front of the vault door. Both steps and area were covered in rotting leaves, twigs and dead birds. Below them the front of the vault was decorated in the classical style popular during the early years of the eighteenth century. The door was flanked by caryatids of sombre bearded men in classical robes gazing across the doorway at each other. On either side of the caryatids were black marble tablets listing the occupants of the vault. Centre-place in the white marble pediment above the door was a cross, beneath which was the word 'Resurgam', the letters made of black marble. The door of the vault, made of smooth bronze, was covered with a patina of verdigris. The three men shuffled down, their feet cautiously feeling for each step, slippery and wet under the rotting leaves. Hurst waited until the other two men had used their boots roughly to sweep away the leaves from the area in front of the door and had lit their hurricane lamps before he inserted the quite small key into the door. "Should have let me oil it first, sir," Mylroie muttered.

Hurst was about to agree as he turned the key but was astounded to find that it moved easily as the tumblers within the lock clicked smoothly.

"Well, I'll be damned," muttered the sexton.

"Bronze don't rust. It's used at sea a lot for that reason," Juan Kewley his assistant and son-in-law stated, flatly.

"That's as maybe, but I bet the bloody hinges are solid."With only the key to use – there was no door knob – Hurst pulled at the door. It swung open smoothly and silently.

"Christ!" said the sexton.

"Enough! Remember where you are! No profanity!"

"Yes, Captain Hurst, sir."

Hurst stared hard at the sexton. The man stared back, but his face was impassive, no trace of insubordination. Lacking much of a sense of humour and inclined to take himself seriously, Hurst was convinced that these Manxmen – his constables were the same – were frequently laughing at him. In fact they had long ago assessed him as a pompous but well-intentioned fool.

The men raised their lamps above their heads, but hung back. The vault was some thirty feet long. It had a black and white chequered marble floor. High on the wall, at the far end, was mounted a gilded baroque cross. Along either wall were tiers of stone shelves, most of which, apart from a few close to the door, held one or two coffins, side by side. A skein of grey dust covered everything.

"Give me your lamp, man." Hurst grabbed a lamp and stepped inside. A faint odour of putrification engulfed him. He sniffed in distaste and walked slowly to the far end."Earliest interments are at this end," he called. "Sir Maitland'll go in where you are, on the left there, just inside the door."

"Shouldn't think so, Captain."

"What, man! What'd you mean, dammit?"

"Should think he'd want to go alongside his wife. She's on the right, here. According to the brass plate, that is."

Hurst walked back and peered at the plate on the side of the coffin that was obviously the most recent addition.

"Oh, yes. Quite so, quite so."

The assistant sexton wiped his sleeve across the glass top of a coffin. "Will you look at that, yessir!" The corpse was that of an admiral in full dress, complete with orders, medals and a magnificent presentation sword. Wiping the tops of more coffins revealed admirals and generals in full dress and ladies festooned in jewellery. On one coffin stood a bishop's mitre with his crozier standing in front of it. The bishop was enrobed and wore a magnificent episcopal ring.

"Here's the first occupant." Hurst stood at the far end gazing at a coffin, the side of which had partly collapsed allowing an arm, with skin like brown paper encased in a yellowing white silk sleeve, to hang out. The claw-like fingers wore several rings while a magnificent gold bracelet set with pearls encompassed the thin wrist. Hurst ran his fingers over the brass plate. "Letitia Alice Coleford-Colley. March 14th 1696 to July 9th 1712." He rubbed again at the plate. "Says ... she ... yes ... that's it. Yes. She died on her wedding day! How sad, how desperately sad."

For a moment or two the three men stood in silence, Hurst wondering why a bride should die on her wedding day as he gazed at the flowing dress, its once white brocade now a rusty yellow. The fragile remains of what must have been her wedding bouquet lay on her breast. He gazed at the face. Once you were lovely, he thought, and I would have kissed you.

Both sextons, thinking along similar lines to each other, were of a more practical turn of mind, and wondered just how much this damn funeral was going to disrupt their quiet lives.

Hurst shook his head. "Right, now I want the entire place

cleaned – and I mean cleaned. The gates to the Eastern Ground and the gates to the vault must be painted. The driveway re-gravelled, grass verges to be cut, and so forth. Those evergreens, shrubs and so on flanking the drive, all to be trimmed. The ivy and bindweed to be stripped from stonework, and fallen statuary and all loose leaves swept up and removed."

Hurst glared at the two men. "It's Monday. Funeral's at eleven on Friday morning. So not much time – got to get cracking. However, I know hard work when I see it, so I'll tell you what I'll do. I intend to go down to Ramsey now and hire two labourers – should be several lounging about Parliament Square. I know it'll be quite dark, but you should be started by seven thirty, and I expect you all to work until it's too dark to see."

"I doubt you'll get anyone, Captain."

"Oh, I will, I will, for I intend to offer them nine pence an hour! What do you think of that?"

"Bloo– very generous, very generous indeed."

"I shall also have a complete roll of bombazine sent up from the dressmakers. On Friday morning – I'll be here early – we can drape it from the cherubs and gates, down, on either side of the steps, to the door. Any slight breeze will cause it to billow gracefully.

"Inside the vault we'll drape the bombazine over those damaged coffins, at the far end. Oh, and get that arm in the coffin again and generally smarten up that area."

"As you say, Captain Hurst, sir. As you say."

Hurst stared long and hard at the man. He snorted, swung the heavy bronze door which closed with a comfortable thud. "Self-closing lock! Very sophisticated indeed." He turned and swished his way back up the steps through the leaves to the surface, followed by the sextons who exchanged knowing smiles.

The funeral went off faultlessly in spite of the weather. A special train was run from Douglas and upward of one hundred men attended. The principal mourners were the Lieutenant Governor, His Excellency Lord Raglan, and Field Marshal Earl Roberts of Kandahar. The Lord Bishop, Dr Thomas Drury, was in fine voice and preached for almost half an hour. Later, the mourners crowding the steps to the vault and the path from the main cemetery could hear his words clearly above the booming of the wind in the trees, as he intoned the Committal. "Forasmuch as it hath pleased Almighty God of His great mercy to take unto Himself the soul of our dear brother ..." Finally, with a nod from the undertaker, the sextons, dressed in their vergers' gowns, slowly closed the great bronze door and the lock tripped into place.

It was later that week, with money on his mind because of heavy losses at cards one evening, that the idea came to Hurst. The Coleford-Colley vault! Of course! All that wealth for the taking!

★ ★ ★

The next big event in the parish was the induction of the new vicar, the Reverend Charles Tillotson. Tillotson, and his beautiful wife, Annabel, caused no end of a stir in society in the north of the Island. The Tillotsons were sociable people – there was nothing sanctimonious about Charles, he was no spouter of Biblical verses or canting phrases. They kept a good house soon known for its hospitality. Further, he was a worker, constantly visiting the housebound and sick and helping the destitute in practical ways. He also taught, when he had time, in the little school just along from the vicarage, in Churchtown. The unemployed found, to their astonishment, that Tillotson would go to great lengths to help them find employment.

Thus Annabel Tillotson came into Hurst's life.

One afternoon in late summer they rode together from Douglas. After the train had left St Johns – they were alone in the compartment – they spoke in general of Church matters. He moved across to sit next to her and she had not objected. Then she remarked, "In the cemetery, Captain Hurst, those big cherubs one can see in the disused area … "

"You're referring to the cherubs flanking the Coleford-Colley vault in the Eastern Ground, Mrs. Tillotson ?"

"Am I? I really do not know, but they're sinister things."

Not having a great deal of imagination he looked at her questioningly.

"Rearing above the shrubbery up there, they make me feel uneasy."

He heard himself say, "There's a great deal of valuable stuff in that vault."

"Valuables, Captain Hurst?"

He was committed. "Valuables, Mrs Tillotson. Jewellery, medals, orders, regalia, all manner of bits and pieces and it'll never be seen again. Sir Maitland Coleford-Colley's funeral, in February, was the last time that the vault would be opened. He was the last of his line. The vault is now closed for good."

He had carried her parcels from Lezayre station to the vicarage. She had half-presented her face to be kissed in the porch of the vicarage. Hurst took the risk by responding to her and attempted to kiss her cheek. At the last second she astounded him by turning and presenting her lips to him.

Thus Hurst and Annabel started to flirt; holding her too closely while dancing, the touch of feet under the card table. It was exciting, stimulating and gave him cause, against all his social and professional mores, to hope that it might develop into something more tangible.

From that afternoon the thought of all that wealth in the Coleford-Colley vault, there for the taking, occupied every moment of his time – when he was not thinking of Annabel Tillotson, that is.

★   ★   ★

That autumn was wild; wild and wet even by Manx standards. It was during the last week of November that Hurst met Annabel in Churchtown. She had been visiting the school and he had been paying the sextons. They stood on the carriage turning- circle at the main gates to the cemetery gazing at the late autumn scene. Annabel remarked that the autumnal gales had completely stripped the last of the year's leaves off the trees. Hurst agreed and they gazed across the sea of headstones, angels, columns and monuments, towards the Old Eastern Ground.

She pointed to the Coleford-Colley cherubs. "There are those things I mentioned to you on the train. Now the leaves have gone they dominate the scene, Captain."

"By this time next year they'll not be visible, the shrubs and trees will have engulfed them again." Annabel nodded, shivered and clutched her cloak tighter round her. "Well, good day to you, Captain." She turned to walk away and paused. "Should you be free on Thursday afternoon I would be pleased if you would call for tea and tell me more about that fascinating vault."

He touched the peak of his uniform cap with his swagger stick. "I would be delighted, Mrs Tillotson, delighted."

He had found it hard to wait until Thursday but eventually it came.

"Charles is usually in Douglas all day on Thursdays and the servants always have Thursday afternoon off, from one to five." She was refilling his cup after offering another piece of cake. It was a wild day and he was glad to be in this pleasant, over-furnished room, sitting on the sofa in front of the roaring fire and sipping tea from this fragile cup, while this beautiful, fashionable woman cut yet another slice of cake for him.

"Do you know this house, Captain?"

"James, please. Only that it is quite modern, built with the church in the late 1830s."

"Quite so. When we've finished, allow me to show you round. We'll start upstairs."

Later, lying on the bed, gazing at the ceiling, she asked him about the 'treasure' as she called it, in the vault. He described it in detail and added his estimation of the value.

In a quiet, breathless, pensive way she whispered her deepest thoughts.

"Two bold people could make a new life for themselves and live very comfortably indeed if such a sum were wisely invested."

He took her in his arms again. "Oh, indeed they could, dearest, dearest Annabel."

* * *

So on this Thursday afternoon, 2nd December 1909, he strode back home with his heart soaring as he anticipated the future, their future. He had planned it all with great care like a military operation, and had shared every detail with Annabel. Every eventuality was covered. He would remove the treasure from the vault on Christmas Eve and store it in the disused hen house at the bottom of the vicarage kitchen garden. This operation would coincide with Charles Tillotson being in the church from eleven o'clock in the evening until one o'clock on Christmas morning. He would then walk into Ramsey, on police duty, of course. On the following Thursday, while Charles was in Douglas, he would transfer the treasure to his own house and pack it in a steamer trunk.

All that remained was to convert the plan into deeds and

he would start tomorrow, in Liverpool, when Walter would give him an estimate of the value of, as he and Annabel had come to call it, their treasure.

The following day as he walked round to the Steam Packet Company's berth in Ramsey harbour, Hurst shivered and cursed both the sailing time and the weather. Why on earth the boat had to sail in the early hours of a winter's morning, was beyond him! He was wearing a flat tweed cap and a heavy overcoat fitted with an Inverness cape. The wind that was booming round the buildings was coming up behind him and every minute or two it lifted him, giving him a sense of weightlessness as it pushed him forward. The rain, driven by the gale, was slashing in great fog-like gusts that hissed across the cobblestones of the quay, streamed off the roofs and steamed on the lantern glass of the gas lamps.

They were loading the last of the cargo and the ship's winches clattered and hissed, discharging great gouts of steam as the ship's derricks lifted and swung cargo from the quay to the ship's holds. Men shouted against the wind thrumming in the rigging while dray horses stamped with boredom and cold. He glanced up at the polished brass letters surrounded by gilded decorative scrollwork under the ship's stern, the *Ellan Vannin*, the usual Ramsey boat. As he approached the gangway Hurst acknowledged the salute by the caped police constable standing over against the Steam Packet office wall. He walked up the steep gangway, groping in his inside pocket for his ticket. At the head of the gangway the purser stood under the shelter of the overhang of the boatdeck. As the gangway muttered, worked and creaked on the deck sill to the movement of the ship, the purser clipped his ticket and bade him good morning. Hurst remarked that the weather was bad. The purser agreed, "Yes, its very bad." As Hurst picked up his bag and turned towards the vestibule, the purser called to say that due to the weather conditions they were serving breakfast now. Hurst thanked him and made for the dining room and the smell of bacon and eggs, kippers, toast and coffee.

The small room was a warm, comfortable haven. The walls were covered in linenfold oak panelling hung with gilt-framed watercolours of Manx scenes. The ceiling was white with mouldings picked out in gold. The portholes were framed by heavy chintz curtains. The mahogany tables were covered in stiff, white cloths and set with silver cutlery and vases of flowers.

Hurst scanned the menu and ordered bacon, eggs, toast, marmalade and coffee from the waiting steward.

There were only six people eating and the man at the next table looked across and said, "We're in for a lively time, I'm thinking."

Just as Hurst agreed, the wind, as if in confirmation, gusted, causing the ship to snatch at her mooring ropes. Hurst enjoyed his breakfast despite the frequent tugging of the ropes causing the crockery and lamp chimneys to rattle, but nevertheless he made up his mind. Draining his coffee and tossing his table napkin down, he stood up and said to his neighbour, "My business can wait another day. I really don't need to cross in this weather."

"Well, having walked in from Andreas I'm not giving up because of a bit of a chop on the sea!"

Hurst nodded, paid, took his hat and coat from the stand, picked up his bag and went outside.

"I'll leave it until the weather moderates, Purser."

The purser nodded. "Need to go to my office for a refund, sir."

They went back into the vestibule and Hurst stood at the gilded grill of the office while the purser scribbled on a pad then rummaged in a drawer and returned the price of the ticket.

Fifteen minutes later Hurst surprised them at the police station by walking in at such an early hour. He was inspecting the log book when they heard the *Ellan Vannin*'s whistle sound a long blast. The duty sergeant looked at the clock, "It's not like Captain Teare to sail late. Thirteen minutes, no less!"

Later that day he met Annabel in Parliament Street. They stood for seconds only, but it was time enough for her to show her disappointment by pointing out that he had allowed a rough sea to stop him getting on with their business.

On Sunday morning the loss of the ship was the talk of the church but, as he whispered to Annabel, "Obviously I was not meant to die, for together we have great things facing us."

A week later he was able to tell Annabel that Walter estimated their business, as he called it, was worth at least seven thousand pounds, maybe more. He would ask a mere four hundred or so for negotiating all of the transactions, and looked forward to doing so in the New Year.

★ ★ ★

Christmas Eve and the midnight Holy Communion service. Charles had left for church at a quarter to eleven. Annabel had watched as he walked from the front door, his shoes crunching on the gravel of the drive, to the path that led through the shrubbery to the church.

"You may go to bed when I leave for church, Greeba." The maid bobbed her thanks.

"As you well know, my husband will require breakfast at seven for there is an eight o-clock Holy Communion on Christmas Day." The maid bobbed again.

Annabel glanced at the clock. She had some forty minutes before she would be expected in her pew. With a circling motion she threw her heavy black cloak around her shoulders and pinned on her tight-fitting round black hat, hurriedly thrusting pins through her hair gathered into a bun. Her 'miniature bowler', Charles called that hat. Then, after tugging on gloves, she picked up her Book of Common Prayer, dropped it into the pocket of her cloak and let herself quietly out of the front door.

Keeping away from the soft yellow light thrown by the windows, she walked on the grass verge, her feet making hardly any sound, up the rear drive that opened on to the Churchtown road. She reckoned that she was far too early to meet any pedestrians or carriages – they would all arrive as usual, minutes before the service was due to start. She was right. She saw no one as she hurried past the school to the cemetery gates. During the day it had grown cold, very cold. She glanced up. Although stars blazed in the bitter night, there was a great bank of cloud building up in the north-east, and the wind carried with it that indefinable smell of snow. To the south the sky was cut off abruptly by the black crest of the Lezayre Tops that towered immediately above the cemetery. Indeed the cemetery occupied the lower hundred yards or so of the Tops, and sloped quite steeply at its far end. Annabel was soon quite breathless as, clutching her cloak and dress, she hurried up the steep paths between the serried ranks of monuments.

As she approached the Old Eastern Ground, the cemetery was less well tended and rose briars that had been allowed to run wild and hang over the path plucked at her cloak and scratched at her boots. Ahead of her, a tangled mass of shrubbery rose beyond the wall that separated the Eastern Ground from the modern Middle Ground. The gate to the Eastern Ground was unlatched, and one half stood partly open. Annabel paused to catch her breath, panting slightly, then eased carefully through the gate. Amid the thickets she could see headstones, tombs and monuments, white in the starlight.

She had walked a few steps along the path, shrubs

encroaching on either side, when, with fear surging in her, she saw a figure crouching under a shrub just off to the right. She recoiled and almost shrieked – but not quite – for in that instant, that split-second, she realised that she was looking at a marble angel kneeling at the head of a grave. Its hands were clasped in supplication, its face gazing sadly to the sky as it seemed to peer through the elder bush that had engulfed both grave and angel.

She was pleased with her self-control when, a moment or two later, on rounding a bend, she was confronted by the great cherubs flanking the gates to the Coleford-Colley vault.

Just as she reached the vault gates she was startled when the tubular bells in the Church tower suddenly started to play, in the slow, ponderous manner of such instruments, the carol 'While Shepherds Watched Their Flocks by Night'. The slow notes reverberated in the clear, frosty night as the sexton, high in the tower, painstakingly pushed down on the big wooden keys.

Below her, Annabel could see that the vault door was standing partly open emitting a dull yellow light from Hurst's lamp. She descended to the area and glanced at three bulging canvas bags standing just outside the door.

She looked in and saw Hurst standing, with his back to the door, part way down the vault, obviously taking one last look round. She must have scuffed her boots in the leaves, for he turned, startled. "Annabel, whatever are you doing! You have absolutely no need to be here, this place is not for you! Just leave everything to me, as we arranged."

As he walked towards her, Annabel said, "The bracelet, the gold and pearl bracelet, have you got it? Is it in one of the bags?"

He shook his head. "No, we've got enough – more than enough without taking that poor girl's bracelet."

"Oh, James! Please. Not to sell, dearest, but as your first Christmas present to me! We can have it cleaned. I'd love to wear it. I'd be the envy of every other woman. Please, James. Oh, please!"

He paused, thought, nodded, turned and walked back towards the far end of the vault and putting his hand through the crumbling side of the coffin, started to remove the bracelet.

Annabel watched until she judged that he was engrossed in what he was doing. Then she drew back and with gloved hands she pushed the door closed. It moved smoothly, far more easily than she had expected, the mechanism of the lock operating with a satisfactory 'clunk' that she could hear above the brazen sound of the bells.

She stood for an instant, then withdrew the key from the door and dropped it into her pocket. After glancing at the bags she hoisted her skirts above her knees and bounded up the steps, two at a time. She ran through the Eastern Ground, dodged through the gate, hurried down the paths and, as she approached the main gates, paused to compose herself.

She had no need to worry, there was no one on the Churchtown road. As she came near to the rear drive to the vicarage, the Five Minute bell started to chime. Keeping in the shadows, she went round to the kitchen courtyard. In the courtyard she carefully slewed the cover of the well to one side, groped in her pocket, found the vault key and dropped it down the well. She heard it strike the brickwork once or twice before she heard a far distant splash.

After pulling the well-cover back in place, she hurried round to the front door, entered and quickly changed her hat and cloak.

She walked into the church just as the congregation started to sing, to Herr Mendelssohn's marvellous tune, 'Hark! The

Herald Angels Sing'. The sidesmen smiled and one of them conducted her to her pew at the front. She smiled back at him gently.

★   ★   ★

By three in the morning the work was complete. Charles had transferred the bags from the vault to the coach house – it had taken him two trips. Now they were locked in a travelling trunk, labelled and ready to go to London.

Annabel and Charles were in the drawing room, sipping brandy. He stood leaning against the piano, she sat by the embers of the fire.

"What still concerns me, Anna, is what you would have done had Hurst not agreed to go back for the bracelet?"

"Oh, there was no doubt that he would get it for me. He would do anything for me – you know that. I learned that fact during those last four tedious Thursday afternoons! Anyway, in the remote, very remote, possibility that he refused to take the bracelet, he would still have gone back to look at it, don't you see?"

Her husband thought for a moment, then nodded. "There will be a hue and cry for Hurst tomorrow, or rather later to-day. Not that that will concern us. Lots of scores will be settled around the harbour and in the alleys and back streets at this time of the year. An Inspector of Constabulary will have made plenty of enemies. It will be assumed that his body has been taken out to sea, weighted and dropped over the side.

"We shall have to remember to be suitably horrified." He thought for a moment. "I shall arrange a perfectly splendid memorial service for him. You know the kind of thing – a hero of the Boer War who has given his life for the sake of law and order. It should go down very well indeed.

"Enough of these thoughts, though! What great good

fortune it is that your father is a renowned antiquarian."

"Indeed, yes. I wrote to papa last week saying that I would be over for a week in early January. He will get us the best possible return on the stuff, no questions asked, have no doubt about that!"

Annabel shuddered and drained her brandy. "Do drink up, Charley, I'm getting cold and you've got an early start."

"Right." He stood his empty glass on the piano. Annabel moved round the room turning down the lamps and blowing down their glass chimneys to extinguish the flame. He opened the curtains to see snow billowing and driving in great coiling gusts. "Snow, Anna, heavy snow. Our tracks are covered!"

At the foot of the stairs he paused, took her in his arms and whispered, "Happy Christmas, Anna dear."

"Happy Christmas, Charley, and a very prosperous New Year to us both."

* * *

In September 1910, Annabel gave birth to a girl, the only child the Tillotsons would have.

According to Crockford's Clerical Directory, Charles Tillotson stayed at Lezayre for four years. In 1914 the Bishop of Rochester offered him the parish of St Michael and All Angels, Yalden, in Kent. Charles was appointed a canon of Rochester Cathedral in 1922. He was to remain in this living for the rest of his life.

Charles Tillotson died suddenly of a heart attack on April 18th 1933. His wife found him dead, sitting at his desk. In front of him was his copy of *The Times*, open at an article headed "Old Mystery Likely to be Solved". The report stated that the roof of a vault situated in Lezayre cemetery, in the north of the Isle of Man, had collapsed. While removing the rubble before re-roofing the vault, the workmen had found the body of a man lying on the floor by the door. Judging by the clothing the body was believed to be that of Inspector James Hurst of the Isle of Man Constabulary.

Inspector Hurst disappeared during the Christmas period of 1909 and was, until now, believed to have been murdered and his body disposed of at sea. It was evident that the vault had been stripped of valuables and it was therefore likely that Inspector Hurst had surprised the grave robbers who had killed him before closing up the vault. The Chief Constable of the Isle of Man stated that they would get to the bottom of the mystery and that Inspector Hurst's killers, if still alive, would be caught and would experience the full rigour of the law. "No stone will be left unturned; the person or persons will most certainly be apprehended," he thundered.

❀ March ❀

Prize-winning novelist **Elaine Aulton** lives in the Isle of Man and when she isn't pursuing her first love, writing, can be found patiently teaching the Island's youth.

As well as being a columnist for four years with the *Reading Evening Post* and a finalist and prize-winner of the *Mail on Sunday* novel-writing competition, Elaine has had short stories and articles accepted by various women's magazines under her own name and under her pen name of Ellan Moore.

Elaine is a member of the Douglas based writing group *Skeealleyderyn*.

The carrasdhoo

Elaine Aulton

There was a sharp crack.

"Jed? Where are you, lad?" Cubbon balanced on the apex of the chapel roof, one arm wrapped around an upright of the bell arch. The rough stone was comfort and safety. As long as he held on he wouldn't fall. Where was his apprentice when he needed him? "Jed!"

"Ah, Mr Cubbon," Jed's voice floated up from the steep slope below the chapel. "You've frit them rabbits, now. That stone nearly got one."

Cubbon peered through the darkness, trying to find the boy. From his vantage point he could still see a little in the dying light on the western horizon. But as he looked back, towards Ramsey, he realised the stars were bright against a blue-black sky. The western glow had fooled him into thinking it was still light enough to work.

He inched round on the chapel roof, scraping his forearm on the rough stone. "Ay, Jed. You'll be for it when I come down at you. We could have called an end to fitting this bell. I need you here to see for where I put my feet."

There was a scrambling, and Cubbon could barely distinguish Jed from the looming tombstones. Jed appeared from behind the blackness of the church wall. "It's fair dark, now, Mr Cubbon. Will I watch you?"

"Ay, lad," Cubbon sighed. "You do that." He squinted at the bell, now a darker shadow against the late March sky that had lost almost all its light. The new moon had less glow than the stars. Cubbon reached out and touched the bell, proud of the work he'd done, but disappointed that it wasn't yet complete. All that was left to do was fix the rope-block for threading, then attach the bell rope. And then, like all craftsmen before him, carve his own sign into the stone. But it was too dark now. He carefully slid a foot along the ridge of the chapel.

Jed said, "A bit more, yessir. I think."

"Think?" Cubbon snapped. "Don't you know?"

Jed's voice whined back at him. "It's right dark. I can see you, though."

Cubbon lowered himself to sit astride the ridge. "I'm getting too old for this," he muttered. He swung his leg slowly, feeling for the roped wood that jutted just above the eaves.

A horse neighed, and far off a dog barked. Cubbon's foot knocked the ladder. "Found him," he said. The ladder creaked under his weight with each downward step.

With the creaks, Jed muttered, "About time. All good folks are in their beds 'cept for us. Ma will be worrit."

"What's that? Eh? Are you talking to me?"

The ladder scraped against the wall, then landed with a bounce that made Jed jump back. "No sir."

Cubbon clipped the back of the boy's head and said, "Come on, then. Walk in my steps."

Their footfalls sounded heavy on the packed earth road that wound down from the chapel, between trees and bushes. Jed could only make out where Cubbon was because he made a darker patch in the darkness. Like a faithful dog he scampered after his master. A horse neighed again. "Mr Cubbon, sir, can't you have a horse and cart?"

"Horse *and* cart? Nary even a donkey. I can barely pay your Ma the ha'penny a day for you."

"But if you did have a donkey, we could ride home."

"Ay, and if the fairies granted wishes I'd be King."

Sea surged, and sighed in the air. Jed sniffed the welcoming reek of a peaty hearth fire. They were very close to the coast road. Jed stumbled as they crossed the rutted cart tracks and aimed towards the cottages on the low part of the cliff. The whitewash of the two cottages almost glowed in the dark, ghostly and unreal. Jed still had a handful of stones, and he threw one at the nearest house. The sharp, high crack proved it was real, all right. Cubbon growled a warning.

"They look like ghost houses, yessir."

Cubbon growled again. Jed saw a curtain twitch at the little window under the thatch; a candle lit up the tiny square opening. He quickened his pace.

Cubbon stopped so suddenly that Jed banged into him. "Hear that, lad?"

"Don't know?"

"The sea."

"Ay."

"Listen, lad."

"Ay."

"It's hitting the rock."

Jed strained to hear what his master meant. The sea sighed, then slapped, sighed, then slapped. "Can we do the shore, then, to get home?"

Cubbon moved confidently forward towards the dip in the low cliff, pushing his way between the gorse bushes that grew closely across the path. Jed stayed where he was, safe between the ghostly cottages. He heard Cubbon curse.

"It's right up, lad. Right up. We left it too late to reach Maughold this way."

In disbelief Jed followed Cubbon's voice. The sea glittered with the reflection of the starry sky, and as he reached the older man he could see for himself the immense spread of twinkling black water that reached to the horizon. Maughold Head looked like a sooty stain, solid and black. A bobbing light far out told of a lone ship on the wide sea.

Cubbon laid a hand on Jed's shoulder, but Jed pulled away; angry with the craftsman for making them so late, angry with want for his bed, angry that they would have to take the long way home, up the valley and across the ford in Ballure Glen.

Ballure Glen. He shivered as a prickle of fear crossed over him. "But it's right dark, yessir."

"I shouldn't have ignored the new moon," Cubbon said.

Jed's anger spilled over. "No sir, because it always brings the spring tide and now we must wade across the river in the devil's dark."

Cubbon was silent for a while and the sea sighed and slapped. Finally he spoke. "Be grateful that there be two of us to walk together then, lad."

"But the Carrasdhoo men!"

Cubbon made a coughing sound, then said, "Are you frit of them stories, lad?"

"Not stories. My ma swears they're true. They hide in the marshes, and if any man goes to find them they slit his throat and throw his body in a bog. It happened to my uncle's friend, yessir."

"Is that so?" Cubbon said, giving Jed a gentle push to get him walking again.

"It is. It is. They never found his body, no, my uncle was telling me."

"He told you that, did he?"

"They draw ships onto the rocks, they do."

"You can talk and walk at the same time, lad. Get on."

They retraced their steps through the gorse and between the cottages, and once again found the rutted track. They marched along as best as they could on the uneven ground, heading for Ballure Glen. Jed's words tumbled over one another. "They make a false light and stand high up at the top of the glen. Many a ship coming from the north veers to their light. The Carrasdhoo bring them to the rocks of Gob ny Rona. They don't stand a chance, no sir. The Carrasdhoo kill anyone alive and take everything off the ships. They do. They take it all back up Ballure Glen, and into the secret road to the marshes."

"That would be the secret road your uncle found, would it?"

"Eh?"

Cubbon laughed. "Your uncle's friend, I mean. Him what was murdered and thrown in a bog? And never found?"

"It's true," Jed answered sullenly. "The Carrasdhoo murder folk."

They tramped on for a while, then Cubbon said, "Do you know where the name comes from?" Jed didn't answer, but Cubbon continued anyway. "You know dhoo means black?"

"I'm not daft." His voice still sounded sullen. "The Moddey Dhoo, from Peel Castle, means 'black dog'."

"Ay. But it's their hearts what is black. And Carras is another way of saying 'curragh'. You know what curragh means?"

"Yessir, Mr Cubbon. Bog or marsh." He breathed in sharply, and added with excitement, "It's true then. It means the black-hearted men of the marshes."

"I reckon."

Trees loomed over the road as it dipped towards the river.

Jed liked it in the daytime, the green gloom was always cool and inviting after the sun. Now it was just blackness before them.

The water spilled down the valley between steep banks. Wild garlic grew profusely, and when Jed trod on the leaves, the pungent scent filled the air. The smell guided them, because in the full dark they couldn't make out what was tree, or bush, or rock, or where the rushing water was at all.

"Eh, lad, my own father told me stories of the Carrasdhoo when I was younger than you." They stumbled resolutely on, their steps becoming more cramped in order to find their way. "Think on, he was told by *his* father. And that would make the Carrasdhoo men mighty old."

"But this is where they live."

"Ay. In stories. But has anyone you know ever seen them? With his own wide-open eyes?" There was no reply. "You know what folks say they did when the wrecking was poor?"

"No."

"Back by yon road into Ramsey, there's an ale-house."

"Ay."

"Well, it is said that the murderous tribe would wait for a stranger to enter through the door." His voice lowered, became more conspiratorial. "They would watch the stranger, and one or two would befriend him. They would fetch him a tankard of ale."

In spite of himself, Jed was intrigued. "But why? I thought they was wicked."

"They would fetch the stranger a tankard of ale, and the one who did the fetching would put something in it. Are you listening?"

"Ay."

"The stranger would fall from his stool. 'Dead drunk,' said the others. And 'Ay,' the Carrasdhoo would say, and drag him away. 'To his home,' they would say." Cubbon paused.

"And, did they?"

"They would drag him away, but not to his home. Oh no. They would drag the unfortunate soul into the back room where the trapdoor opens into the deep, dark cellar. Then, they would … shhht! Slice his neck from ear to ear."

Jed halted, sudden fear making his heart pump. Cubbon continued, "They robbed the stranger of all he had, then pushed his murdered body through the trap. So my father told me."

"But," Jed's voice came out as a whisper, "if they catch us in their glen, we're done for."

Jed jumped when Cubbon suddenly grabbed his shoulder. "We need to stay close, lad. Two pairs of eyes."

Anger towards Cubbon prickled under his skin, and he deliberately stepped forward without knowing how safe his step would be. His foot dipped far lower than he thought and if it hadn't been for Cubbon holding on to him, he would have sprawled headfirst into the river. He stood with water swirling almost up to his knee. The shock of it dissolved his tension. "We're at the river, yessir."

Cubbon chuckled, and said, "Ay, the splash you made told me that. Good thing there's two of us. How deep?"

"To my knee."

"And the next step?"

Jed dutifully stepped forward. "Below."

"Stand there, lad. I'll come and lead."

Cubbon stepped heavily into the water, still keeping a hand on Jed's shoulder. "By, it's cold," he complained. He splashed past him, and then pulled him on, slowly.

"Now, lad, we can't use us eyes."

"No."

"So feel the water on your legs."

"Ay?"

"Turn about," Cubbon said, putting pressure on Jed's shoulder to show what he meant. "Feel the water agin your shin?"

"Ay," realisation showed in Jed's voice.

"Good lad. You won't end up wading up or down river and losing the bank."

"Yessir," Jed said with enthusiasm. "That's clever."

"When I was a lad I was not. I learned my lesson the hard way, and got a thrashing for my pains."

They laughed together as they crossed the ford.

It was a steep climb and Cubbon was winded before they breasted the rise. Jed's feet and legs were cold and ached, and he was grateful to stop for the older man. They leaned against broad tree trunks, listening to the scurrying of unseen animals in the undergrowth. An owl hooted, and then they heard a commotion.

Muted voices, indistinguishable from each other, low whistles and rustling.

"What – ?"

Cubbon put his hand across Jed's mouth. "Shh," he whispered, "take care."

Jed whispered back, "But who … ?"

"Ay, lad, who indeed?" He pulled Jed down into a crouch, and they crept as quietly as they could towards the people making the noise.

As they climbed higher they saw figures silhouetted against the skyline. One of them was swinging something that flamed.

Jed's teeth chattered and he groaned, "The Carrasdhoo."

"It can't be."

"Mr Cubbon?"

"I don't know, lad."

"No. Look out there." Jed clutched the man's elbow. The lights of the ship he'd seen earlier were bobbing about on the sea, close to the inky black rocks off Maughold.

They peered at the ship, and then Cubbon pulled Jed down into the undergrowth. "They're misdirecting the ship."

"What?"

"They're wreckers. If the ship comes this way it'll hit the rocks."

Jed stared back up the slope to the men silhouetted there. And gasped.

"Mr Cubbon," he whispered. "Look at them. Look."

The fiery lantern still swung, but as each man stood against the starry sky the stars could be seen through them. Jed watched them as if hypnotised.

"Jed," Cubbon whispered, "get help."

"But ... how?"

"I don't understand how the Carrasdhoo men are here, but the ship is real enough."

"You said they weren't real," Jed pleaded.

The sounds from the men on the rise changed. Jed watched in horror as two dozen transparent faces turned towards their hiding place.

Hot breath whispered into his ear. "Hurry, lad. Save that ship."

Jed slithered backwards, allowing the undergrowth to swallow him. His heart hammered as he saw the phantom Carrasdhoo sweeping the hillside with their gaze. Menace rolled through the air and turned Jed's skin to ice.

He slid, scrambled and fell downwards, scraping skin from his hands, knees and chin. The river splashed loudly, covering the sounds of his escape, for Jed knew he was running for his life. But Mr Cubbon? He had to find help. The two cottages.

Jed's foot caught in a root and he hurtled forwards. He flung his hands out, but instead of hitting the ground he landed in the river, taking a mouthful and choking for air. He scrambled onto his hands and knees. The water forced past him. How was the river this close? He drew in a ragged breath, and stood. He'd lost his bearings. He waded a step, then kicked a submerged rock and fell into the water again. No. He must get help. He held his arms out for balance and remembered what Cubbon had said – the river was racing up the back of his knees, so that meant he was facing towards the sea. He made a half-turn and took a hesitant step, the sound of the river crashing in his ears. Had the Carrasdhoo men followed him? In panic he took another blind step, feeling the rush of water coming from his right.

Wrong way.

Jed turned to face the opposite direction. When the river tried to push him from the left he plunged forward, confident of making the Ramsey bank. He slipped and skidded, and then fell into the muddy ruts of the coast road.

His breath came in quick gasps as he tried to hurry along the barely visible track. The cottages. Get to the cottages.

Long stems whipped against his shins, brambles snared his skin and clung there. Time and distance became confused. He became deadly certain that he'd been stumbling along much further than he should have. Had he missed the cottages? He stopped, bewildered, made a slow turn trying to force his eyes to see a landmark. He heard a hooting that no owl ever made, and that made him lurch forwards. Somehow, Jed lost the track. His legs told him he was going upwards, and he stumbled over hummocky grass, praying that he was heading the right way.

Up ahead, glooming palely in the starlight was a wall. A cottage. Jed ran forwards and smashed into a drystone wall that stood between him and the whitewashed building. Pain shot through his face like lightning, and the iron taste of blood filled his mouth. He spat, then cupped his hands over his nose. It was bleeding. His knee burned. Fighting back tears of pain and fear he held his bloodied hands out sightlessly. The wall curved away. Confused, he followed it, the rough stone edges grating his palms. A rabbit hole twisted his foot, and he fell against the wall. Could he climb it? With effort he pulled himself up and got one arm across the top of the wall. Jed almost screamed, and jumped back down.

The Carrasdhoo were waiting for him. They were standing there. On the other side. Just standing there. He was dead. He tried to hold his breath to listen for them coming, but there was nothing. Nothing. Except his ragged breathing. A memory nudged, and he realised where he was. Back at the chapel. It was the looming tombstones he'd seen.

Jed sobbed out in frustration. From here he'd have to find the path down the other side of the hill, then find the cottages – and what was happening to Mr Cubbon? And the ship? And the ghostly Carrasdhoo men?

Jed used the wall to guide him, chanting, "Please God, Please God," with each snatched breath. The wall curved sharply towards the door of the chapel, and ended. Jed moved between the tombstones, heading for the porch. The bell. That would wake the families in the cottages. The bell would call for help.

Jed grabbed hold of the iron ring that lifted the heavy latch. And stopped. The cold iron soothed his painful hands, but he barely noticed because he'd remembered. He sagged against the door, defeated. "No bell rope," he mumbled. "No-o-o."

Tears sprang to his eyes. "Please God, help us." He dragged himself out of the chapel porch in the direction of the winding path and kicked Cubbon's ladder that lay on the ground. He fell awkwardly, landing on his hands and knees, his palms grating on loose stones.

Stones.

"Thank you," he said as he clenched his fist around them. Jed weighed some of the biggest, ignoring the stinging in his palm where it was scraped raw. He climbed over the ladder and followed the wall. Nearly there.

As he reached the corner of the chapel he pushed his way into the bushes, where the ground sloped away. There it was. Outlined against the starry sky, almost like a doorway above the chapel roof, was the bell arch. Inside it, in solid silhouette, he could see the bell. This was no phantom. In the dark night, with his eyes fixed firmly on the bell, he pushed further back into the gorse until he was satisfied he was at the right distance. To one side of the bell arch, on the horizon, the distant flaming lantern glowed orange. Jed roughly swabbed the blood from his nose and wiped his hand on the front of his jacket. He took one stone, aimed, and with a flick of his wrist, threw.

★ ★ ★

Cubbon could barely breathe. "I'm not frit, I'm not frit," he kept telling himself. Above, the Carrasdhoo were whistling and owl-calling to one another. Cubbon could hear them thrashing about, getting closer. Sweat poured down his face, stinging his eyes. He heard a whisper. A laugh. A swish of something cutting through undergrowth. And still the flaring lantern swung back and forth on the skyline. Suddenly, one of the Carrasdhoo hooted, very close to his hiding place. Cubbon crossed himself – how could phantoms be this real?

He tried to hold his breath. Fear made sweat trickle down his back, down his sides. Jeering laughter. He trembled as the ghostly hooting came closer. Closer. A deep, sinister laugh sounded only inches away from him. Cubbon shrank away, covering his head with his arms.

A bell rang out. One note.

The sounds stopped. Cubbon cowered, waiting for the inevitable. They'd found him.

★   ★   ★

The bell rang out again, clear and pure. And again. And again.

Jed, at the chapel, whooped with elation, throwing his stones in victory. He'd seen the swinging flame on the hillside wink out when his first stone hit its mark. The feeling of menace disappeared too. When his last stone rang the bell, Jed limped painfully back the way he'd come. He had to find his master.

The cart track seemed longer and rougher, but the night seemed softer, somehow. Each time he licked his sore top lip the metal of his blood made his stomach jump. The Carrasdhoo had come – and he had sent them back. Tiredness in his body made his feet heavy, but his heart was light with excitement.

The heavy garlic scent told him when he approached the ford. This time he was confident. He let his nose, ears and feet lead him across, and when he gained the Maughold bank he grinned and spat blood.

"Mr Cubbon, sir?" he called. He stopped to listen. Above the sound of the river behind him, he heard a faint moan.

"Is that you, Mr Cubbon? It's me, Jed. Come back."

The moan came again. Jed followed the sound, and found his master crouched in the bushes at the base of the trees. He reached out to touch him.

"No," whimpered Cubbon.

Jed squatted down in front of him. "It's all right now, yessir. The Carrasdhoo have gone. Vanished away, they did, when the chapel bell pealed." He gently touched the old man's trembling arm. "They've gone."

"You ... *you* did ring him?"

"Ay," Jed said. "Like skelping rabbits. I skelped a stone to the bell."

Cubbon cautiously raised his head. He peered first at Jed, then he twisted around. There was nothing on the skyline. Nothing except the vast expanse of stars.

"Shall we get home then?" Jed asked.

Cubbon nodded, but didn't move. Jed wrapped an arm around the old man and helped him up. Cubbon cleared his throat and croaked out, "With my own wide-open eyes, I saw. Didn't I, Jed?"

"We did, yessir. We did." They scrambled together out of the undergrowth. Jed said, "Shall we get us a drink of water from the river?"

"Ay."

At the ford they scooped up handfuls of water and splashed their faces, then drank. Cubbon said again, "With my own wide-open eyes. I saw, didn't I?"

"Nowt but phantoms." Jed put his hand on his master's shoulder. "We have us own story, yessir. Now, let's get on. Will you walk in my steps, Mr Cubbon? We'll set our feet for home."

Cubbon patted the hand on his shoulder. "Ay, lad. Ay."

* * *

The chapel at Ballure has been called St Mary's, and St Catherine's, and it's been neglected to the point of dereliction. A few years ago an enterprising builder bought it from the Church and converted it into a house. The workers found a craftsman's sign carved into the bell arch, but no one knew when it was carved. Or who had carved it.

There are many tales of the chapel being haunted. Ghostly singing in the early hours; footsteps that sound the length of the floor and stop at the wall; faint organ music that stops the second the door is opened.

Yet, every year, in the month of March when the new moon is the slenderest sliver in the sky; when the last glow of setting sun has gone; when full dark has descended upon the Isle – the bell rings.

April

Steve Westcott lives in Sulby on the Isle of Man with his wife and two children. He began writing ten years ago and is currently in the process of completing the third book in the Black Dragon trilogy. His first book *Reluctant Heroes*, originally published in 2003, has recently been reprinted by FrontList Books and the second book in the series *Cronan the Librarian*, also published by FrontList, was launched in March 2008 and is available online and from all good bookshops. The prequel to the trilogy, *Bruvvers in Arms*, is scheduled for release at the end of 2008.

Steve is gaining a growing reputation amongst fantasy sci-fi fans both in the UK and the USA and has contributed to two other print anthologies, *Deeper Magic* and *A Twist of Fate*. He has also sold a number of short stories to net-based e-zines.

April's Fool

Steve Westcott

A wave of white heat blasted from the furnace as the secondary burners ignited. Standing on the observation deck, high above the controlled conflagration, General Dawson shielded his eyes with a hand. Even three layers of tinted plasplex screen could not fully protect him from the effects of the burner. "Is it always this hot?" he asked the military scientist standing beside him, feeling moist patches spring to life beneath his arms. He tugged a finger under the collar of his shirt.

The scientist nodded, then pushed thick-rimmed spectacles back to the bridge of his nose with the pencil from his clipboard. The bald expanse of flesh on his head, fringed by woolly brown hair, glistened with perspiration.

Turning his head, General Dawson fixed him with a penetrative stare, smirking as the man shrank back. "Is that the last of it?"

The scientist nodded. "That is the last of the returned stock, General. Destroyed, as ordered."

The General nodded, then frowned. "That is not what I asked, Sheldrake. Is that the last of it?"

Giving a nervous smile, Sheldrake avoided the General's gaze. "It would appear ... that is to say ... erm ..."

"Out with it, man! I haven't got all day!"

Sheldrake swallowed nervously. "I am reliably informed there is another consignment out in the field. One that was ... ah, overlooked."

Overlooked? General Dawson was momentarily dumbstruck. His orders had been most specific. All stock of MTX was to be returned at once, for immediate disposal. And now it would appear that a consignment had been overlooked? It could prove calamitous, especially if the damn stuff became unstable. Heaven only knew what the consequences would be if that happened. Leaning forward until his face was merely inches away from Sheldrake's, he jabbed him in the chest with a forefinger. "Well you had better un-overlook it immediately – understood? If not, it will be you roasting in the damn furnace!"

Without waiting for a response, he strode to the door to punch in the access code. As soon as the smoked-glass panel slid open, he stepped outside and turned to face Sheldrake. "You have a week to get it here and destroy it, otherwise looking for another form of employment will be the least of your problems."

Sheldrake breathed a sigh of relief as the click of the General's boot heels faded. After a quick glance in the direction of the furnace he rammed his pencil into the top pocket of his lab coat, then quickly made his way to the room's wall-mounted telephone. The fingers of his left hand beat an impatient tattoo on the smoked-glass wall as he waited for the receptionist to answer. When she eventually did, he snapped, "Get me Captain Selbourne, immediately! I don't care what bloody time it is. I want him now. Understand?"

Before the girl had a chance to say 'Yes, Sir,' he slammed

the receiver back into its cradle. The plastic holder snapped on impact. With a clatter, the receiver bounced against the glass wall and began to swing on its flex. Sheldrake stared at it in fascination as an image of a body dangling from a noose sprang to mind. A hand rose to rub at his neck. Not usually given to superstition, he hoped it was not a premonition of things to come.

★ ★ ★

Headlamps blazing, the covered Bedford TM hurtled along the mountain road, kamikaze moths splattering against its windscreen, drums of redundant chemicals crashing around in the back. Twin beams of light bisected the darkness and illuminated the road ahead, but did little to aid the cloud-shrouded moon in lighting the surrounding countryside. Willy Clague did not need daylight to tell him what awaited them should they leave the road, however. He had travelled this way many times and knew that to their left was a large embankment, to their right a steep drop to the valley below and directly ahead, a sharp ...

"*Slow down, Juan!*" Willy gripped the handle above the door with his left hand and braced his other against the dashboard. "*There's a bleedin'–*" He screamed, cringed and squeezed his eyes closed, fearing the worst as the wagon slewed around the bend. The wheels screeched in protest as they fought to maintain traction.

Cigar clamped between his teeth, Juan cackled in delight, gripped the wheel more tightly and wrestled the wagon back into line. "What's the matter? Not scared of a little speed, are yer, feller?"

Willy had to shout to make himself heard over the roar of the engine and the pounding of his heart, which threatened to burst through his ribcage. "N-n-no. Bend caught me by surprise, is all."

"Glad to hear it!" Juan cackled again, and floored the accelerator.

The wagon increased its speed, to bounce and career along the undulating surface at a terrifying rate. Willy groaned. They had at least another twenty minutes to travel before they reached the ferry and he was already feeling ill. Juan 'Madcap' Maddrell was living up to his name on this run, that was for sure.

When the lads on the yard had been told one of them had to accompany Madcap on the 'night-run' they had drawn lots to decide which poor mug would be the one to go with him. As the only luck Willy ever seemed to have was bad, it was he who pulled the ace of spades from the pack. He glanced at Juan, the owner of the haulage business, whose eyes were bright and unblinking as he gunned the Bedford down the mountain road, and grimaced. Out of fifty remaining cards, he had to have drawn the one that placed him with this maniac.

As if reading his thoughts, Juan looked his way and grinned, the dull glow of the cigar reflecting off tartar-stained teeth. "Bet you we get there and back before the Easter Bunny visits. What's the wager?"

Willy swallowed the bile that had risen in his throat at the thought of chocolate. He felt nauseous and was sure he would puke instead of speak if he answered. Even so, he managed to croak, "Eyes on the road, gaffer," before gagging.

Madcap laughed. "Don't worry, I drive by Braille. I'll know soon enough if we get near the edge. Now, what's the wager?" His arctic-blue eyes held a manic gleam as he waited for an answer.

Before Willy could respond, something caught his eye; reflected light in the middle of the road ahead. He turned to look. His mouth dropped open. *"Juan!"* he yelled. "Watch out for the –"

thud!

"Rabbit."

Madcap hammered on the brakes and the wagon skidded to a halt, trails of burnt rubber marking the road behind. Hands still gripping the wheel, he stared blankly ahead. "What'd I hit?"

"A-a-a rabbit."

The cigar dropped from Madcap's mouth to the footwell as he turned to stare at Willy. "Y-you mean I killed a … a rabbit?"

Meeting his gaze, Willy swallowed, and hesitantly dipped his head.

Tears formed in Madcap's eyes and his mouth dropped open. Leaning forward, he lowered his head to the steering wheel. "I killed a rabbit," he murmured, shoulders shaking. He began to tap his forehead against the wheel. "I killed a rabbit."

Unsure what to do, Willy stared at the shaking figure for a moment, then said, "You all right? It was only a rabbit."

Madcap shot upright and glared at Willy, eyes wild, face contorted by rage. "Only a rabbit?"

Although softly spoken, the words held a hint of hysteria, and Willy slunk back against the door in fear.

"Only a rabbit? As a devout vegan and me being the Grand Master of Ramsey's Power to the Animals Brigade, how do you think that makes me feel? Hey?" He leaned forward menacingly. "Sick, that's what. Sick to the bloody stomach!"

Willy gulped, and gave a nervous smile. "With any luck it might just be stunned."

Madcap's eyes widened and his demeanour relaxed. "Stunned? You're right. It'll be stunned." So saying, he leaned away, stamped out the smouldering cigar on the dash, and pushed open the driver's door. "Come and help me look for it.

It'll need help. Grab the first aid kit before you come out." Snatching a torch from behind his seat, he thumbed on the light and began to trek back the way they had travelled, the narrow beam of light from the torch flicking to and fro across the road.

It took a moment before Willy could summon the will to move. Madcap's mood swings had unnerved him. Realising that dallying might encourage further demented behaviour, he opened the door, stepped out and grabbed the torch and first aid kit from behind his seat before following.

The moon, having partially escaped its shroud, lent its assistance to the search by casting a pale, silvery light across the road. Under its ghostly glow, Willy spotted Juan's portly, broad-shouldered figure twenty paces back down the road, stepping slowly forward, head lowered as he scanned the road for sign of the injured rabbit.

Quickening his pace, Willy caught up with him and added his beam to the search. Two minutes later he spotted a still form. "Over there!" He shone the light on the small, furry, prostrate bunny.

A strangled groan escaped Madcap's lips and he darted forward. Kneeling, he placed his torch on the ground before scooping the rabbit to cradle it to his chest before looking up, eyes gleaming. "It's alive."

Willy breathed a sigh of relief. Perhaps now they could continue to the Steampacket in peace. He frowned as he stared down at the duo. Something was not quite right. "Juan?"

Madcap looked up. "Hmmm?"

"Why's the bunny wearing a bonnet?"

"A bonnet? You been at the whiskey, boy?"

Willy shook his head and shone his torch onto the rabbit's head. Confident his eyes had not deceived him, he said, "Definitely a bonnet. Look for yourself, if you don't believe me!"

Madcap looked down, and gaped. Perched between the rabbit's ears was a white bonnet, tied under its chin by a red ribbon.

"You're bloody well right. It must be someone's pet. Good job we came back for it. Some poor sod will be missing this feller, that's for sure." He rubbed a calloused finger against the rabbit's cheek. "Cute, isn't he?"

Willy frowned. The only rabbits he'd ever appreciated were in a stew, but he somehow doubted Madcap wanted to hear that.

Madcap rose to his feet, the rabbit still cradled to his chest, and began to walk back to the wagon. "Grab my torch. We'd best get this one to the vet."

Willy stooped to pick up the torch, and paused in the act of straightening as the beam shone on a battered lump and some smaller objects scattered in the middle of the road some ten paces away. Puzzled, he went to investigate. "*Juan!*" he yelled, once he'd identified the objects. "You'd better come and see this!"

Waiting for Madcap to join him, he surveyed the objects again, just to make sure he was not seeing things. But he wasn't. On the tarmac before him lay a squashed wicker basket, and ten small chocolate Easter Eggs. The silhouette of a bonnet-wearing bunny was stencilled on each foil wrapper.

Twenty minutes later they arrived at the harbour, the remainder of their journey having been completed at a relatively sedate pace. To Willy's surprise, two armed soldiers greeted them, and directed them to an enclosed compound across from the offices. Once inside, Juan killed the ignition and vaulted out to sprint to the rear of the wagon.

Willy closed his eyes and leaned back in his seat to breathe a sigh of relief. They were here, and in one piece, which was more than could be said for the rabbit. He very much doubted whether the creature still lived. He shook his head. Madcap would never forgive himself if it died. A crooked smile formed on his face. And wouldn't that look good in the Indy? He could picture the headlines now: 'Ramsey's Grand Master of Animals squashes Easter Bunny'. Chuckling, he opened the door and slid out of the seat to the ground. Forcing a solemn expression onto his face, he walked to the back of the wagon and peered inside.

Swaddled in some old blankets and surrounded by the drums of redundant chemicals they'd picked up from a hangar at Jurby, lay the Easter Bunny. Madcap sat on the tailgate beside it, stroking its ears. The rabbit's nose twitched at the attention, and Madcap smiled. "It's alive," he murmured, looking up.

Willy gave a hesitant grin. "What's that green ick around its mouth? It's not rabid, is it?" He stepped back, just in case.

Madcap peered at the rabbit and frowned. After unfolding the blankets that enveloped it, he wiped its mouth with a finger and then lowered his head to sniff at the goo. "Smells like Metatrixacote. But how the hell did that stuff get here?" He sniffed it again and grimaced. "It bloody well is." He wiped his finger on the edge of a blanket. "It's bloody dangerous, that stuff."

Metatrixacote? Willy had never head of it. "Why? What's it do?"

"Army stuff. Top secret like. Some sort of nerve reagent, I heard. But it proved too unstable so the army decided to destroy all the stock." He scowled. "Yet another expensive balls-up swept under the carpet. And the island used as a convenient dump – again. There was uproar when we found out some of the stuff had been sent over here. Thought they'd shipped the lot back years ago."

Willy's eyes were drawn to the metal drum immediately

behind where the rabbit lay. The central seam had corroded and, from a point near its top, green slime oozed. Faded letters on the side of the drum read, 'Metatrixacote Concentrate – handle with extreme caution'.

"Er, Juan."

Madcap looked up, and Willy nodded toward the drum.

Squinting, Madcap mouthed the words to himself, then said, "Bloody hell. No one told me we were hauling this stuff." He peered down at the rabbit. Light reflected off the green slime staining its mouth.

As if sensing it was being observed, the rabbit opened its eyes, and Madcap grinned, green slime momentarily forgotten.

Whether it was a trick of the light, Willy was not sure, but the rabbit's eyes appeared to glow with a luminous green radiance under the floodlights, the pupils a darker green and in the shape of what looked like a flattened rabbit. Willy frowned. A flattened rabbit? All thoughts of the strange phenomenon fled, however, when the rabbit emitted harsh barks and leapt from the blankets to launch itself at Madcap's throat.

Screaming in alarm, Madcap tumbled from the back of the wagon, hands attempting to tear the bunny from his neck as he thrashed around on the ground. But the rabbit clung on, teeth firmly embedded in flesh, and refused to be budged.

Willy was frozen with shock at the ferocity of the attack. Shaking off his paralysis, he grabbed the nearest weapon available, and advanced. Had he paused to think through his action he would have searched for a more appropriate club before launching his attack, but seeing as time was of the essence and reaction had kicked in, he was stuck with what he had grabbed. Adjusting his posture so that the target was in the middle of his stance, he squared his shoulders to the objective – a clear parcel of land some ninety yards distant – kept his head still and eased his arms back. Ensuring that the club connected at the right instant, he powered through, completing his arc to perfection.

A shrill cry escaped the bunny's lips as it looped through the air to land slightly right of the intended landing area. Willy cursed. He thought he'd cured his slice.

Madcap groaned.

Tossing aside the pitching wedge, Willy scrambled to Madcap's side and eased his hands under the man's head. Blood pumped from a wound to the side of his Adam's apple. Willy swore. It was a deep one, edged with green slime.

"What's goin' on 'ere?"

Willy looked up and met the steely gaze of one of the guards who had been at the gate. His hand rested on his holstered pistol, and he surveyed the scene with narrowed eyes.

"It's Madcap. He's been injured."

"Injured?" The guard moved closer and peered down. He frowned when he spotted the wound, then glanced at the discarded pitching wedge whilst easing the flap free of the holster. "How?"

Willy gulped. How could he explain this one? How would anyone believe what he had just seen without having seen it themselves? Nervous, he licked at dry lips and glanced to where the bunny had landed, but it had gone.

The pistol slid clear of the guard's holster. "Move away, son. I don't want to have to use this."

By the look in the man's cold eyes, Willy knew that, in reality, he did. After laying Madcap's head on the ground, he slowly straightened and backed away, arms raised. "It's not what you think. Honest!"

The guard waved his pistol, indicating for Willy to step further back. Willy complied, and the guard knelt on the ground to press fingers against Madcap's neck. At his touch, Madcap's eyes flew open. A feral snarl escaped his lips and he launched himself at the startled guard, who shrieked as teeth sank into his neck.

For the second time that night, Willy stood immobile, transfixed by the attack.

Alerted by the shout, the second guard sprinted into view, fumbling with his holster. On spotting the assault he grabbed his pistol and fired into the air, its sharp retort echoing through the night.

"Get yer filthy hands off him or the next shot's for you!"

At the sound, Madcap looked up, blood staining the fur around his snout, nose twitching in annoyance.

Willy felt his jaw drop. Agape, he stood and stared. Since when had Madcap had long pointy ears, a snout and buck teeth?

A series of short, sharp barks issued from Madcap's mouth. Then, turning, he flicked out his legs in contempt before making good his escape.

Too stunned by what he had seen, the second guard could only stand and stare as the six-foot white rabbit, bob-tail poking through ripped trousers, hopped rapidly from sight. And so the tableau would have remained if the attacked guard had not cried out in pain.

Willy looked down, and shrank back in fear. The man's ears were growing longer and white fur had appeared on a previously clean-shaven jaw. Low growls came from the man's mouth which, strangely, seemed to be altering position on his face as his nose flattened and grew. With a shrill cry, the guard rolled onto his stomach. His back arched and he bunched his legs beneath him, the seam of his trousers splitting to reveal a fluffy white tail. With a powerful thrust of his legs, he too bounded away, turning once to bark at the two men before following the route Madcap had taken.

"W-what's happening?" asked the second guard, staring at

the spot where the two men had hopped from sight.

Willy staggered a pace and dropped to his knees. Leaning forward, he pressed palms to the ground and took deep, calming breaths. Even after witnessing the night's events firsthand, he could not believe what he had seen. And he somehow doubted anyone else would. There were not many people over the age of ten who believed in the Easter Bunny; what chance them believing he now had two six-foot assistants?

* * *

Standing stiffly to attention, as he had seen his escort do, Willy stared at the photograph hanging on the wall behind Captain Selbourne's desk, waiting for the explosion that was bound to come. A bead of sweat ran between his eyes. Suppressing the instinct to wipe it away, he concentrated on the picture, but it did no good. It was of the Captain himself, taken next to a shelled-out building, and the image returned Willy's gaze with cold, haunted eyes. The caption under the photograph read, 'Bosnia'.

The silence stretched uncomfortably and still Captain Selbourne gave no indication as to his thoughts, even though Willy could feel his eyes boring into him. The bead of sweat was joined by another. The swelled droplet rolled down to dangle off the end of his nose where it stopped, contemplating suicide. At Captain Selbourne's sudden, sharp command, it made its decision and splashed to the timbered floor.

"Corporal! Report confirmation?"

Standing beside Willy, Corporal Davis snapped to attention. Eyes staring straight ahead, he said, "Report correct, Sir! Corporal Johnson and Juan Clague are now bunnies, Sir!"

Captain Selbourne's chair clattered back as he rose to his feet to lean forward, hands splayed on the desk top, to glare at the soldier. "Is this a joke, Corporal?"

"No, Sir!" he answered, reddening.

"Permission to speak, er, Sir!" said Willy.

Captain Selbourne nodded.

"Before he … Juan changed, he mentioned Metatrixacote. And the Eas– … er … rabbit had swallowed some before he attacked him."

Captain Selbourne's eyes widened and he visibly wilted. Breathing heavily through his nose, he slumped to his seat. "At ease." He shook his head and raised his hands to rub at tired eyes. Then, steepling his fingers, he tapped at pursed lips and gazed into the space between Willy and Corporal Davis. After a second or two he came to a decision and rose. "Davis, don full chemical protective equipment and mount the truck. Take my aides with you" He turned to Willy. "You, come with me."

"Sir?"

"What is it, Davis?"

"What do I tell them, Sir?"

Captain Selbourne considered the question for a moment, then said, "Tell them we are tracking down two thieves, Corporal. Tell them that two drug-crazed hippies dressed in rabbit costumes broke into the wagon and stole dangerous bio-chemicals. Warn them that on no account are they to allow themselves to be bitten by these two … druggies, that they should approach with caution and, if unable to subdue, shoot to kill. We do not want this, this … contamination to spread."

Willy was dumbstruck. Contamination? Shoot to kill? This was the Isle of Man, for heaven's sake, not the Wild West. "Sh– sh– shouldn't we inform the relevant authorities, Sir?"

Captain Selbourne fixed him with an icy glare. "And tell them what? That a group of towering, vampiritic rabbits are on the loose?" He shook his head. "I think not. In this instance, *we* are the relevant party."

★   ★   ★

George Harris was unaware he was being observed as he piled the last of his Easter eggs on the central display stand. Stepping away from his creation, he placed knuckles in the small of his back and stretched. His shoulders popped. Wincing, he rolled them to ease the pain. He was getting too old for this. Running a shop was a young man's work; it was getting near time he retired. He stared at the massive pile of Easter eggs, and sighed. He would never shift that little lot in a day. Yet again he would lose out. Running a small shop was not the profitable enterprise it was before the supermarkets snaffled all the trade. He was hard-pressed to earn a decent wage, never mind a profit. Maybe the 'three for two' offer would shift them. Or maybe the Easter Bunny would hop by and buy the lot off him. Chuckling at the thought, he shuffled to the counter to retrieve the key from inside the till. It was eleven-thirty and way past time he was closed. Not that he had anyone to go upstairs to. Mrs Harris had passed away years ago.

Arthritic fingers fumbled with the key as he scrabbled to remove it from its compartment, and it dropped to the floor. Cursing, he bent to retrieve it. The bell above the entrance tinkled. In rising to see who entered, he cracked his head against the counter. Stars danced before his eyes, and he winced, a hand rising to massage the injured spot. "Can I help you?" he asked, taking care to avoid the counter as he straightened to meet the luminous green-tinged gaze of ... a rabbit?

"Give ush your Eashter eggsh!"

It *was* a rabbit! A rather big one at that. Standing at least six feet tall, it towered over George who, at five-foot-four, was used to staring up at people. But a rabbit? Smoking a cigar? This was a totally new, if not unique, experience. "P-p-pardon?" he heard himself say.

"Give ush your Eashter eggsh! Now." The rabbit took a toke on the cigar and exhaled the acrid smoke into George's face.

"I got 'em!" another voice chimed in.

George looked across the small store to where he had built his Easter egg mound. His jaw dropped as he saw yet another towering furry bunny.

Just when he thought things could get no worse, a more conventional sized bunny came into view, wearing a rather fetching white bonnet. It hopped toward the egg pile, chittering and squeaking. The larger bunny looked down. "Yesh, bossh!" Turning, it said, "Need bagsh. Lotsh of bagsh. Carry Eggsh."

"Bagsh!" said the bunny at the counter.

This was too much for George to take. His eyes rolled into his head and he swooned. The last thing he saw before darkness claimed him was a small white rabbit, white bonnet awry, pink nose twitching as it peered down at him.

Some time later – maybe an hour, maybe two, George had no way of knowing – he felt rough hands grip his shoulders to shake him, but he refused to be roused. He much preferred the safety of unconsciousness. At least there the rabbits could not get at him. The hands shook him again. An image of a towering, man-eating rabbit sprang to mind, and he screamed. He screamed again when he opened his eyes and saw the alien stooped over him, silver suit sparkling in the shop's fluorescent lighting and a large, single black eye in the middle of its headgear. Scrambling back, he sought refuge against the shelves behind the counter.

"Easy," a muffled voice said to the alien that had been stooped over George. "He's scared."

Scared? Too right he was scared. Who wouldn't be? Another silver-suited figure strode around the counter. "W-what do you want with me?" George heard himself ask, flicking his gaze between the two figures.

"Information," said the second alien.

George gave a hesitant smile, convinced it came out more like a grimace. "You got the wrong man. I'm just a poor shop-keeper. I don't know nothing." His head shook from side to side as he said the words, to emphasise his point.

One of the aliens sighed, then said, "I am Captain Selbourne and this" – he pointed to the man who had previously been stooped over him – "is Willy."

George flicked his gaze between the two aliens – men – again, and sagged in relief.

Moving forward, Willy helped him to his feet.

"Now, the information. Have you seen anything strange? Something that seemed …" He appeared unsure as to how to continue. "Abnormal?"

"Like six-foot bunnies?" George offered, with a nervous laugh.

"You've seen them?" said Willy.

George nodded.

"When?" demanded the captain.

George glanced to the clock on the wall at the rear of the shop. It said twelve thirty-five. "About an hour ago." His gaze fixed on his display stand, now devoid of anything resembling Easter eggs. "They've gone!"

Willy looked around. "What's gone?"

"The eggs," wailed George. "They've taken all the Easter eggs." He leaned on the counter in dejection and buried his head in his hands. "Five hundred pounds worth of stock gone, just like that."

"Eggs?" Captain Selbourne turned to Willy. "You know what this means?"

Willy shook his head.

"They mean to contaminate the eggs and feed them to the

86

kids."

Willy gasped. "Why?"

"Contaminate?" queried George, looking up.

Without answering either question, Captain Selbourne turned and made his way to the entrance, gesturing for Willy to follow him. Before leaving, he turned to George, and said, "Drug addicts. Fancy dress, and all that. You understand?"

George didn't, but nodded anyway.

"Send the bill for the stolen eggs to the nearest army base. I will see that it is paid, plus a bonus for your trouble."

Now that part George did understand. When the door closed on their exit, he grabbed the key for the door and hurried across to lock it. After this night's escapade, he did not fancy having any more late night callers. Turning off the lights to the shop, he made his way up the stairs to the flat above. So it was drug addicts in fancy dress, hey? That explained a lot, especially their slurred speech. He frowned as his thoughts turned to the small bunny with the bonnet. How on earth could someone fit into a costume that small, unless they were a pygmy? Shaking his head in mystification, he shuffled along the corridor to his bedroom. It must have been his eyes that deceived him. Things like that happen when you got old, he decided. And at the moment he felt very old, very old indeed.

★ ★ ★

Captain Selbourne's jeep led the way with Juan's truck following, they sped from George's shop and along the promenade leading past Port Jack.

"Where are we going, Sir?" Willy asked, his voice muffled by the chemical headwear he wore.

"Onchan!" came Captain Selbourne's equally muffled response. "That is where they will be heading." He cursed as the jeep hit a rock on the road, causing the vehicle to jerk off line. "Loads of kids there. Plenty of targets for them to in-fect."

Willy was mystified as to how Captain Selbourne could sur-mise that from the information they had. "How can you be sure?"

Captain Selbourne grimaced. "Metatrixacote. I know what the damn stuff does. Let's just hope we capture them rabbits before they do some real harm. I doubt very much whether they will have reached the village yet, so we may come across them along the road. Use the headset and tell Davis to put on high beam and to keep his eyes peeled."

Within moments, two sets of headlights illuminated the road. Bushes, trees, hedgerows and fields were bathed in light, which completely buggered the antics of a young couple in a campervan, who fled, naked, into the night.

"That'll teach them," muttered Captain Selbourne, shak-ing his head. "Keep your eyes peeled, those rabbits could be anywhere."

Willy gasped. "Like in a field by a camper van, Captain?"

"Exactly." The horror evident in Willy's voice penetrated, and Captain Selbourne hammered on the brakes. The jeep slewed to a halt, whereupon he turned his head to peer into the field, and cursed. Behind, the following truck barely avoided a collision as it took evasive action.

"Davis!" Captain Selbourne bellowed into his headset. "The field, now! There's two kids in there, and they're about to be attacked by rabbits."

"At once, Sir!"

Willy heard his response in his headset and craned his neck to peer into the field. What he saw made his blood freeze. The naked couple from the camper van were backed against a tree, staring fearfully at the two man-sized bunnies carrying bulg-ing black sacks who hopped slowly towards them, led by a smaller version with a white bonnet on its head.

"They've nearly got them, Captain," Willy cried.

Before the captain could respond, the truck behind smashed through the low, wire fence that separated the field from the road. Engines roaring, lights blazing, it hurtled toward the rabbits and their prey.

Alerted by the bright, noisy intrusion the rabbits formerly known as Madcap and Corporal Johnson turned. Green-tinged eyes widened in surprise when they saw the truck hurtling toward them. Like startled rabbits, they stood and stared in fascination at the approaching doom and, like startled rabbits, they were still standing there when the truck mowed them down. Following behind in the jeep, Willy felt the double thud, and winced.

"That got them," murmured Captain Selbourne, in grim satisfaction. After bringing the jeep to a halt behind the now stationary truck, he pushed open the door and got out, ignoring the naked couple who clung to each other in terror to make his way to where the two bunnies lay. Hands on hips, he stared down at the prostrate forms, centred in the beams from the truck's headlights. "Are they alive?"

Rising from where he stooped over one of the bunnies, Corporal Davis said, "Yes, Sir. A few broken bones, but they appear to be all right."

Captain Selbourne nodded. "Truss them up and put them in the truck. Best get them back to base before" – he glanced to the naked couple – "someone else sees them." Turning his attention to the young couple, he removed his hood from his chem-suit and wandered over to them, leaving Willy to help Davis truss the captives.

"Any sign of the Easter Bunny, Sir?" asked Davis.

Captain Selbourne shook his head. "Seems like it ran off as soon as the trucks appeared on the scene. The kids saw it go but were too terrified to take much notice of where it went." He frowned. "Although they did say it appeared to have a happy smile on its face when the other two got run over." He gave a small shrug and pursed his lips. "Wherever it's gone, it will not cause us any more problems."

"But what if it attacks anyone else?" asked Willy, aghast at the thought of it running free, spreading its gene-altering germs. He was not as convinced as the Captain that it would not be seen again.

Captain Selbourne met his gaze. "My view is that it attacked Juan Clague through fear. It will not attack again. And remember, it was Juan Clague that bit Johnson, not the rabbit. By now it will be well away from here, doing what bunnies do. You travel back with Davis while I make sure the kids are – attended to." Turning, he addressed Davis. "When you get back, you know what to do."

Davis nodded. "I'll call them in as soon as we make base, Sir."

Once seated in the truck and out of earshot of the Captain, Willy turned to Davis and asked, "Call who in?"

Meeting his gaze, Davis gave an enigmatic grin. "The men in white. That's all you need to know."

Hidden amongst a clump of long grass, a pair of green eyes watched and waited for the vehicles to depart before emerging from view. Standing on its hind legs, nose sniffing the air, the Easter Bunny tried to fix on the scent of chocolate. Its search yielded nothing, and he dropped to all fours. Cursing the loss of its eggs, it hopped into the undergrowth. Revenge on the race of bunny-squashers would have to wait. While sniffing the air it had detected another scent, one that called to it, one that it could not ignore, one that it did not want to ignore. And what was a bunny to do when the female of the species sent such an appealing invitation?

Twelve months later

Elbows resting on his bedroom windowsill, chin nestled in cupped hands, Tommy Radcliffe peered into the garden below. Silvery light bathed the neatly tended lawn, shrubbery and borders, the darker outline of his climbing frame standing stick-like against the backdrop of moon-kissed fields, where grass swayed gently on the night breeze. He glanced to his bedside table. Red numbers glowed in the darkness of his room. Two-thirty, and still no sign of the Easter Bunny. Last year it had visited while he lay sleeping and deposited five chocolate eggs around the garden for him to find. It had taken him most of the morning, but he had found them all, with a little help from his dad. This year would be different. He was a big boy. He had been six last birthday and would show his dad that he could find the eggs all by himself, which was why he waited at his window. If he spotted where the Easter Bunny hid them, he would have no problem finding them.

A movement in the field attracted his attention. Stalks of grass were being thrust aside as something short and wide made its way through. It appeared as a ripple of devastation, flattening the stalks as it swept forward. Surely the swathe was too big for one bunny? Tommy thrust the thought aside and held his breath. Heart racing, he followed the flattening trail, wide-eyed in excitement. By the time it reached the wooden fence that separated the garden from the field, he could scarcely contain himself. He was about to see the Easter Bunny!

The sight that met his eyes when the ripple moved into his garden made him gasp out loud. There was more than one of them! There were at least fifty bunnies, each wearing a pretty bonnet and carrying a basket of eggs. As he watched, spellbound, all bar one of the bunnies peeled away to visit the neighbouring properties. Tommy ignored them, eyes fixed on the remaining rabbit that was busy depositing eggs around the garden. One under a bush, another next to the apple tree, another on top of the climbing frame and yet another inside his father's greenhouse.

Giddy with excitement, he memorised each hiding place, ready for when he hunted them out in the morning. What a tale he would have to tell his mates when he went back to school. He knew not one of them would wait up like he had done. He looked forward to seeing their faces when he told them that there was not one Easter Bunny but hundreds, and that they had magic green eyes that glowed in the dark.

May

Paul Quaggan was born on the Isle of Man and lives in the north of the Island with his wife Angela. Before retirement he had his own decorating and sign-writing business and was at one time the proprietor of two local hostelries and a private hotel.

Since retiring Paul has had time to concentrate on his two main loves, writing and watercolour painting.

one Day in May

Paul C. Quaggan

Long before I could see her, the sound of that squeaky, rusty old wheelbarrow being pushed around the yard told me that Florence Carberry was busily carrying out her daily task of cleaning up, in and around the stable.

"Good morning Mrs Carberry."

"Good morning," she replied without as much as a glance in my direction. "If you're looking for Robbie, I think you'll find him down in the bottom field."

"Right. That's fine," I replied, as I continued on my way up the lane with Roly, my slightly overweight black Labrador, at my side. How I looked forward to the weekend, especially at this time of year. Gone were the cold winds of March and the "can't make up it's mind what to do' weather, so peculiar to April. During the icy cold winter months, the stuffy atmosphere in the back office at the Bank could just about be tolerated, but now we were well into May, with the evenings stretching and temperatures rising daily. All around, the birds were singing. In the hedgerows, daffodils and bluebells had given way to small bouquets of wild primrose, whilst tall stems of the local "fairy flower" Red Campion were forcing their way through the tufts of long coarse grasses growing on the roadside verges. No one could be left in any doubt that Spring had finally arrived.

Roly had already raced ahead to the entrance to the public footpath. "That's it boy," I shouted. "Down we go." He has always loved it here. That goes for me as well. No cars, no wagons and no tractors! Roly hates tractors. Making our way along the narrow, leafy pathway, bordered on either side by a profusion of bright yellow gorse, interspersed with the occasional hawthorn, its clusters of delicate white, vanilla-scented blossom just waiting for the right moment to burst open, we turned a corner and there he was. Robbie, Florence Carberry's brown and white Shire horse, waiting patiently for his regular weekend treat of peppermints. Over the past couple of years or so, this big, strong stallion with legs like tree trunks and hooves the size of giant flower pots, had always followed the same routine. Reaching over the gate, he would gently consume three or four mints, one at a time and then, after a short fuss, would return to his endless task of endeavouring to rid both fields of every blade of grass in sight. But today, something about him appeared to be different. There was a weird, faraway look in his eyes. The kind of look that stared right through you as if you weren't there. "All gone, Robbie lad." I held both hands wide open to confirm that there was nothing else to eat. Still, he stared. Now I too was starting to feel weird. "Cheerio Robbie," I said. "See you soon." Suddenly, without any warning, he reared back on his hind legs, whilst both front legs pawed the air vigorously. Turning sharply, he galloped a short distance up the field, swung round and charged straight at me!

"Look out Roly!" I shouted. "He's never going to stop!"

I need never have worried about Roly. He may not have

had the lean physique of a greyhound but he most certainly covered the ground like one. He had travelled at least fifty yards down the path in no time at all. As for me, I wasn't so lucky. In a state of sheer panic, I fell backwards and soon realised that, along with primroses and Red Campion, it had also been a very good year for nettles! Two things I learnt from this experience. One, that falling into a bed of lush green nettles is not recommended and two, whoever said that dock leaves were the perfect antidote for nettle rash, was either having a laugh or didn't know what they were talking about. Finally, pulling myself together, I was astonished to discover that Robbie had gone. He had completely disappeared! I began to continue my journey down the path to join up with a still shaking Roly. That was when I heard it. A deep-throated voice coming from the other side of the hedge.

"Sorry about that, yessir. Hope the jinney nettles didn' sting yer!"

I turned sharply. "Hello," I called out. "Is someone there?"

"Aye, me," came the reply. "I'm up here by the gate."

"Me?" I asked, making my way back up the path. "Who's me?"

"Robbie of course. Who did yer think it was?"

"Robbie!" I exclaimed. "Is this someone having a joke? Besides, I can't see anybody."

"That's 'cos I'm invisible and believe me, it's no joke," said the voice.

"You expect me to believe, that not only am I speaking to a talking horse, but one that's invisible as well?"

"Oh, I know it takes a bit o' swallowin' boy but, to cut a long story short, each year, on just one day in May, somethin' mighty strange comes over me."

"Blimey!" I retorted. "You can say that again. But what's so special about May?"

"It's jus' the way it works. I can be struttin' around the field, mindin' me own business when all of a sudden, I come over all twitchy, like. Before yer know it, I'm rearin' up on me hind legs, gallopin' round like a madman and chargin' head down towards the gate. That's when it all happens."

"How do you mean, it all happens?"

"I become invisible, don't I?"

It sounds ridiculous I know, but without thinking, I reached out and attempted to stroke this so called "invisible horse". "Hold on!" I exclaimed. "I can't feel anything."

"Ah, ha," said the voice. "Yer goin' t' have to jump on me back for that to happen."

"*What!* Jump on your back?"

"Aye boy," said the voice. "Then you'll become invisible too. That's when we'll both be able to see and touch each other, yet no one else will even know we exist."

For the life of me, I couldn't even begin to understand why I was leaning against a five-barred gate having a conversation with a horse that, to all intents and purposes, didn't exist! One thing was certain. Wild horses would have their work cut out persuading me to go galloping around on a nag I couldn't see. What was required was a good excuse and I had one, if only I could persuade him to come back to me. "Sorry," I said, rather smugly. "Afraid I won't be able to take you up on your offer." I pointed to the now slowly returning Roly. "Can't leave the dog, you see. Not used to being left on his own, but thanks all the same."

"Ah, don't worry about the dog," came the reply. "See that bit of ol' orange-coloured twine wrapped aroun' the post? Tie him to the gate with that."

For reasons I couldn't explain, I did as I was told.

"Right. Now, climb up on top o' the gate, put yer legs over the other side and when I give the word, let yerself go, onto me back."

No one in their right mind would jump from the top of a gate onto an invisible horse but then, I wasn't feeling in the right frame of mind. Some strange inner force was urging me on.

"Now!" shouted the voice and without thinking, I closed my eyes and jumped! When I opened them, to my utter astonishment, I was sitting on Robbie's back!

"How's that, yessir? Can yer see me all right now?"

"Yes," I replied, "I can see you clearly."

"Now, I don't know whether you've noticed or not, but there's no saddle or reins or any o' this fancy stuff."

"Well, no," I replied, "I hadn't noticed but, now you come to mention ..."

"No problem boy. Jus' press yer knees in hard and grab hold o' me mane."

I didn't need asking twice. "You won't go too far, will you?" I asked rather nervously. Roly, still tied to the gate, was looking up and down the pathway as if to say "Where's he got to?" It was plainly obvious that now, I really was invisible. "One more thing. Don't forget I'm riding bareback, will you?"

"Course I haven' forgotten." He half turned his big, broad head and casually remarked. "How are yer at flyin', like?"

"Flying," I exclaimed. "What has flying got to do with anything?"

"Everythin', boy," came the sharp reply. "No use havin' wings if yer not goin' t' fly!"

"*Wings!*" I screamed. "What do you mean, no use having wings?"

Too late! Robbie was already galloping as fast as his "tree trunk" legs could carry him.

"Look behind yer."

Look behind me? It was taking me all my time to look ahead,

let alone behind. Gripping his mane as tightly as possible, I managed to pluck up sufficient courage to take a fleeting glimpse to the rear and – lo and behold – he was right. Sprouting out from his body, just to the rear of my legs, were the most magnificent pair of enormous white wings I have ever seen. Then it happened. Hesitantly at first but then slowly and steadily we began to take off. Higher and higher as his wings flapped faster and faster.

"Hol' tight. We're away!"

Beneath us, everything was getting smaller and smaller. I could just about make out the figure of Roly, still looking around in sheer amazement at the fact that both his master and that ruddy big horse had, without any warning, completely disappeared.

"Do yer fancy a trip down the South?"

"Er ... well actually, if you don't mind, I would prefer to go back."

"South it is then, yessir," interrupted Robbie. "I like the terrain down there. It's nearly all flat yer see and that makes it a lot easier for a novice flyer like meself."

"A *novice!* You're a novice?"

"Well, put it this way boy. Yer can hardly expect me to perform miracles when I only fly once a year and even then, for no more than an hour or so."

By now, we were flying over Robbie's stable where Florence Carberry was still trundling around the yard, pushing that squeaky old wheelbarrow and totally oblivious to what was happening overhead.

Robbie was now, literally, in full flight. Gripping hold of his long silky mane as tightly as possible, I managed to pull myself forward and shout in his ear, "Doesn't Mrs Carberry know anything about your annual flights?"

"My Gawd no," he replied, shaking his head wildly from

side to side. "Have yer not seen her fillin' those sacks and puttin' them out near t' that sign on the gate?"

I had. At any one time, half a dozen large plastic sacks, filled to the brim, were placed against one of the stone pillars. Fixed to the gate itself, was a big white board with bold, black lettering which read

FOR SALE
Top Quality – Well Rotted
HORSE MANURE
£1.00 per Bag – 3 for £2.50
Satisfaction Guaranteed

"So what?" I asked.

"C'mon. Think about it. If she's keen enough to charge a quid a bag for me waste stuff, there's no tellin' what would happen if she found out I could fly as well!"

I had to admit, he did have a valid point. "But if Mrs Carberry doesn't know anything about it, aren't you just a little bit worried she may come down the field and discover you're nowhere to be seen?"

"There's not much fear o' that, at all. She'd never walk that far."

"Ah," I said. "What about the big maroon and silver four-wheel drive I've seen sitting outside? She could always drive down in that."

"What?" Robbie, gave a half-hearted horse laugh. "An' end up gettin' mud all over the wheels? Yer mus' be jokin'! Besides, if she gives me a shout and gets no reply, she'll jus' think I'm hidin' behind that big gorse bush down the bottom o' the field an' actin' a bit strange, like."

At that point, I was tempted to make a very sarcastic comment, but thought better of it.

"Anyway," he continued, "Unless there's one o' them

Agricultural Shows on, she never takes me out before eleven o'clock, so I always make sure I'm back before then."

"But Robbie," I shouted. "What would happen if …?"

"Sorry t' interrupt yer, boy. Can I ask yer a favour?"

"No harm in asking," I replied. "What is it you want?"

"Yer promise not t' laugh?"

"I promise."

"The truth o' the matter is this." He hesitated for a second or two, then continued. "When I'm flyin', I like to be known as … Godred!"

"*Godred!*" I struggled to stop myself from laughing out loud. "Why Godred?"

"Well, now. Have yer never heard about them Greek horses and fellas with wings?"

"Do you mean Pegasus?"

"Aye, that's him and then there's that fella, Mercury. Yer know the one. Him with the wings stuck to his ankles."

"Yes," I said. "But *they* both came from the Mediterranean. Godred came from the North."

"Hol' on , yessir!" exclaimed Robbie. "Surely, he didn' come from Ramsey, did he?"

This time I couldn't stop myself from laughing. "Actually, I was thinking more of Scandinavia. Besides, you still haven't told me why you want to be known as Godred."

"Let's face it. What with Pegasus and Mercury and all those other fancy names, who ever heard of a flyin' horse called Robbie!"

"So?" I queried, while trying my hardest to keep a straight face. "When you turn into a winged horse, you think of yourself as more of a mythical creature?"

"Mythical? No, not really. I picture meself as more mystical than mythical."

"Well," I confessed. "I'll say one thing Robbie, er … sorry,

Godred, at least you're honest!"

By now, we were travelling some two or three hundred feet above the south of the Island. In the distance, the airport was clearly visible and beyond it, the vast expanse of the Irish Sea. Oh no!

Up to this point, I had begun to enjoy myself. The "flight" had been a great deal smoother than I had imagined it would be. But as for flying over water – now, that was something I didn't relish. "We're not going out to sea, are we?" I asked, with some trepidation.

"No, yer all right," came the reply. "Too late today boy. Maybe nex' time."

"Talking of next time," I enquired. "Does this ability to fly occur on the same day in May, every year?"

"Good Gawd no! It can jus' happen on any day throughout May and without any warnin' as well."

"That seems rather odd, doesn't it?"

"Not really," came the quick-fire response. "After all, what about Easter. That's never held on the same weekend, two years runnin' now, is it?"

It would have been very easy to have argued over the "whys and wherefores" of Easter but suddenly I remembered that old adage that you should never argue about religion at any time, let alone while riding bareback on a clumsy Shire horse, a few hundred feet above the parish of Malew! As it happened, that was something I was curious to find out about. "By the way, Godred. Have you any idea how many feet we are flying above the ground?"

"Search me, yessir. Not very well up in feet an' inches, or them centimetre things either, if it comes to that, like." He paused for a second or two. "Now ask me about hands and I'm a bit of an expert, even if I say it meself."

"All right then. Roughly, what is our height in hands?"

"Why ask me?" he joked. "You're the one with the hands. All I've got is hooves!"

We continued to circle over the southern countryside when, without even as much as a word of warning, we started to descend. "Hold on!" I shouted. "What's happening?"

"Over t' yer left. Near to the clump o' trees in that big field."

That's when I realised the reason for Robbie's rapid descent. Half a dozen or so horses, a couple of them grazing peacefully, the others were lying down enjoying the warm morning sun.

"Are you planning to land?" Although he seemed competent enough at flying, I wasn't quite as optimistic regarding his ability to land safely.

"Aye, hol' tight. Prepare for landin'!"

As it happened, apart from a few worrying moments when we appeared to bounce up and down rather erratically, the landing was reasonably smooth.

"You've done this before," I joked, more with relief than jollity.

"Oh aye," he replied smugly. "Every year for the last eight, apart from one."

"When was that?"

"Three years ago, or maybe it was four. That year we had a really wet Spring."

"Was it too wet for you to fly?"

"No, it was ol' Florence, wasn' it? Didn' take me 'Rambo' horse rug off 'til the beginnin' o' June."

"That prevented you from flying?"

"C'mon now, boy! How was I expected to get me wings out, with a damn big waterproof sheet strapped around me middle?"

"Ah, well," I remarked. "At least you've got a fine day for it this year. Now, will it be all right if I dismount and stretch my legs for a minute or two?"

"*No!*" bellowed Robbie, turning his head sharply. "Yer can't get down, yessir! Not 'til we're back home an' I gives yer the word." He shook his head. "If, for any reason, we part company, you'll stay invisible for the res' o' yer days!"

"For the rest of my days!" I exclaimed, gripping his mane even tighter than before. "But what happens if I fall off?"

"There's only one answer to that one. Don't!"

By now, Robbie was casually strolling up and down among the group of horses who, for their part, seemed totally oblivious to our presence. Even to the untrained eye, it was obvious that these tall slender animals were no close relatives of his but were, in fact, showjumpers.

"I wouldn't have thought they were your cup of tea, Godred."

"No. Yer only have t' look at the legs on them. Like matchsticks with the wood shaved off, that's what they are!"

I said nothing, but must confess that, alongside these fit and sporty-looking creatures, Robbie seemed distinctly heavy and cumbersome.

"Don't appeal t' me, anyway," he continued. "When yer go t' these Agricultural Shows an' things like that, they're so stuck up. They won't even look at yer."

"What you need to do, is find yourself a nice friendly Clydesdale mare. One of your own kind, so to speak."

"When yer say 'mare', I expect yer mean 'female horse'."

"But I thought a mare was a female horse?"

"Oh no, not any longer." Slowly, Robbie shook his head from side to side. "Nowadays, we all have t' be known as horses. It's all t' do with this equality thing, like!"

"Equality! Amongst horses?"

"Aye, boy. Political correctness gone mad, that's what it is. We had a bit of a get t'gether at the Southern a couple o' years ago an' it was agreed that, in future, we'd have t' refer to each other as horses. Male horses, female horses, big horses, lil' horses, you name it, we're all grouped t'gether now."

"Good grief!" I said. "This is all news to me. What about donkeys?"

"Donkeys? Oh, I've got yer now. Is it dunkeys yer on about?"

"Er, yes. I think that's what I mean."

"Well now. They did send a delegation t' the Show but they weren't very keen t' join us."

"Why was that?"

"Partly our fault, I'm afraid. Yer see, we wanted them t' be known as 'long-eared lil' horses' but they didn' go much on that idea, at all."

"So what was the outcome?"

"Now," said Robbie, "I don't know whether you're aware o' this or not, but officially, dunkeys come under the headin' of 'asses'."

"Er, yes," I replied. "I did know that."

"Well, after a lot o' heein' and hawin', they decided they would stay as they were. Apparently, most o' them took the attitude that, once an ass, always an ass!"

I decided to remain silent. After all, there was no answer to that one!

"Now, then. I think we're jus' about ready for take-off." With that, Robbie turned, proceeded to gallop for all his worth and before you could say "Godred", we were airborne.

"Heading back home now, are we?" I enquired, optimistically.

"Good Gawd no, yessir! Couldn' come this far without a sight on the airport."

"Why the airport?"

"Surely, yer can work out the connection. Down there, it's all t' do with flyin' and today boy, that's what I'm all about."

For reasons I couldn't quite put my finger on, flying around a busy airport whilst invisible, on an equally invisible horse, didn't strike me as the most sensible pursuit to be indulging in on a fine Spring morning. "Won't it be rather dangerous to be hovering around that kind of area, what with aircraft coming and going all the time?"

"Hoverin'! There won't be much hoverin', at all." Robbie gave a casual shake of the head. "Keep yer eyes open and yer wits about yer. That's all it takes. Besides, I come down here every year and I haven' had any problems up to now."

So engrossed was I, trying to hold on tightly and at the same time, take in what Robbie was telling me, that I failed to notice which direction we were travelling in. Until I happened to glance beneath my feet. "*Water!*" I shouted. "I thought you told me we wouldn't be flying over water!"

"Hol' yer hosses, boy." He gave a hearty laugh.

If he thought the situation was funny, I certainly didn't, "But I can't swim!" I cried.

"Not t' worry," he said and without more ado, veered sharply to the right and headed straight for the main runway. "Sit tight. We're goin' down."

"Going down! Surely, you're not going to land in the middle of the runway?"

"No, no. More a practice landin', like. Jus' let me feet touch the groun' an' then it's up, up and away again."

I could see the ground beneath us getting closer and closer. Down, down we went until I could hear the "clip-clop" of hooves on the tarmac. After galloping along for a short distance, we were off again. Up, up and away, just as Robbie had promised. Except for one small detail. We may have been going up but we weren't going away. Far from it. Having taken a wide circle, he was now dropping down once more to carry out the same manoeuvre as before.

"Hope yer don't mind," he said. "Jus' like t' keep me hand in. Practice makes perfect an' all that, or so they say."

"If you only do it once a year, is there much point in trying to be perfect?"

Robbie hesitated for a second. "Well now," he laughed. "I suppose when yer put it like that, it does seem a bit of a waste o' time. After all, it's not as if I have t' do it on regular basis, is it now?"

"No," I agreed. "It isn't," at the same time hoping it would deter him from performing any more "practice" landings.

"Jus' a bit o' fun, really. Tell yer what. We'll do it once more and then we'll be off. How'll that suit yer?"

I was just about to say "if you must" when suddenly, without as much as a word of warning, Robbie dived sharply to the right. I gripped hold of his mane even tighter than before, if that was at all possible and held on for dear life. With my heart in my mouth and legs that were rapidly turning to jelly, I managed to pull myself forward and bellow in his ear, "What do you think you're–!" My words were dramatically cut short. At first, I could hear it. Then I could feel the draught from it. Finally, I could see it! Big, bold and far too close for comfort, I could *see* it! Overtaking us, no more than a few feet away on our left hand side, was a gleaming, silver-liveried passenger plane.

"Phew!" exclaimed Robbie, the sweat starting to run in rivers down the back of his neck. "That was a near thing, boys!"

"Near thing?" I replied, still quivering from the biggest fright I've ever experienced. "That's putting it mildly."

Robbie tried to put on a brave face. "Yer know what's happened, don't yer? That was the incomin' flight from Gatwick." He gave a loud sigh. "Some stupid idiot's only gone an' altered the timetable, hasn' he? Doesn' normally get here for another half hour, yet."

"Never mind," I said, having regained a slight sense of normality. "At least there is one consolation about being invisible. Even if we hadn't been able to get out of the way, it would have gone straight through us and no one would have been any the wiser."

"Ah, well now." He paused for a second or two. "Not quite as simple as that, I'm afraid."

"What are you trying to say Robb– er ... Godred?"

"It's like this, yer see. True enough, nobody can see us, or hear us. In fact, if it comes to that, nobody can smell us either and comin' from me, that's sayin' a lot." His ears pricked. "But ..."

"Yes?" I asked. Why did I have a funny feeling there was going to be a "but".

"The fact o' the matter is, I still haven' perfected the art o' touchin'. Or to be more precise, the art o' not touchin', like!"

"Do you mean to tell me ...?"

"Afraid so, yessir. If somethin' was t' come into contact with us, we'd feel the full force of it and vice versa. If we were t' run into somethin', look out!"

I couldn't believe what I was hearing. "So what you're saying is, if that plane had struck us, we would almost certainly have been killed!"

Robbie gave a snigger. "Well, put it this way. It wouldn' have done us much good, that's for sure!"

After what we had just experienced, I was finding it difficult to understand his "happy go lucky" manner. However, there was one consolation. Our "near miss" had seemingly, convinced this unbelievably mad horse that practising aerobatic skills over and around a busy airport, was not to be recommended! "I think I've had enough for one day, Godred," I shouted forcefully in his ear.

"Had enough!" Don't yer want to see some o' me other

skills?"

My knees went weak at the thought of this big, clumsy animal attempting to show off his other flying skills, especially with me clinging for dear life to his back.

"Other skills?"

"Aye. I might need t' gain a bit o' height if I'm goin' t' show yer how t' loop the loop."

"*Loop the loop?*" I bellowed. "You can't do that. I'll fall off!"

"D'yer think so?"

"I *know* so!" Whether he was called Robbie, or Godred, or even Einstein, it was plainly obvious I was riding one big lump of brainless horse with not an ounce of common sense in his head.

"How about a victory roll, then?" Clearly, he was not going to be easily put off. "Are yer up t' chancin' one o' them?"

"Good grief, Robbie … er … sorry, Godred. That will be equally as dangerous!"

Robbie was not perturbed. "It'll only take a second."

"*Yes!*" I screamed. "About the same time as it will take me to lose my grip and go plummeting to the ground!"

"Ah, well. Fair enough, boy." He half turned his head. "Have yer ever seen them fellas in the lil' red jets that come over durin' Race Week?"

"Do you mean the Red Arrows?"

"That's them!"

I was tempted to ask why he wanted to know the name of an aerobatic flying team but, something deep down told me that I would not fully appreciate the answer. How right I was!

"Now," he continued. "There is one thing we can do without yer fallin' off." Without any further explanation we were away. Climbing at an unbelievably steep angle!

"*Godred!*" I yelled. "Where are we going now? I'm sliding backwards!"

"Have yer not seen them performin' that manoeuvre where they go right up into the clouds, turn sharp, like and then wheeeeee ... drop like a stone till, jus' when yer think they're goin' t' nosedive straight into the ground, they bottom out and go whizzin' pas' yer?"

"You're having a joke, aren't you? Besides, there are no clouds today!"

"Not a problem t' me," he replied, rather smugly. "When we reach the point where the air starts t' get so thin, that we can hardly breathe, then I'll know it's time t' start the descent."

"*No, no,*" I shouted. "Supposing I can't hold out as long as you? I could have a blackout, lose my grip and that would be the end of me!"

"Tell yer what. As soon as yer start t' feel a bit faint, give a couple o' tugs on me mane an' dig yer heels in like mad. Then I'll know it's time t' think about comin' back down."

We climbed and climbed until finally I could stand it no longer. Pulling as hard as I could on his mane and pressing my heels into his side so firmly that even he flinched, I yelled "Enough! I've had enough. Turn back!"

"All right," replied Robbie. "Goin' down."

Big dippers and rollercoasters had never really been my scene but compared to this experience, they bore a strong resemblance to a leisurely ride around a fairground on a miniature railway! Not that I remembered a great deal about our rapid descent. With eyes tightly shut, a firm grip and a heart that seemed to disappear halfway down, the only option left to me, was to pray!

"There, now," he remarked, as we levelled out, no more than a few feet from the ground. "What did yer think o' that, then?"

Oh, how I would love to have told him what I was really

thinking but the words would not come out. I was speechless! However, there was one consolation. We were now flying along at a more leisurely pace and, more importantly, away from the airport.

With a casual glance, Robbie remarked, "It's a pity I hadn' known in advance that you'd be comin' with me."

"Oh!" I said, "Why is that?"

"Well, I could have asked yer t' try an' get hold o' one of them canister things."

"Canister things?"

"Aye, yer know. Like them lil' red jets have."

"What would you do with one of those?" I asked.

"Simple. Yer could o' fixed it t' me back and then, jus' as we were about to descend, swung round and switched her on." He shook his head and laughed. "Jus' picture it, yessir. Swoopin' down from a great height with red, white and blue "smook" comin' out o' me back end. Now that would have been a sight worth seein', don't yer think?"

The mind boggled! The thought of having to swing round, a few thousand feet above the ground, in order to turn on a canister of coloured smoke, didn't bear thinking about.

It was at this point that Robbie uttered words that sounded like music to my ears. "Time we was makin' tracks for home."

"Yes," I agreed, with a broad smile. "I think we've had enough excitement for one day, Godred." Strange as it may seem, I was beginning to feel quite pleased with myself. At last, I was remembering to call him by his "stage name"!

"Aye, boy. The missus will be lookin' t' take me out later an' if I'm not t' be found, she might begin t' smell a …" He stopped in mid sentence and gave a shrill, piercing whistle!

"Blimey," I remarked. "I didn't realize horses could whistle."

"What?" Robbie tossed his head around in disgust. "With these teeth yessir, if I was t' put me mind to it, I could whistle so loud, they'd hear me down at the Ayres!"

In the far distance, I could just about make out Florence Carberry's cottage and stable. "Almost home," I said with a sigh of relief, at the same time trying my best not to hurt the big Shire horse's feelings.

"Look at her." Robbie nodded in the direction of the yard. "The missus is still hard at it. What d' yer say, we give her a bit of a fright?"

"Oh, no!" I exclaimed. "I don't think that's a very good idea."

"C'mon. Nothin' serious. Jus' a bit of a laugh, like!"

As we got closer, I could see Florence Carberry, complete with brush and shovel, finishing off her clearing-up operations. That was when Robbie swooped! Heading straight for the overloaded wheelbarrow, he managed to catch the handles with one of his front hooves. For once, the rusty old barrow actually moved without squeaking, as it fell sideways, tipping its contents all over the cobbled yard! Mrs Carberry swung round quickly, just in time to catch the full benefit of a strong draught, caused by the "flying horse" and his rider as they flew past at close quarters. Her big, brown, floppy hat didn't stand a chance! It took off, bounced a couple of times on its brim, rolled across the yard and finally came to rest, sitting proudly in the middle of the large heap of Florence's fully guaranteed, top quality manure!

"What in the name of ... ?" She looked around in astonishment, but there was nothing to see.

As for Robbie and I, we were now back where we had started, circling over the bottom field. "Fasten yer seat belts," he shouted. "Prepare for landin', yessir and keep an eye out for pheasants getting' in the road." You had to hand it to him. He really did take this flying business seriously!

"Pheasants?" I remarked. "Judging by the numbers of them

down there, I would have thought rabbits were a bigger
problem when trying to land."

"Not at all. Yer know where yer are with the bunnies, boy."
He nodded towards the far hedge where a family of pheasants
were busily pecking away among the long grass. "They're the
fellas I haven' got much time for."

"Why? What have they done to upset you?"

"Throughout the whole o' the year, I only have one day in
May to go flyin', whereas those 'bird brained' pheasants were
born t' fly an' yet, for all that, what happens when they hear
the least bit o' noise?"

"I don't know. What happens?"

"What *happens!* Unlike other birds that would jus' take t'
the skies and fly off, these idiots run backwards and forwards,
up an' down the field like a load o' headless chickens!" Robbie
shook his head. "No sense in them at all."

Within seconds, we had touched down and the big brown
and white horse was standing alongside the gate. "Right," he
said. "That's us. If yer climb on t' the gate, throw both legs
over the other side and everything'll be back t' normal."

Rather warily, I did as I was told and … whoosh! It happened! Or, to be more precise, two things happened. Roly, who
apparently had been fast asleep, now woke up and began to
leap up at me with sheer excitement, while Robbie, who had
momentarily disappeared, quickly re-emerged and was now
making his way back down to the gate.

"Everything all right Godred … er … sorry, I mean Robbie?"

He trotted over to the gate and proceeded to lick my face.
"Robbie!" I laughed. Or is it still Godred?" Whichever it was,
he took no notice and continued licking. I attempted to step
back but to no avail. I was rooted to the spot. "Robbie! Robbie!
Will you stop …?"

Suddenly, I was interrupted by a familiar voice! A very

familiar voice! "What have I told you about letting that dog of yours lie on the bed!"

"Ma! Is that you, Ma? What are you doing here?"

"The same as I am every Saturday morning. Trying to wake you up! Don't you know what time, it is?"

"But, Ma. I thought I was …"

"Never mind what you thought. Get yourself out of that bed before this dog of yours licks you to death."

So startled had I been by Ma trying to wake me, that I hadn't noticed Roly sitting alongside me with his head on the pillow.

"Besides, why have you started calling him Robbie? Heaven forbid. It's bad enough trying to get him to answer to Roly without confusing him even further!"

She turned and started to make her way downstairs but not before asking, "As for Godred, well, wherever did you dig that name up from?"

Fortunately, she didn't bother to wait for an explanation.

Breakfast over and with a tube of peppermints in my pocket, Roly and I made our way up the lane. Approaching Florence Carberry's cottage, I heard something that made me smile. The sound of the squeaky wheelbarrow, although I was convinced it was nowhere near as noisy as the one in my dream! "Good morning Mrs Carberry."

"Good morning," she replied and to my astonishment, looked up. Putting down the barrow, Florence pointed towards the bottom field. "Ah, it's all right," she said with a sigh of relief. "Robbie's down there now." She shook her head. Her bare head! What had befallen her floppy hat?

"When I came out here, earlier this morning, I called and called him but he ignored me completely *and* he was keeping out of sight as well." She shook her head and smiled. "Sometimes, I'm convinced he makes himself invisible!"

"Yes," I laughed. "It does make you wonder."

"Ah well, I must crack on." She ran the back of her hand across her brow. "What with Robbie playing me up and then that sudden gust of wind."

"Gust of wind?"

"I know it seems hard to believe now, but earlier on, there was such a strong gust of wind, that it tipped the wheelbarrow over on it's side, spilling the contents all over the yard."

"Oh no!"

"Oh yes, and what's even worse, my hat blew off and before I could grab hold, it had landed right in the middle of the heap of fresh manure!" She turned her head and nodded in the direction of the stable. There, balancing on the corner of the door, was her big, brown, floppy hat! "I've had to give it a really good wash. Only hope it dries out all right." Grabbing hold of the wheelbarrow's handles, she started to make her way across the yard. "Never mind," she joked. "We all get days like this, don't we?"

"Oh yes," I replied. "We most *certainly* do!"

❀ June ❀

Although **Kate Stokes** now lives in London she still retains strong connections to the Island and visits as often as she can. Kate graduated from the Royal Holloway University of London with a BA Hons in English/Theatre Studies and started her theatrical employment appropriately enough at the Gaiety Theatre in Douglas. She has since worked as a Deputy Master Carpenter at the Aldwych and Piccadilly Theatres and also with the RSC during their London seasons. Kate currently works as a freelance theatre technician.

Althelbrede and the Battle of Poyllvill

Kate Stokes

Al sat, dangling his bare feet in the breathtakingly cold water, and allowed himself a moment of contentment. Summer had triumphed over the bluster and false promises of spring to settle, glowing, over the land. The chill winds that had blown northerly past Milner's Tower onto Mull Hill had softened and swung round to the south-west, bringing with them the sweet scent of gorse and heather from Spanish Head.

A light sleeper, Al had woken before the midsummer sun and had climbed the Howe road to enjoy the first slanting rays of the morning in his favourite spot by Poyllvill; sheltered from the wind by the long dry-stone wall that marked the boundary of Norman Bridson's farm, and by an unruly tangle of gorse bushes, from any other early risers making their way down the Darrag into Port Erin, or up, towards Cregneash or the Sound. There would be few distractions this morning, though. The annual frenzy of the Tourist Trophy races had entered its second week, so the swarms of leather-clad bikers, who had spent the recent days shattering the peace with their brutish machines and their indignant cries to each other of

"*Links fahren*" whilst hurtling down the middle of roads discreetly deserted by local traffic, would be safely ensconced behind bales of hay and in pub car-parks along the TT course. This carnival of Bushy-fuelled, fume-laden gaiety deterred those holidaymakers who came to the Island seeking tranquillity, unspoilt coastal walks and opportunities for extreme picnicking, so their stout boots and windburnt faces were prudently absent at this time of year, creating a temporary oasis of quiet around the hillsides of the south as the Island's tourist industry focused its attention elsewhere.

Not totally quiet, though. In the absence of humanity's din, Nature's raucous cacophony could rise unchallenged, swelling with the strengthening sunlight of the morning. A colony of greenfinches, squabbling incessantly as their territory expanded with the arrival of the next generation of quarrelsome fledglings. Insects hurtling around the murkier corners of the pond, living out their condensed lifespans at breakneck speed. The ewes and lambs on Norman's farm conducting their familial dramas at a distance and volume that showed little regard for discretion. Even the gorse responded audibly to the warmth of the sun, the vivid yellow blooms opening with a delicate 'pop' accompanied by a waft of heady fragrance.

Al sighed contentedly and wiggled his toes to see if he could still feel his feet in the cold water. Apart from having his trouser legs rolled up and his shoes on the ground beside him, he was impeccably dressed in a dark green suit over a spotless white shirt. His waistcoat hung open, showing a lining that shimmered darkly and matched the sheen of his tie. He ran his thin, pale hands over his head, smoothing back the long, grey hair that still showed no sign of thinning despite his advanced years, replaced his hat, a curiously shapeless affair that nonetheless complemented the overall sartorial effect, and started to think about breakfast. He thought he still had a couple of eggs knocking around from yesterday. They'd do nicely, and then perhaps a spot of fishing for the rest of the morning, to try and catch some lunch.

With such pressing issues resolved, Al lifted his feet out of the water. He picked up his shoes, a very elderly and battered pair of brogues, and was about to stand up when he heard voices. Al was extremely shy; he disliked most company at the best of times, even more so when he was unprepared, so he decided to stay quietly where he was, hidden among the taller reeds and bushes of the pond, in the hope that whoever the owners of the voices were would pass by. He could make out two voices, a man and a woman, walking down the Darrag from the direction of Norman's farm. As they drew closer, Al recognised the man's voice as Norman's, but the woman's voice was unfamiliar. Despite his shyness, Al was a little on the nosey side, and his curiosity was aroused. Norman's wife was a broad woman with a broader Irish accent, and this was definitely not her. So who was Norman out walking with this early on a sunny Monday morning?

The conversation continued, but they seemed to have stopped moving. Al very gently pushed a clump of gorse to one side to see if he could catch a glimpse of the mystery woman.

They were sitting on a bench, with their backs to him. There were a few benches like this along the Darrag, affording resting places and views, either out to sea, towards Bradda Head or the Calf of Man, or across the heather-clad hillside of Mull, to the sweep of Gansey beach away towards Scarlett Point and, on a clear day, Derbyhaven. The placement of the benches was often sentimental; most of them carried an inscription to a departed friend or relative, each bench capturing a view that had been favoured by the remembered loved one. The one upon which Norman and his companion now sat had always been a bit of a puzzle to Al, seeing as it faced toward the rocky hill and away from a gorgeous panorama of craggy cliffs, crashing waves and sublime sunsets, but he was glad enough of that now, as it meant he could edge a little closer without being noticed, to eavesdrop on their conversation.

"... so full of rocks that I can't grow anything on it, so I mainly use it for storing the pens when we're not lambing."

"Well, the museum would only need to use it until September, so the rest of the year wouldn't affect that."

She had a low, earnest voice, a local accent partially masked by some years away. All Al could see of her was a smartly tailored coat, topped by an unnecessarily thick scarf for the season, and a cascade of immaculately coiffured blonde curls. He leaned down a little and glanced appreciatively at the pair of slim ankles and low-heeled, elegant shoes visible beneath the bench. Next to her, Norman looked decidedly scruffy; workclothes patched and frayed, boots encrusted with mud and God knows what else, and the ubiquitous cap covering his unruly hair. Al turned back to the ankles, leering slightly to himself, before remembering that he was meant to be listening to their conversation and should probably be paying more attention.

"So what's this bird, then?" asked Norman, the apparent change of subject making Al wonder how long he'd been staring at the ankles.

"The Arctic Rock Bunting," the woman replied with genuine-sounding enthusiasm. "It's very exciting. Been on the protected list for over a decade, no sightings anywhere in the British Isles for years, and now it looks like there's a breeding pair nesting in the quarry. Beautiful birds. Slightly larger than our native Rock Bunting, and the male has these white tail feathers with a bright orange flash at the base which they use for their courtship displays. Of course, we're not making too much noise about it quite yet – we don't want hordes of twitchers descending on us and scaring them off, but once the eggs have hatched, who knows?"

"So it'll just be for this summer, until they've gone back to … wherever it is they go in the winter, will it?" Norman sounded less excited at the prospect of nesting birds, but the woman's enthusiasm was unaffected.

"No, no, not at all! That's what's so great!" She was becoming quite animated now. "The Arctic Rock Bunting will return to a successful nesting site for years … start a colony … generations of them. So using your field for the coach-park will be a long-term solution. It's perfect. Far enough away from the village for the coaches to be out of sight, close enough for the older visitors to manage the walk. Of course, we'll have to think about access – perhaps a pathway through here, some kind of rustic bridge over the pond, maybe even drain part of it, refreshments, perhaps extend the museum site. Of course, this is all off the top of my head, we don't want to get too far ahead of ourselves."

Al heard no more. At the words 'rustic bridge' he had felt all the blood leave his already pale face, and at the mention of draining Poyllvill, a terrible rushing sound had filled his ears. The spectre of mechanical diggers ripping up the gorse swam before his eyes, the thundering of a thousand feet rang mockingly in his ears. He had to find out more. When would this start? How long did he have?

Norman and 'that museum woman', as Al had mentally dubbed her, had lowered their voices again, presumably discussing Norman's payment for his part in this rape of the landscape, thought Al bitterly. He tried to calm himself enough to listen, leaning forward through the gorse, straining to hear.

"Aa-al."

Hearing his name called out so loudly made him jump and

he was savagely poked by the tougher thorns of the gorse in which he was lying.

"Aa-al."

It was Sam, possessor of the loudest voice on Mull Hill, strutting up the Darrag from the direction of Port Erin, looking very pleased with himself. Birds scattered, Norman glanced round and Al froze, trying to blend into the gorse bush. Norman didn't seem to have noticed the interruption, however, and after a moment, he turned his attention back to the blonde woman, and they stood up to leave.

"Aa-al."

Al wished he could scream at Sam to shut up, but he bit his tongue until Norman and his companion had moved off. Sam, meanwhile, had threaded his way through the brambles by the dry-stone wall until he emerged by the side of the pond.

"There you are," he said, a touch huffily. "Didn't you hear me calling?"

Al rounded on him furiously.

"Hear you?" he hissed. "The whole chuffing island heard you!"

Sam was not known locally for his sensitivity or perceptiveness, but something about Al's tone made him wonder if everything was OK. He sat down, heavily, next to his friend.

"Go on then," he said gruffly. "What's up?"

Al outlined, briefly and bitterly, the conversation he had just overheard. As the echo of his last expletive drifted away over the hillside, Sam looked thoughtful.

"So," he mused, "there's a bird's nest in the quarry where they usually park the tourists' coaches, and they want to park them here instead."

"Yes."

"And to do that they'll have to drain the pond."

"Yes."

"Because of the birds."

"Yes." Al was doing his best not to sound testy, but his best wasn't quite up to it.

"So kill the birds."

"What?"

Sam looked at Al patiently.

"Kill the birds. No birds, no new coach park, no pond draining, no problem." He sat back, waiting for Al's outpouring of gratitude at this simple yet brilliant solution.

"Oh, shut up, you psychopath. That's your answer to everything. You can't just go round killing things ..."

"Yes you can."

"... if they get in your way. No you can't. Well, I can't." Al suddenly felt tired and alone. "You may be able to go through life eating, fighting and copulating, but some of us have responsibilities." He looked sternly at Sam, who seemed hurt. Al immediately regretted his outburst. Sam had tried to help, and Al had known him for too long to start pointing out his personal limitations. He put a hand on Sam's broad back and patted him gently. "Look, thanks for listening, Sam. I'll work something out, don't worry."

Sam sulked for a moment, pointedly looking at the dry stone wall. Then his eyes widened as a thought struck him. He stood up excitedly, almost knocking Al into the pond.

"Let's ask Jim. Jim will know what to do."

Jim Quine was a local historian who, living in one of the only houses in Cregneish not owned by the Manx National Trust, was one of a dwindling number of residents not contractually obliged to wear a shawl from April to September. Sam had shared the house with him for many years, since before Jim's wife had died. Although they both missed her, they rubbed along happily enough together, meeting mainly at mealtimes, or sitting quietly together in the front room during winter evenings, Jim poring over some recently acquired Victorian land register whilst Sam dozed contentedly by the fireplace. Sam was secretly of the opinion that there was very little Jim Quine didn't know, and he couldn't imagine a person better equipped to tackle this particular issue.

Al waited until Sam's enthusiastic tribute to Jim's problem-solving abilities had slowed enough to make interjection possible, and ventured, "Yes, but Jim won't even know about it yet. It's still a secret."

Sam barely paused for breath. He was on a roll; nothing was impossible.

"Easy. Nice day like this, he'll take a stroll this evening. I'll accompany him, all casual-like, bring him past here, you introduce yourself, start chatting, sorted. Jim Quine on the case, two dead birdies."

"Sam!"

"I mean, problem solved," Sam corrected hastily. "Problem … responsibly solved."

Al didn't quite know where to begin listing the pitfalls of this course of action, and he still hadn't had any breakfast, so he decided to let it go. He supposed that the local people would be involved sooner or later, and it would be better to put his point across sooner. Maybe Sam's plan had possibilities. If change was inevitable, he thought morosely, better to be its architect than its victim. He sighed, feeling the weight of decision settle in his empty stomach like a bellyful of cold water.

"OK," he said.

Sam beamed with pride.

"Great!" He was trying to sound nonchalant and failing. He stretched, yawned and stepped past Al onto the road. "Right then, I'm off for a nap. See you this evening. And don't worry, Al, with me and Jim on the case, you've got nothing to worry about."

He sauntered off up the Darrag, head held high, leaving Al staring moodily into the dark, ancient waters of Poyllvill. He had plenty to worry about.

★ ★ ★

The sun had dropped behind the Calf of Man, framing it with hues of pinks and oranges that promised another fine day tomorrow, and still there was no sign of Sam or Jim. Al leaned against the bench, feeling his ears grow numb as the night's chill descended, moodily watching the first stars prick through the sky spreading inky blue from the east. They weren't coming. Al wasn't sure if he was relieved or disappointed. After Sam had left him that morning, he had considered raiding his wine-larder and spending the rest of the day in an insensible fug, but then had decided that probably wasn't the best way to make a good first impression. Instead, he had shaved, trimmed his hair, cleaned and pressed his suit, polished his shoes and even managed to coerce his hat into a tangible shape. Now he was wishing that he'd stuck to Plan A. He glared up the road. Behind him, a pair of baby rabbits, lulled by his stillness, broke cover from a bramble bush and approached the bench, lured by the long juicy grass that grew around it.

"Bugger off," he snarled, and they did.

Well, he thought to himself, so much for the great Jim Quine. Next time he saw Sam, he'd tell him straight, not to go getting people's hopes up, making promises he couldn't keep, offering help then just fading into the background, leaving him all alone to face whatever the future might throw at him, friendless and isolated in an uncaring world.

"Evening," said Sam.

A moment passed in which Al didn't open his mouth in case he let out the shriek that was in there. Eventually he managed a nearly noncommittal high-pitched sound that may have passed for a greeting. If Sam noticed, he didn't mention it. Instead, he looked back up the road.

"Right," he said briskly, "Jim's just a minute or two behind me. Good luck."

Al felt a little ill. He peered round the bench as a tall, slightly stooped figure came into view, carrying a walking stick but not leaning heavily on it, stopping occasionally to take in the magnificent view, the clean, cool air, the deepening silence of the gathering twilight. Sam nudged Al gently in the back.

"Go on," he urged. "I'm right beside you."

Al took a deep breath, stepped out into the road, swept off his hat and bowed.

"Good morrow, Jim Quine. My name is Althelbrede of Poyllvill, also called All-Heal, also called Marsh Woundwort. Our friend Sam hast told me of thy wisdom and compassion and so I come unto thee to ask for help. These are dark times, great villainy abounds and mine own wit hast been found wanting. Therefore, I seek thy counsel and do profess in return mine own gratitude and allegiance to thee and thy Clan."

He heard Sam make a noise that sounded suspiciously like a snort, and straightened up. "Too much?" he asked out of the side of his mouth.

"No, no," Sam said reassuringly. "Just … unexpected."

They both stared at Jim, waiting.

Jim Quine had always considered himself a reasonably open-minded man. In his youth, as a sailor in the Merchant Navy, he had travelled extensively and witnessed many strange customs. As a historian he had heard myths and legends of dazzling variety. As a man in his seventies, he had seen acts of generosity and malice from the entire spectrum of human fear and desire. Apparently, he was now looking at a man slightly less than eight inches tall standing next to Sam, his black Manx cat.

He rallied magnificently.

"Er ..."

Al put his hat back on.

"Er ... hello."

Al's eyes narrowed slightly.

"Er ... d'you mind if I sit down?"

Jim sat, slightly more quickly than he'd intended, on the bench. One part of his brain was leaping and fizzing with the sheer joy of the moment, whilst another was telling him he'd just gone totally insane and should keep as still as possible until help arrived. As a result, the part dealing with standing, sitting and the bit in between was being largely ignored. Gradually, as the eight-inch man continued to be standing there (starting to look slightly cross, Jim noticed) instead of vanishing, the voice of insanity quietened down, and Jim realised he should probably make some kind of formal greeting in return.

"Er ... good morrow to you ... er ... to thee," he started. This was too much for Sam, who disappeared into the gorse bushes laughing. Al lost his temper.

"Oh no you don't!" he snapped. "This was your bloody idea, Sam, so don't think you can wander off and leave me with this, this ... well, look at him. How the hell's he going to help me when he can't even get a bloody sentence out?"

"All right, hang on a minute." Jim had collected his wits sufficiently to start feeling insulted. "Right, let's start again. Your name is Marsh what?"

"Marsh Woundwort. Also called All-Heal, also called Althelbrede."

"Marsh Woundwort, that's a kind of plant, isn't it? So you're a kind of plant spirit." Jim had a flash of inspiration. "Like flower fairies!"

Al fixed him with a malevolent glare.

"Not exactly," he said coldly.

"Right. Sorry." Jim decided to try another tack. "So, you said you wanted my help with something?"

Al gave Jim a long, appraising look. Despite his apparent derision, he was in fact impressed with Jim. The last man he had introduced himself to had fled, screaming, down the hillside. In comparison, Jim had taken this in his stride. He climbed onto the bench next to him and, as twilight turned fully to night, lit only by the light of the thumbnail moon, once again recounted the events of that morning. Jim listened, frowning, nodding occasionally, and shook his head sadly as Al finished speaking.

"I'm so sorry. I don't know what to say."

Al looked him in the eye.

"Say it can't be done. Say Poyllvill is a protected area that can't be disturbed. Say it's illegal."

Jim pinched his lower lip between finger and thumb, thinking hard.

"Well, Norman's land is his own to do with as he pleases. The Manx National Trust own a lot of Cregneish, the Sound, Mull Hill, most of the Darrag…Poyllvill certainly falls within their boundaries. Technically speaking, as long as they're enhancing the area, or protecting it, there's not much room for legal argument."

Al visibly wilted. Sam, who had been quietly listening whilst having a quick wash, couldn't bear it. He had to say something positive.

"Maybe it won't be so bad." Al didn't even look at him. "No, I mean it. If it's just that far corner, just a little wooden bridge? The reeds will still be fine, and you spend most of your time at this end. You said yourself that it's all a bit frogged up at that end. And how many people would it be, really? A couple of coaches, a few times a week? And only during the summer. Most of the time you probably wouldn't even know it's there ..." his voice faded as he saw the look on Al's face.

"Won't know it's there?" Al was ashen-faced. "Thousands of tourists traipsing around at all hours of the day and night. Clattering over some rustic sodding bridge first thing in the morning. Burger wrappers and Coke cans clogging everything up, poisoning everything. People taking pictures, what about that? What if I can't hide in time? I'll be trapped indoors all day. Dogs jumping in and out ..."

It was too much. Al covered his face with his hands and sobbed.

"How long have you lived here?" Jim asked quietly. Al took a deep, shuddering breath, and wiped his eyes and nose, hurriedly.

"I don't know." he said quietly. "A long time. Since the Quarterlands."

Jim raised his eyebrows. The Quarterland system of land division was over nine hundred years old. He put a hand, gently, on Al's arm. Al looked at him, bleakly.

"Althelbrede of Poyllvill, also called All-Heal, also called Marsh Woundwort. We will not let your home be destroyed. I promise."

His tone was so gentle, so serious, that Al completely and sincerely believed him. He nodded, gratefully. Jim shivered, and stood up. "Get some rest, my friend. I'll come back tomorrow with a battle plan. Come on Sam."

He stood, a little stiffly, and waved farewell before turning back towards the village. Sam shivered from his ears to the stump of his tail, but not from the cold.

"I told you he was good." And he ran after Jim, leaving Al alone on the bench, weary, yet comforted, as the light from a billion stars threw the contours of the hillside into unfamiliar shadows, and reflected in the waters of his pond, his home.

* * *

The red sky of the previous night had not brought shepherds' or sailors' delight, unless the shepherds and sailors in question enjoyed being out in cold, slanting drizzle and a thin, cruel wind. The Calf was gone – veiled in featureless white mist and Spanish Head and Bradda were both truncated by low clouds. A heavy silence lay over the hillside, as the birds and beasts of Mull roosted and nestled in whatever shelter they could find, a silence broken only by the drizzle collecting on the plants around the water's edge forming droplets that plip-plopped into Poyllvill, creating a concentric chaos of ripples.

Al's mood was as grey as the sky. Whatever comfort Jim Quine's words had brought him had seeped away during the night. He sat, gloomily, among the fleshy stalks of his name-sake herb, not even bothering to wring out his hat as it absorbed the rain and dribbled cold water down his neck.

He didn't know how long he had sat there when he was startled by a damp and disgruntled Sam blundering through the wet undergrowth some feet away, wearing an expression of supreme martyrdom.

"Jim said to fetch you up to the house. This weather brings on his rheumatism, apparently, so he thought you'd both be more comfortable indoors. Coming?"

Al perked up a little.

"Great. Thanks, Sam."

"Don't thank me. It wasn't my idea to come out in this. Completely blown my cover, we have. Now he knows I can understand what he's saying, it'll be 'do this, Sam, do that, Sam'. Like he's the only one with rheumatism. I should be on a rug in front of the fire on a day like this, not traipsing around running errands." He sneezed and shook himself, spraying Al with discarded rainwater, then began to pick his way disdainfully over the wet ground back to the road. Al dutifully plodded after him, glad that the rain was keeping everybody inside so he could move about unobserved, his spirits rising despite the stream of peevish muttering that Sam managed to keep up all the way to the village.

The first house on the left was small and neat; recently whitewashed and in good repair. A cat-sized gap in the stone wall surrounding the back garden afforded them a discreet entry point, and Sam led the way past a large sycamore, in which hung the remains of a swing, not used for many years, to a cat flap in the back door. Al eyed it doubtfully, but scrambled through as Sam held it open for him.

Al couldn't remember the last time he had been in a house, but it was long enough ago for it to have been made of stone with holes for the doors. He took his hat off, wrung it out absent-mindedly, and then tried to disguise the resulting puddle of water by standing in it. They were in the kitchen, a warm, vast-seeming room containing table and chairs, a cooking range and a dresser covered in crockery, knick-knacks and books. There were lots of books. In fact, almost every surface in the room seemed to double as a bookshelf.

Jim entered the room, seeming much taller in the confined space, and stared at Al, who stared back. Overnight, they had each forgotten just how momentous their meeting had been, now they both seemed lost for words again.

Sam dispelled the awkwardness of the moment by rubbing his wet flank along Jim's trousered shins.

"Oh, don't do that, Sam, you're all wet." Jim exclaimed. "All right, all right, I'll get your towel."

He went to the back door and returned holding a fluffy brown towel, with which he proceeded to vigorously rub Sam's head and body. Sam was delighted; purring, leaning this way and that, pretending to bite the towel, in what was obviously a well-established ritual of bonding. Al felt a little uncomfortable and wasn't sure where to look. Eventually, Sam remembered that Al was in the room, and belatedly tried to regain some dignity by stepping away from Jim and sniffing nonchalantly, but it was no use. His hair was bouffant from head to tail-stump, and Al couldn't help laughing as Sam stalked, pointedly, from the room.

Jim smiled at him.

"It's odd. You seem more real today. Out of your natural habitat and into mine, I suppose. Come through to the front room, I've found some local maps that might be useful." Al followed him into a larger room, full of books, papers, prints and maps, with two comfortable chairs, what might have been a desk, under piles of paperwork, and a freshly laid fire, in front of which Sam was stretched, trying to smooth down his fur and studiously ignoring both of them. Al climbed onto a chair, and Jim rifled through the topmost layers on the desk, finding maps, pencil and paper, and sitting down.

"See here," he said, indicating to Al a line on the map. "this is the wall that runs down the side of Norman's farm. This is Poyllvill, here, and this is the Darrag. So," he pencilled in two parallel lines across the western corner of the pond, "this would be the most obvious place to put a bridge, as it's closest to Norman's land, and would join this path, here, into the village. See?"

Al saw. He looked at the map and understood how easy it would be to plan roads and paths and bridges over these soulless symbols, when all you had to look at was a dotted line, instead of lichen-encrusted, weathered stones, selected and placed with such skill and care so long ago, or a misshapen circle, instead of Poyllvill, teeming with such varied life, that he had nurtured and tended for so many generations. He shrugged, feeling out of his depth.

"Any ideas?"

"Well," Jim leaned back in his chair. "the most obvious thing would be to declare Poyllvill as a heritage site, as it's home to a mythological Norse sprite, I imagine that would pull rank over a couple of rare birds, but I think that's a bit of a non-starter. We'd either be stampeded by scientists or consigned to a loony bin."

"Any other ideas?"

"One or two. I can go to the MHKs for Rushen. We can start a petition, get the locals involved, have a 'Save Poyllvill' campaign." Al was looking at him warily. "Don't worry, I won't mention your name. It's an ancient landmark, that should be enough to generate some interest. We can talk to the Manx National Trust, too, I've dealt with them over the years. Who was the lady Norman was talking to?"

Al described the woman as best he could, leaving out the ankles. Jim nodded. "That sounds like Wendy Caine. I've met her before. I'll make an appointment to see her."

The sun chose that moment to break through the cloud cover, sending a beam of light into the room. Jim looked out of the window. "Looks like it's turning into a nice day," he said.

Al jumped out of the chair.

"I'd better get back. There'll be people." He ran towards the back door, before remembering his manners and turning back. "Thank you, Jim Quine. See you later, Sam." And he was gone, past the sycamore and through the hole in the wall, leaving the cat flap swinging behind him. Jim sat, for a moment.

"Quite a surreal morning, eh, Sam?" But Sam was asleep.

* * *

Al crossed the road carefully, clambered up the grassy bank and dived into a patch of last year's heather, cursing as the

135

wiry sprigs dug into some tender places. He paused a moment, before peering, cautiously, up and down the Darrag, but it was still deserted. A few finches twittered along the line of gorse bushes opposite, enjoying the break from the rain. The shelter of the pond was only a hundred yards away, and Al had started to extricate himself from the heather, when someone close behind him exclaimed.

"Hello, there."

He froze, convinced that he'd been spotted, but another voice replied, "Hi. I was just coming to see you."

Al turned, slowly. Norman Bridson and Wendy Caine were approaching each other along the road, he from the direction of his farm, she from the quarry road, still smartly dressed, but with binoculars slung round her neck. If he'd been a moment later, Al thought, he would have run right into her.

"Been to see your arctic whatsits?"

"Rock Buntings, yes. Just keeping an eye on them. The eggs should be hatching any day now. We shall have to close the quarry off soon, to make sure they're not disturbed. I've brought some paperwork for you to have a look at, if you like."

Norman turned, and they started to walk back towards his farm. Al crept after them, quietly.

So you'll be going public soon enough," Norman was saying.

"Hopefully there'll be a press release this week."

"Do you think there'll be much opposition?" Norman sounded apprehensive, and Al felt a surge of hope. Maybe he wasn't keen on the plan after all. His spirits plummeted, though, at Wendy's reply.

"Oh, nothing much. There'll be the usual 'Stop the Museum' campaign, I shouldn't wonder, but they usually fizzle out once thay realise that the planning permission has already gone through. It's often just some old dear hanging around the library with a petition, anyway."

Al sank blindly into the nearest cover, a dense, rambling briar. They were scuppered. He had been so naïve, to think that a sprite, a man and his cat could take on such an organisation. He made his way slowly back to Poyllvill. The sun had retreated behind the clouds, and the rain had started again, but in earnest this time. Great, fat droplets pelted the vegetation, battering the newest growth to the ground. Normally, Al would be busily rigging shelters over the tenderest shoots, but what was the point? It would all be gone soon anyway.

As the day passed, he grew more morose, and found himself getting angry, however unjustifiably, with Jim Quine. Petitions and meetings! That was no way to fight a battle. In his youth, Al would have stood firm against all invaders, to the death, if necessary. When he remembered some of the bloody encounters of the early days …

Al blinked. That was it. An ancient landmark, Jim had said. Well, thought Al. An ancient landmark deserved an ancient champion, and he knew just the fellow. He stood, the light of bygone battles in his eyes. Just you wait, Norman Bridson, he thought. I'll show you opposition.

* * *

Moonlight glinted on each aeon-smoothed surface of the white stone circle on Mull Hill. The air crackled with the charge of age-old mystical incantations. Al's tiny frame shook as the circle magnified his power, calling through time and space, reaching beyond the boundaries of nature, beyond life itself.

A low rumbling filled the deathly silence of the night. It intensified, the ground juddering, dislodging the dust of ages from crevices in the standing stones, the stones themselves creaking and yawing, like teeth lining the very mouth of Hell.

A shimmering light erupted from the ground – a longboat, hung with shields, pennants flying, a great, bearded, fur-swathed figure wielding a sword and laughing triumphantly.

Al wondered if this had, in fact, been such a good idea after all.

The unearthly light faded, and Godred Crovan found himself standing in a stone circle on a not entirely unfamiliar hillside. He looked around, trying to get his bearings, peering into the darkness to see who had summoned him. He heard an apologetic cough and swung round, sword aloft, ready for battle.

"Greetings, mighty Godred, Gorry the Dane, King of Man, Slayer of ..."

"Althelbrede?"

"Yes, Sire."

"What in Odin's name are you playing at? Was this you?"

"Er ... yes, Sire."

Godred stuck his sword in the damp, loamy soil, exhaled heavily, and sat down on one of the flatter stones.

"Well, you'd better have a bloody good excuse. What's on your mind?"

"I request of you a boon, Sire."

Godred frowned.

"Let me get this straight. You reached beyond the boundaries of time and space and summoned me here to ask a favour?"

"Well, you *did* say you owed me one, Sire."

Godred thought for a moment.

"Yes, yes, you're right, I did. So what can I do for you?"

Al explained about Poyllvill, and about Norman Bridson. Godred seemed unimpressed. "I don't do parlour tricks, Althelbrede," he said sternly. "If you're asking me for some cheap Hop Tu Naa tomfoolery I shall be most displeased."

Al quaked under Godred's gaze.

"N-no Sire." He tried to keep his voice steady. " I just want you ... that is ... I was just wondering if you would be so gracious as to consider ..."

"Oh, do get to the point, Althelbrede, I can't abide crawlers."

"Just talking to him, Sire? Just explaining?"

Godred stroked his beard thoughtfully.

"Is he Manx, or Norse?" he asked, finally.

"Manx, Sire. They're ... um ... all Manx nowadays. Well, apart from the English. And the Irish. And the ... rest. It's been a while since you were last here, Sire."

Godred narrowed his eyes.

"How long, exactly?"

"Oh, about nine hundred years or so. Give or take." Al tensed for flight, ready to dodge the lethal swipe of a Norse sword, but Godred just raised his eyes heavenward.

"Fine, well, I hope you know what you're doing." He picked up his sword and stomped off down the hill, leaving Al to scurry after him. "And after this, we're even. Agreed?"

They disappeared round the corner to Norman's farm, and Sam peeled himself away from the shadow of a large rock. His ears were flattened against his head and his fur stood straight out from his body. On his way down to Port Erin for the night, he had heard a noise and come over to investigate. Casting his mind back, he could not remember a more terrifying experience. He had to let Jim know, at once. He set off as fast as his trembling legs would carry him.

★   ★   ★

Norman was in his kitchen, finishing off his library book, when he heard the doorbell. His wife was away visiting her sister in Belfast for the week, and he wasn't expecting visitors. He marked his place and went to answer the door.

"Norman Bridson," boomed the Viking apparition on his doorstep. "I am Godred Crovan, Gorry the Dane, King of Man, Slayer of … hang on a minute, have we met?"

Al peered round the doorframe. This was an unexpected strategy even by Godred's standards, and he'd always been aware of the tactical advantages of misdirection. Norman just looked nonplussed.

"I don't think so."

"Are you sure?" Godred leaned closer, studying Norman. "You're not related to Aufrica of Galloway, are you, your face is ever so familiar?"

"I think I would remember," said Norman,

Al felt that the moment was slipping away.

"Sire," he urged gently, "the incantation doesn't last long."

"What? Oh yes. Mind if we come in?"

Norman stood aside, and Godred and Al stepped into the hall, Al looking decidedly uncomfortable. Norman looked from one to the other. The silence lengthened.

"Tea?" he offered eventually.

"No thanks," said Godred. "We can't stop. The thing is, Althelbrede here is concerned about your plans for Poyllvill. Wanted me to stop in and have a little chat, see if we couldn't come to some other arrangement."

Another, potentially even longer, silence was prevented from developing as the doorbell rang again. He stepped past Al and opened the door to reveal Jim Quine and Sam, both out of breath, Jim carrying a sheaf of maps and papers. His eyes widened when he saw Godred and Al in the hall.

"Evening, Norman, mind if I come in?"

Norman had decided to go with the flow until further notice.

"Sure, come on in. Are we expecting anybody else?" he

asked. Jim smiled,

"Well, it might be an idea to call Ms Caine. I think she would find this meeting useful."

Norman moved to the telephone as if in a daze, picked up Wendy's card from the table and took four attempts to press the right buttons. Meanwhile, Jim smiled at Godred.

"May I introduce myself? My name's Jim Quine, I'm a friend of Althelbrede's. Am I right in thinking that you're King Orry?"

Godred glowered at Jim.

"What? Who *dares* call me Orry?"

Jim looked taken aback.

"Sorry, no offence meant. It's just – the history books, the boats, the grave ..."

"What?"

Norman prevented the conversation from deteriorating any further by hanging up the phone, "Right, she's on her way over. Now, what exactly is going on here?"

Godred was still glaring thunderously around the room, so Jim decided to take the floor.

"Well, I just wondered if everything was all right. Sam saw ... I mean, *I* saw Althelbrede and King O– this gentleman coming over, and thought you might need a little help."

Norman thought so too.

"Godred here said something about Poyllvill. About the little fellow ..."

"Althelbrede," they chorused,

"... being worried about it?" Norman was beginning to see the light. "Is this about those birds?"

Sam had had enough. He'd been scared half to death, forced to humiliate himself with a passable feline Lassie impression to drag Jim over here, and he was damned if he was going to stand around listening to them argue about birds all night. He turned and stalked off into the darkness.

Moments later, a crunch of gravel announced the arrival of Wendy Caine. She rushed into the hallway, looked at Norman, Jim, Althelbrede and Godred, swayed, gathered herself and smiled the smile of a woman in complete control.

"Everything all right, Norman?" she asked in a tense voice.

Norman had no idea. He looked helplessly at Jim, who looked uncertainly at Godred, who glowered at Althelbrede, who sighed.

"The thing is," he said reluctantly, "I heard you talking about moving the coaches from the quarry to Mr Bridson's farm, and using Poyllvill as a pathway for the tourists, and I wanted to stop it, because I've lived there my whole life, and so Mr Quine said he'd help me with a petition and then I heard Ms Caine say that there was always an old dear with a petition and it never made any difference so I summoned Godred Crovan to scare Mr Bridson into changing his mind and he just started on about how Mr Bridson reminds him of his daughter-in-law and then you all turned up and … and …" his confidence failed him, and he stared at the floor.

There was a moment of silence as they each considered their roles in the saga. Norman spoke first.

"I didn't know anybody lived there. I just thought it would be good to use that field for something, maybe make a bit of extra cash, I mean, the lambs don't bring in half of what they did, and it's an expensive place to keep up. If it'd mean you losing your home, Althelbrede, then we'll just forget it."

Wendy interrupted,

"But you can't just back out now, Norman. I'm sorry about the pond, Mr Althelbrede, really, but if you look at the bigger picture, you'll see Cregneish is a snapshot of Manx history, and if we can expand that to the surrounding areas, the better that is for everyone."

"Rubbish!" Jim Quine was still smarting over the reference to old dears with petitions. "You're talking to a Norse sprite, two born and bred Manxmen and one of the founding Kings of Man about the bigger picture? If you go ahead with this then you're destroying the real past and replacing it with a fake. Poyllvill is a thousand years of history, right there, not some daft rustic bridge."

"Why not use the other path?" said Godred. He was looking at one of Jim's old maps.

"What other path?" Norman peered over Godred's shoulder, Jim crowded over the other one.

"See here." Godred traced a line with his finger. "This other path goes along a fair way to the west of Poyllvill and joins the road on the corner."

"I didn't even know there was a path there," said Norman. "How old's that map?"

"1868," said Jim, beginning to smile. "And room on that corner for a refreshment stand, eh, Norman? Sell a few Manx Ices to the visitors."

"May I see?" Wendy looked, and nodded. "If we widened the verge along the road, I don't see why not."

Al thought he might cry. He bowed low to Godred.

"Thank you, Sire." He turned to Jim, "and thank *you*, Jim Quine." He smiled happily at Norman and Wendy. They were already poring over the map, discussing the excavation of the path. Godred picked up his sword.

"Come, Althelbrede, I must return home."

"Yes, Sire." Godred led Al and Jim out. Jim paused to ask Al, quietly,

"Just one thing. Why was he so upset about being called Orry?"

Al hung back a moment so that Godred wouldn't hear him.

"It was a nickname that he got on the way over from Norway.

He suffered terribly with seasickness. That was why I came with him, you see, the Woundwort did the trick." Jim shook his head. He still didn't understand. Al continued, "The lads on the boat called him Orry because that was the noise he made over the side from Flekkefjord to the Hebrides." Al winked. "Keep it to yourself, though."

Jim laughed.

"Come *on*, Althelbrede!" Godred was becoming impatient.

"One minute, Sire, I just want to tell Sam the news." Al looked round, but couldn't see him. "Where did he go?"

"Here he comes now," Jim nodded down the road, where Sam was walking, very slowly, towards them. As he got closer, they could see that he was wearing an evil smile.

"Problem solved," he said happily. He belched, coughed and spat out two long white feathers with distinctive orange splashes on the base. Jim and Al looked at him, aghast.

"What?" he said.

july

Vivienne Higgins is Manx born and lives in Douglas with her husband and young daughter. After leaving the Isle of Man College in 1985 with a BTEC National Diploma she worked as a manager for the Isle of Man Treasury.

Vivienne now works as a freelance writer with a specific interest in Manx history, herbalism and the flora and fauna of the Island.

voices

Vivienne Higgins

Erin was worrying about 'moving day' tomorrow, restless in the heat of the July night. She woke, then slept again, but her dream was unsettling.

A small child was gathering blackberries and wild strawberries in the hedgerows with her mother. Golden gorse clothed the hedges, and the gentle sun warmed her hair in the stiff breeze. Her bonnet hung down and her snowy-white pinny was stained deep red and purple, holding her harvest. Her mother stayed in the lane, but kept a close watch over her daughter as the child climbed a stile to search in a field. Hooves thudded dully on the dry track, a horse whinnied as it was reined in. The child peeped round the hedge and saw a handsome rider – a stranger with fine clothes and a black hat. She carried on picking her berries.

A cry of alarm whistled by on the wind. She hurried back to the stile and saw her frightened and upset mother, held tight at the wrist by the big, rough man. Her mammy struggled, then glimpsed her daughter hiding nearby. The child screamed when he tore her mammy's dress. He spun around, giving the woman a vicious push, then swung quickly up onto his horse and thundered away.

Wild-eyed, the young woman stumbled backwards into the deep ditch, smashing hard against the dry stone wall. Her daughter squealed and scrambled to her. There was strawberry juice in her mammy's hair and a deep, red gash across her cheek. Her emerald eyes fluttered open, wet with tears and she reached to stroke the small, anxious face. They held hands tight.

"Mammy loves you," she whispered, before the smile tightened and her grip went slack. Her eyes were open but she couldn't see. Her lips were pale, her head floppy. It was blood that trickled to mix with the final tear on her white face. With a shaky hand the little girl wiped it away, then nuzzled her mother's still-warm neck. She sang a lullaby until her voice faltered, breaking into great, wretched sobs. Mammy hadn't yet taught her how it finished. Now she never would.

A woman found them, on the track from Ballasalla to Castletown, the child still nursing her poor, dead mother, singing over and over again, a lullaby without an end. The little girl had woven buttercups and pale pink thrift through her mammy's flaxen hair before crowning her, tenderly, with a circlet of daisies.

Erin whimpered. Always the same dream. Would this never stop?

* * *

The cottage seemed much smaller than Erin remembered at the viewing. Spuds and Herring, freshly released from their cat box, were tentatively stepping about, examining every dusty nook and cranny they could find. Three loud thumps on the front door sent them scampering to hide amongst the packing cases. Sunshine, and a salty-sea smell flooded in as Erin answered the door.

A man of about seventy was doing his best to skeet past her into the sitting room. "*Moghrey mie!*" he said, a crinkly smile making his tanned face crumple like a brown paper bag. He held out a weathered hand. "Charlie Kelly, next door neighbour." He bobbed his head, blatantly taking in all the stuff on the sitting-room floor, including, to Erin's dismay, the box marked 'bras and knickers'.

"Pest Control came round yesterday, aye, left some stuff in the back yard. Longtails! I'd watch them kittens if I were you. Your side, not mine. *Slane lhiat!*"

Tugging his cap politely, he walked off up the road. Erin was left open-mouthed but smiling at his Manxness – dying out now of course. She hadn't even had a chance to introduce herself!

At six o'clock she ate quiche with broccoli and a jacket potato on the sofa, a kitten snuggling against her on each side.

"I've got to get things sorted out tomorrow, and get some coal for that fire", she thought aloud.

Although it was July, the cottage was chilly. She scowled at the Manx stone fireplace dominating one wall of her tiny sitting room, sucking all the heat up the chimney. She heard a scratching noise over the partition into the kitchen. "And mouse traps too," she groaned, "or are you two going to make yourselves useful?" Spuds and Herring didn't move, snoring contentedly.

Next morning, Erin woke at ten fifteen, horrified she'd slept so late. Jumping out of bed, she stood on a nail sticking up from the floorboards, then nearly fell down the stairs – she'd forgotten how steep they were. She stopped dead at the bottom. Gas! She sniffed again. Yes, definitely gas. One minute later she was frantically rattling Charlie's 'Three Legs of Mann' brass knocker.

149

"Hold on there, girl!" Charlie arrived in the street behind her, a paper under his arm.

"Gas leak, Charlie! Can I use your phone?" She felt ridiculous in her pink dressing gown and fluffy slippers. Charlie ushered her to the phone, then disappeared to put the kettle on.

Two hours later, they waved off a stony-faced gas man, who had given Erin time to go and get dressed before giving her a stern lecture on wasting his time, and about *real* emergencies.

"How was I to know it was only last night's broccoli, in the pan on the stove?" she mumbled, sheepish now in front of Charlie.

"I'll have to get going!" he said, looking at his watch and deftly sidestepping the question. "You need curtains up here before tonight ... the Ghost Walk comes past this way. You don't want them all seeing you in those jim-jams of yours now, do you?". Erin agreed, and hurried upstairs to do her make-up in the cosy bedroom. She tidied her glossy, strawberry-blonde hair then dashed out with her purse.

The market was quiet, but she found everything she needed, then she ordered a cup of tea at the refreshments van and sat down at a rickety table.

"Live 'ere, do you?" asked the woman curiously, placing a scalding cup of the weakest tea ever seen on the Island, in front of Erin. The table wobbled, slopping the tea. "Well, only since yesterday. I'm starting a new life! I've just retired at the end of the summer term."

"Never! Well, you're certainly not sixty!"

"No – fifty!" Erin cringed inwardly, wishing she was only twenty-one.

"Well, you don't look it!" laughed the woman. "We're here most Thursdays – market's been going for years. Used to do the executions 'ere too! See you then!"

Erin sipped her tea and grimaced. Yuck! Was it execution by tea, she wondered? Then she made for home, struggling with all her bags.

Walking back, the old, familiar loneliness crept around her like the cloak of Manannan's fog and she was glad to reach her own front door.

"Weather's turning!" called a passing fisherman.

"Is it?"

"Aye. I can taste it. You get to know…"

"I expect so," murmured Erin, as the man walked on, looking as if he had saltwater in his veins.

Later, she woke on the sofa, stiff and uncomfortable, a kitten licking her ear. She could hear a man's voice outside. The fire was low, the room chilly. She got up and opened the front door. A man was perched precariously on her windowsill, surrounded by a crowd of about twenty people. He was telling a story. He pointed his stick towards her door just as it creaked open. A few people screamed and everyone else laughed. Erin dived back inside quickly, aware her hair must look as wild as a witch's!

At bedtime she lay in a warm, lavender-scented bubble-bath, her eyes closed. She was nicely relaxed when she became aware of faint voices. She wasn't afraid, just strangely reassured. She thought about why she had retired early. 'Over-stressed,' the doctor had said, but Erin knew it wasn't that. She'd simply pleaded the need to do other things, and had gone happily on her way.

It was the dreams that plagued her every night, and she 'saw' things in the daytime too. Not frightening things, just scenes, like watching a snippet of a play. Fleeting and simple. They were such a normal part of her life now that she barely noticed them. She had never told her doctor about these little vignettes – he'd only send her for tests!

Later in bed she felt rested, cocooned in the small, low-ceilinged room. She realised, as she snapped off the lamp, that she hadn't felt so happy for a very long time.

* * *

September 1st 1796, and an old woman shuffled into Castletown market-place. Clothed practically in rags, she sat down and opened up a sack. Inside was an array of small cloth bags, tied at the top, and a selection of tiny brown jars with fat, cork stoppers. People pretended not to notice, but all had seen her come. There was an air of unease, and folk instinctively began to move away.

When her wares were laid out, she raised her head, lifting her hood a little. Her face remained hidden. She sat very still, just watching. Then she shifted, and poked all her pieces with a bony finger. Once satisfied with her display, she began to rock steadily, backwards and forwards, singing a wistful song in ancient Manx. Women whispered,gathering together, buzzing, like flies to a cowpat. The men were bolder and some ventured near, but none approached her.

It was Aalish Kerruish who went to the woman, leaving her grandmother selling their eggs and cheese. There was a strong, musty smell on the old woman's clothes.

"*Moghrey mie!* What are you selling?"

"Cures and herbals for all and any ills," she answered without looking up, "and an eye to tomorrow or words from beyond."

Aalish held her breath for a moment, gathering her wits about her.

"I'm sorry. I need nothing from you." But suddenly, the old crone grabbed her wrist -the grip as tight as an iron cuff. Aalish cried out.

"Wait! I can cure your broken heart, and these rough hands.

Soft hands suit a soft heart."

Aalish looked at her hands. They *were* rough from all the hard work at home. "Thank you," she said, meaning to add that she didn't have a broken heart.

"Shh!" the old woman hissed, then quickly set to work. She chose a small pot and measured out a scoop of golden salve, before handing it to Aalish.

"And for my broken heart?" teased Aalish, lightly.

Lifting her hooded head slowly, a single, glimmering, black eye was suddenly visible.

There was no other. Aalish gasped. The woman answered the question with one of her own.

"What do you see?" Her voice was velvety.

Aalish tried to speak, but found she could not – her own voice was caught fast in her throat. She tried again, never taking her green eyes from that piercing black one.

"Someone ... someone looking for my soul!"

"Aye," nodded the old woman. "Can you read and write? You got any learnin'? The truth now! I'll not want to be wasting my time."

Aalish nodded.

"You're Voirrey Kerruish's grandchild." She wasn't asking, she was telling. "Aye, you're like her. She's a good 'un. The fruit don't fall far from the tree." Then, more gently, she said, "She teached ye', did she?"

Aalish nodded again, aware that the old woman was looking her over, like one of the calves at market.

"Your broken heart will mend quicker with knowledge."

"Knowledge? I don't understand. And I don't have ..." she didn't finish. The old woman put a finger to her lips.

"Mine! The old ways. I could teach you. Tell me at noon what you say."

Aalish was speechless. She rubbed her arm, red now where

153

she'd been held, then snatched up her salve and turned to drop a few small coins onto the sack.

"Noon – mind you don't go forgetting now." The voice trailed to a wheezing cackle as Aalish fled.

She dodged around the stalls and townsfolk with their raggedy children, pushing through people carrying bread and sacks of apples. She was glad to find her Gran still selling cheese.

"Aalish! Where've you been girl? Did you get that fish I sent you for?"

Aalish grimaced. Her errand had been completely forgotten. "Sorry Gran."

"God bless us! Tsk, tsk …be off with you and fetch it quick. Too much of this *traa-dy-liooar* with you sometimes!"

Aalish did as she was bid. She returned with the herring, then set to work at the stall,all the while watching the clock on the walls of Castle Rushen.

There seemed to be a natural lull at about eleven, so Gran opened a tied cloth revealing a meal fit for the Lords of Mann. Bread, cheese, even a bit of mutton and some apples. Aalish fetched drinking water from the nearby well and as they ate, she showed her grandmother the salve and told her what had happened.

"Old, did you say?" Gran asked, sniffing suspiciously at the little pot.

"Yes. With so many cures as I've never seen, an' bent double she was. And somethin' else …"

"Tell me, child."

"She had just one eye! Well, I think she did." Then she told of their conversation, and her appointment at noon.

"Well I never!" Voirrey Kerruish shook her head, whistling through her teeth, as she chewed on a gristly bit of meat. "That'll be Nana Comaish then."

"Nana who?"

"Nana Comaish. She's not seen out much these days. She must be a good age by now ... no doubt folk still call on her though!" The woman clearly had a shady reputation, given her grandmother's snort of disapproval. "'September," she mused, "nearly Autumn. A time of maturity, then decline. And she wants to teach *you*?"

"Yes. But what? And why me?" Aalish was wide-eyed at the very thought of it.

"Because she knows," said her grandmother mysteriously, gazing away, far across the square, to where the crowd milled around the old woman. Then, as she squinted into the low sun she added, "She's come a-lookin'."

It was impossible of course. Aalish was needed at home – she could not be spared even if gran had wanted her to go, which she didn't. So when noon came, she was sent back to the old woman.

A boy was playing Aalish's favourite tune on a whistle and, as the melody washed over her, she watched the people swarm around Nana Comaish. A farmer nearby was selling potatoes, and the smell of freshly dug earth made her yearn for home and Gran's blazing hearth. The old woman had spotted her and raised her hand, only to drop it down, slowly, as she got back to her work. It was a sign that she already knew Aalish's answer. The girl hung her head, ashamed that the old woman would believe her to be a coward, surprised too at how relieved she was to be able to turn and walk away.

Voirrey Kerruish died the following September. She had been failing after a fall, up Snaefell, cutting peat. No one was surprised when she finally slipped away.

No one except Aalish.

Within a week, the girl was turned out of the cottage she had lived in since she was a child. Despite her pleas, the landowner said she was too young, at seventeen, to run the smallholding. He had a young farmer in mind who was ready to work the land. And so Aalish found herself back at Castletown market-place, at the Michaelmas Fayre, 29th September 1797, looking for work and lodgings for the coming year. She did not join in the traditional dancing, but just listened to the soulful tunes, played on the whistles by the ruddy-cheeked girls. She ached for Gran and feared the future.

A chill wind blew through the square, and Aalish pulled her thin shawl tighter around her shoulders. Then her heart missed a beat. An old woman shuffled into the market-place, dressed practically in rags. Aalish watched as she sat down, opened her sack, then carefully laid out her wares. After a moment of stillness, she began to rock slowly, backwards and forwards, and her haunting song began.

Aalish was drawn to the old woman, pulled almost against her will, by some invisible thread until, standing in front of her, she said "*Moghrey mie*. What are you selling?"

"Cures and herbals for all and any ills, and an eye to tomorrow or words from beyond," was the answer.

Aalish said, as before, "I'm sorry. I need nothing from you," only to hear "I can cure your broken heart and these rough hands. Soft hands suit a soft heart."

This time Aalish didn't smile. Last year's conversation was being replayed. Nana Comaish spoke the truth, and had foretold her present heartbreak a whole year earlier. Terror choked her as hot tears spilled, unchecked, down her bone-white cheeks. The old woman watched, with her glinting, all-seeing eye.

Aalish's tongue thickened in her mouth and blood rushed in her ears. Tiny, tiny stars danced before her eyes. Her knees buckled, and she stumbled down, into a dense blackness. She was caught, falling in a dead faint, by Nana Comaish herself –

small and quick as a wren, yet strong as an ox.

She woke on a narrow bunk in a warm, windowless room. Someone was singing far away. Her eyes felt so heavy. She could see nothing, until a candle threw ugly shadows onto the rough walls. Footsteps shuffled nearby. A lamp was lit. Then a tin cup was pressed to her lips, and she swallowed something bitter.

"Gran?"

"Hush child ... rest now." She was pressed back firmly against the scratchy pillow, and a musty smell wafted over her.

Nana Comaish came back a few hours later and sat on the bed. She watched Aalish in the candlelight.

"So ... I never got a chance to ask. Just fainted away, you did. Shall I teach you the old ways?" She paused. "Do we have a bond?"

Aalish rubbed her eyes and considered everything for a moment. Grans' death, her home gone, no work to be had. She drained the cup and shyly handed it back. "Aye, we have a bond."

Nana Comaish gave a toothless smile and patted her hand.

Aalish was made to rest all day, aware that many visitors called at Peggy Comaish's door. Mostly women, some with babes in arms, all in need of the wise-woman's remedies, or her advice or ... something else.

'They can't all be sick,' Aalish thought, as the door rattled shut again. Castletown folk were as hardy as any Manxmen. Out in all weathers, living off the sea and the land in times of hardship and plenty.

"What do they all want?" she asked Peggy later.

"They're after what they're needin', that's all!"

Suddenly, she said "Hush! Look, can you see it?" and she pointed a stabbing finger into the gloom on the stairwell.

Aalish peered, but could see nothing in the shadows. And

then – a wisp, a shape.

Wavy and dark. Then it became more defined as though a fog was clearing. A beautiful lady was staring down into the cellar. Her clothes were odd, not rough wool like Aalish wore, but more colourful and in a strange style. Her red-blonde hair gleamed in the lamp light. She seemed to wait a moment, like a cat at the edge of a strange garden, then descended. She approached one of the cupboards and leaned forward, trying to read the labels on the jars. Aalish held her breath.

"She'll be gone in a minute," whispered Peggy. "She can hear us – she's listening.

Just look at her!"

It was true. She was standing perfectly still, eavesdropping on the past.

"And one day she might see us. She's from the time to come, when we're dust probably. She might even be livin' here for all we know. She could be learnin' our secrets too."

Aalish had no idea what Peggy meant about secrets. When she turned to look again the lady was on the stairs. Then the woman turned, and shock creased her face as she saw the two women below. She fled. Peggy turned to Aalish, triumphant and smiling. She was nodding and Aalish felt as though she might cry.

"I knows … Your Gran, God bless her – she told me once, when you were a little 'un. How you sees things and hears things – like me. You've got to nurture it. Don't be afraid. Use it! The craft, well, that's long in the learnin' but you'll do well, I know it now. You proved you're ripe for it just then – no fear, just accepting it." Peggy took a deep breath. "Listen," she hissed, a knobbled hand on Aalish's arm, "you must take and learn from the past, enjoy the present and add your voice to the future. Are you ready?"

Aalish closed her eyes, breathing in the dry, mustiness of

the cellar, and the pungent scent of hanging herbs. She heard her own voice say "Yes ... yes I am"

They did not notice the lady still listening at the top of the stairs.

★ ★ ★

By mid-September, Erin was depressed. School had been her way of life, every minute accounted for, bells going off regularly, specific break-time allotted. Now she found herself struggling to fill her days. She'd wander aimlessly around the old streets of Castletown, coming back along the quayside to feed the ducks and swans.

Today, she watched the boats bobbing about on the water in the low September sun. It was a perfect autumn morning, with a cloudless sky and fresh, salty breeze. *Search Beneath* was the name of one brightly painted boat and, as she turned for home, the name danced around in her head.

Crossing the swing bridge, she veered along the harbourside, cutting up the narrow back street adjoining hers. She was met by three Manx cats, all friendly but full of fleas. They squirmed as she bent to tickle them. Then she noticed that each house had a tiny window at floor level. Cellars. She wondered if her little cottage had one – there had been no mention of a cellar in her deeds.

Straightening up, she stopped dead. Everything was different. Their cottages were still there, but changed almost beyond recognition – changed back to the old times. The street itself was little more than a lane, the mud dotted with fist-sized stones from the shore, giving a rough, cobbled surface. The smooth render of the cottages was gone, showing the common grey stone which emphasised the poor, huddled look.

The door of Erin's cottage opened and a tiny old woman stepped out, broomstick in hand.

A long pinny covered her heavy woollen dress, she wore clogs on her feet and a shawl hung around her shoulders. Erin stared, fascinated yet uneasy. After sweeping the front, the woman turned to go back inside, looked up and saw Erin. She smiled right at her, nodded, then went inside.

Erin froze. She rubbed hard at her eyes, opening them to find the scene gone, and the street back as it should be. She looked around, as if seeing the place for the first time. Creamy cottages, Charlie's dirty red door next to her cornflower-blue one, house numbers, letterboxes, road, pavement. A nerve began to twitch under her left eye. The seagulls' screams were too loud, mocking her. Had they seen it too? One gull chose that moment to make a direct hit on an unsuspecting Erin, literally adding insult to injury. She gasped as the warm deposit ran through her hair and down her cheek. But still she didn't move, seemingly glued to the pavement.

The little sightings had happened a few times before but never like this. No one had ever seemed to be aware that they were being watched. This was different – the old lady had clearly acknowledged her presence. Erin didn't like it – not one bit.

A door began to creak open. This time it was Charlie's. He stepped out, fixing his cap, then saw his neighbour. He gawped at her, standing so still in the road, awash in bird droppings.

"*Moghrey mie!*" he called cheerily.

When she didn't answer he stepped over and touched her arm. She jumped, as if she'd stood on a jellyfish. Charlie stepped back, peering at her closely. She got a waft of soap and his porridge breakfast.

'It's only seagull muck, love, it'll wash off! By golly you *are* a real townie, aren't you? Hardly know what's hit you!' and, well and truly tickled, he chuckled all the way to the newsagents.

Erin glanced down, noticing the white splash beside her on the pavement. She felt quite shaken. Then, remembering the cellars, she looked for a small window but didn't find one. With a trembling hand, she put her key in the door, trying to ignore the prickle of fear as she stepped into her home. Into the unknown.

Everything seemed to be all right inside, so she cleaned herself up, lit the fire and put the kettle on to boil. What if there *was* a cellar? There didn't have to be a window. Where would you access it?

It didn't take long to find the forgotten trap-door in the understairs cupboard. She tugged the iron ring gingerly, and saw the steepest stairs she had ever encountered. She fetched a torch. When she was halfway down, an icy chill and eerie silence wrapped around her. Her torch cast gruesome shapes up the walls. Sweeping the weak light around the cellar, Erin gave a long, low whistle before continuing. There were wooden dressers lining three walls, shelves laden with jars. Each bottle and jar had been carefully labelled and those labels were now yellowed with age. A wooden bunk, with a straw mattress and blanket, was placed against one wall. As a teacher, Erin had visited many folk museums, but she had never before seen such a display, untouched and forgotten in the passage of time. This could easily rival Harry Kelly's cottage at Cregneish. She examined the jars on the shelves. Dried herbs, tisanes, bottles of mysterious potions and remedies, all thick with dust and cobwebs. But she didn't linger long. This was no museum; it was her home, her property. And however impressive it all was, Erin knew one thing for certain – all this junk would have to go.

As she stood there, she heard voices, soft as a dove, in the dim light. Her scalp tightened as she hastily made for the stairs. Something made her look back, and she strained her eyes to scan the depths of the cellar, immediately spotting an old woman, bent nearly double. The one she had seen outside. Then she noticed a girl lying in the bed. Clutching the cold iron stair-rail, she scrambled back to the safety and normality of her cosy kitchen.She made a cup of hot, sweet tea and tried to calm down until she felt ready, an hour later, to brave the descent to the cellar again. It was sort-out time!

Erin was leaning over the open book, struggling to see in the torchlight. 'Take three times, as the first helpeth not,' she read. Giving a sigh, she closed the book and decided to go back upstairs to reality, and to get warm. She had seen enough for today. It was nearly six o'clock, so she carefully laid the heavy book on the lumpy mattress, her head buzzing. Ways to make cider, methods to make nettle beer and cough syrups, earache remedies, soothing salves and poultices, all with strict instructions for their use. All these things and many, many more, written in tricky-to-read script, with sketches too. All skills unknown for generations, yet carefully and precisely recorded here.

Back in the kitchen, Erin thought about the book. Rough, handmade paper, leather covers, smooth from years of use. Who had written it? Those two women? They had called it 'A Household Herbal – A Record of the Old Ways'. Fascinating. And all still intact, in the very place it belonged, where it had been used, and even with the apparatus used by its scribe or scribes. Erin knew it was quite a find. Now she just had to decide what to do about it.

She took her time over dinner. Yesterday, the rather alarming chasm of retirement had gaped ahead of her. Now, she felt short of time because she had a purpose, a mission. A very important one.

After her meal, Charlie called and persuaded her to go on a Ghost Walk – his treat.

She felt nervous at five minutes to eight, waiting beside Charlie in the square. He grinned at her in his gummy way. He was not in the habit of putting his teeth in, even on a big night out, but he had popped a clean jumper on under his anorak. Erin wished she hadn't come. Her pulse was quick, and she felt as though a moth was fluttering at the base of her throat. She tried to make an excuse to leave, but Charlie made such a fuss she had to stay.

Despite her initial reservations she found, almost immediately, that she was enjoying herself and really having fun. The storyteller was good, clearly relishing the job, and there were some spooky surprises along the way. Then they arrived outside her cottage. She held her breath.

"Not far from here is the market square where witches were hanged. And here is the home of a Manx woman named Peggy Comaish. She reached the ripe old age of ninety-three. Some records say she was a witch, and notorious in the south of the Island. Others say she was just a wise-woman, healing the sick and helping the townsfolk. She taught a young girl, Aalish Kerruish, her craft of herbalism. Rumour has it that they once helped the Castletown Witch Finder, and it was widely believed Nana Comaish may have struck a bargain with him, to spare them both from persecution. But she was arrested, once, along with Aalish Kerruish – and imprisoned on suspicion of witchcraft for some days in Castle Rushen. They protested their innocence, and many, many local people vouched for their good character and kind deeds. With such support from the locals and no clear evidence of wrongdoing, they were released.

Erin closed her eyes at the back of the crowd .She felt a bit sick. That poor old woman and the girl, imprisoned in Castle Rushen. On suspicion of witchcraft. She couldn't bear to think about it. So many other innocent women were put to death if suspected of such things. And now it seemed worse – because now she knew their names.

She saw them later.

Hearing voices whilst on the moon-blanched landing, she looked into the bedroom. *Their* bedroom. Gloomy, with the same sagging floor, but the ceiling open to the roof joists. Plainly furnished, with little thought for their comfort. They didn't hear her. The girl, seemingly a little older now, was doing the bidding of the elder, labelling bottles. At first their voices were muffled, like a distant radio programme, but slowly they grew louder.

"When you've done this, you can write some more in the book," said Peggy.

"It doesn't do to be idle!" Aalish laughed.

Trapped in a pocket of time, like two insects in amber, they played their story out for Erin. Peggy prattled on. Erin watched until she got pins and needles, wondering why they were staying so long. Was it she who was trapped in time? She carried on listening.

"Knowledge. It needs passing on, or many skills learned will be forgotten. Ought to write it all down, see, the old ways. It's sad when skills of our grandparents are learned only to be forgotten, lost with time. It's a waste, a sin. We need to treasure the old ways, our traditions. If we don't they'll be gone, lost forever."

The girl nodded, and Erin realised she was nodding too. Seconds later, they had gone.

★ ★ ★

One night in late September, they had a caller after Aalish had gone to bed. Next morning Nana Comaish was troubled.

"We've a visitor to tend to. You'll have to see to the work and I'll see to him. Nasty business. Keep your own counsel, do you hear?" Aalish merely nodded and went out to pick some herbs.

But next day, Peggy was agitated. Fever was rising, wound could go bad, she said. Aalish had heard him, wailing and screaming all night, down in the cellar. They nursed him night and day. In the parlour at dawn, Peggy had a haunted look about her."He's a grand gentleman. Someone'll hear him, with all his noise. Been up to no good, he has! And ranting about a murder. He did it, he's saying, over some stuff smuggled in!"

"A murder? But what's to be done?" Aalish was frantic. "We can't keep him here!

And he's a smuggler too?" Aalish was horrified at the thought of a murdering smuggler under their roof. She could barely believe it.

"We have to, Aalish. There's no movin' him. Might die, see?"

Later, Aalish took over more of his care, fearing Peggy would exhaust every bone in her tired old body. The knife wound was nasty, deep in his left shoulder, and his breathing and colour were bad. It took all their skills to keep the wound from rotting, with constant bathing and applying poultices. They controlled his fever with herbs and potions and, at last, the fever broke.

Two days later, Aalish watched him sleeping. His face, once handsome, was spoiled with lines round his eyes and mouth, showing temper and stubbornness. His beard was short, his hair raven-black and long. Gimlet-eyed when awake, he showed no charm, never smiling or showing gratitude for the care he was given. He unsettled Aalish and she, like Nana Comaish would be glad when he was gone.

* * *

As she was putting some of her tomatoes onto the kitchen windowsill to ripen, Erin turned around and there they were, behind her at the fireplace, whispering. "Black Jack, he's known as, and his heart's black too, so they say. Should've left 'im where he fell – I would have."

"Who brought him though?" asked Aalish, "You've not said."

"Him! The Witch Finder!"

Aalish gasped, and choked on the crust she was eating. The old woman thumped her back, and handed her a ladle of water from the bucket. She explained she'd made a deal that if they got him right they'd have no trouble.

"And you trust him?" Aalish was close to tears. Peggy took her hands.

"Listen, my love. The way things are, well, we'll just have to."

Often now, they'd look right at Erin when she saw them, aware they were being seen and heard. Erin sometimes wondered if they changed the talk for her benefit – giving precise instructions for this, and samples of that. If they did, she took heed, and the very first chance she got, she wrote everything down.

* * *

Peggy was working at the spinning wheel by the fire and Aalish was at her feet, carding wool in the firelight. They were both tired but relieved. Black Jack had gone at first light. Aalish was thinking about how he'd caught her eye for a moment, holding her gaze with a queer, penetrating look, as if he knew her somehow. Then he had left.

Suddenly, with a gasp, she dropped the wooden brushes, and slumped forward like a wounded animal.

"What is it, child?" Peggy scrambled out of the chair to hold her close. Aalish was white with shock, her eyes wild. "Aalish! What is it?"

"Black Jack ..." She whispered at last, through pale, numb lips. "It was him, Peggy. Black Jack! *He* killed my mother." Then she cried as though her heart would break.

Peggy sucked in her breath. Now she understood her own instinctive dislike of him.

They talked about that day, when Aalish's mother had died, and about what Aalish had seen. They talked about Black Jack, and their work, and the risk they'd taken to nurse him in their very midst. They decided to take action. Peggy was worried Black Jack might still make trouble for them with the Witch Finder, despite having *his* word they would be left alone.

"Only place he could leave 'im see? What with him being in with the smugglers himself. Couldn't risk anywhere else. This would be the very last place anyone would think the Witch Finder would come – to the wise-woman's cottage!'

He had certainly been clever. Nevertheless, they hid everything they could. Aalish tucked the book behind a stone, deep in the chimney breast.

But they had a witness to their actions. Erin, shocked and afraid at all she had heard, watched unseen from a dark corner of the room.

Two weeks later, Aalish waited until after dark before stealing out of the cottage, through Castletown, and along the cliff path. She knew the way well. She found a part of the path where the gorse stopped, showing the cliff edge, and waited, crouched in a hollow, where rabbits liked to play. There would be no games tonight. Black Jack was in the alehouse and would come back this way.

The moon was full, the sky clear. Everything was bathed in a shimmering silver light. He was coming, cantering along on his huge, black horse. Hatred burned within her, bubbling through every vein.

As horse and rider passed by she sprang, with a terrifying

screech. The horse reared up, his shrill scream tearing the silence. Black Jack, full of ale, cursed and struggled with the terrified animal.

Aalish dodged the trampling hooves. Black Jack was unsure of the path. The edge crumbled, as Aalish knew it would. Scrambling for a foothold, the horse threw his rider. Black Jack's scream was cut short with the crack of his bones on the rocks below.

Aalish caught the horse. She whispered and soothed him and,when he was calm, she walked home without a backward glance.

When she slipped through the cottage door, not a word was said about where she had been, or what she had done.

★　★　★

After breakfast Charlie called at Erin's. It was a cool September morning, not yet eight o'clock, but she was out and about already, gathering this and that as usual.

"*Moghrey mie!*" she called to Charlie, as he turned from her unanswered door.

"Aye, *Moghrey mie*. Just off for the paper. Want anything?" He noticed she was a beauty still, even ten years on.

"I'll have a paper too, please."

Erin unlocked the front door, and put a wooden chair outside. Spuds and Herring were asleep on the sunny windowsill, two fat old gentlemen now. She took the opportunity to sweep the sitting-room floor, then sat, picking over the blackberries.

"Paper boy's back!" called Charlie, ten minutes later. "You were busy yesterday! You know where I am if you need any help."

"Thanks Charlie. Cuppa?"

"Aye, and a cup of that potion you take too, please!" Erin raised an eyebrow. "The one you use to keep young and beautiful!" His leathery face, thinner now, broke into a wide, gummy grin. Erin gave him a hug.. "Sorry Charlie, I just don't think it would work!"

Later, she turned the sign outside to 'Open'.

'Witch Ways' had been established seven years ago, after three years of intensive study. She had a real gift for herbalism and had made other changes too. The parlour was now a perfect copy of Peggy's and a cauldron hung over the fire, which was rarely allowed to go out. Customers were invited in, and even 'down below' to the cellar, to see where Erin worked, amongst the dressers brimming with bottles of tissanes and tinctures. They snapped up her organic remedies, along with her home-made bonnag, jams, pickles and chutneys.

She ran a market stall every Thursday, selling her wares much as Peggy Comaish once had. She had even studied palm reading, and 'read' for folk now and again, when she wasn't too busy on the stall or making potions. She was just what the market needed.

Now she placed her hand over the book she was reading. It was Peggy and Aalish's 'Herbal' with all their wise ways – she never tired of reading it. She glanced at the other book on the table, and felt the hairs prickle at the back of her neck. It was much smaller, wrapped in the soft goat's leather she'd found it in, deep inside the chimney breast. A very different book.

A secret book of potions, spells, rituals. Scary, even to Erin. They had always maintained a veneer of respectability, concealing a much darker truth. She'd been shocked to find a tiny doll with it, all stuck with black iron nails, along with clippings of human hair. Erin cherished the things, despite knowing the truth, often wondering what had become of the women. Perhaps one day she would find out. She opened her paper. Good, the advert was in. Modern times called for modern means. Well, so be it. This could take time, years maybe, and she had to be sure. It was her turn now. She was ready. She'd learned from the past, was enjoying the present – now for adding her voice to the future. She was sure they'd approve. She read it again:

WANTED
Girl to learn the Old Ways.
Serious enquiries only please.
Tel. 820001

'The Craft so long to lerne', they had written inside the front cover of the spell book. And they were right. Yes, she needed someone who could be trusted. Trusted to learn and keep their secrets. Peggy's, Aalish's and hers. Each and every one of them.

If she dared.

❈ August ❈

Jacqueline Shirtliff lives in Douglas with her husband and three children. She obtained a B.Ed. Honours degree in Education and Religious Studies at university and now works parttime as a primary school teacher around the Island.

Jacqueline is a keen writer and has had several articles published by *The Lady* and *Woman Alive* as well as being one of the editors of *Magnet*, a magazine published by the Methodist Church.

As well as writing, Jacqueline is also a keen musician and plays the tuba with the Isle of Man Wind Orchestra.

perfectly ruined

Jacqueline Shirtliff

Richard Tomkins was a property developer. A very wealthy property developer. He had made his fortune buying up derelict old buildings in desirable locations, renovating them and then selling them on at a handsome profit. Not that he was a particularly handy man himself. In fact he hardly knew one end of a hammer from the other. But he knew a few men who did. So whenever he bought another property he called in his team of workmen and, hey presto, that ramshackle old hut was miraculously transformed into a luxury residence.

But Richard Tomkins had made his fortune and he was ready to settle down, and so he was on the lookout for a very special property in a very special location. A place of his own for his team of workmen to renovate, and then he'd settle down and live off his profits. It had to be individual in character, in a quiet, unspoilt location, not too rural, not too far from the sea, nor too far from the hills either. Within easy reach of London. Everywhere he went he kept a lookout for the ideal ruin and then one day he spotted the perfect place.

He was on a brief business trip to the Isle of Man. He'd flown into Ronaldsway airport and was due to meet up with a contact at a restaurant along the Peel Road, to discuss the purchase and transportation of some rare-breed Loughtan sheep that an English customer was very keen to have wandering around the grounds of his newly restored farmhouse. It was as he approached the restaurant that he saw it, standing alone in a field, half hidden behind the avenue of beech trees that lined the road to Peel in one direction and Douglas in the other: a derelict church.

He mentally went through his checklist and ticked off every requirement. It fitted the bill exactly. A bolthole on the Isle of Man. Perfect. A tax haven too! He glanced at his ornate gold Rolex wristwatch. Still twenty minutes to go until his meeting. Just time to take a closer look.

He climbed out of the hire car and carefully locked the door behind him before making his way along the edge of the road and through the gap in the wall that must once have marked out the churchyard. It was a fine summer's day and as he strolled up through the long grass and meadow flowers, insects buzzed and chirrupped lazily around him. He reached the church and inspected the walls. Hmmm ... good strong stone and sturdily built. He found a doorway and went inside. Plenty of space. He could already imagine an open-plan design, with a gallery at one end. Without the roof there was plenty of light, and he made a note to try and keep as much of that light as possible, perhaps by incorporating glass panels as they replaced the roof. He looked at his watch again. Cripes! Was that the time? Must hurry or he'd lose the advantage and end up late for his meeting.

He was already seated with a glass of fruit juice in front of him when his business contact entered.

"Morning, Charles. Over here!"

Charlie Kissack turned and made his way across to Richard Tomkins's table.

"Good morning, Richard. Good journey?"

"Not bad. Left London City at eight. Here by nine. Pleasant drive over. Even time for a quick stroll around that old ruin before I came in."

"St Trinian's? Yes, could have been a fine church if they could've kept the roof on. You're not wondering about ...? No, don't even think about it, Richard."

"Oh?"

"Some old legend associated with the place. I should steer well clear if I were you. I'll tell you about it sometime. Anyway, time to get down to business. Coffee?"

The two men settled down to their discussions and the ruined church was temporarily forgotten. But that evening, as Richard Tomkins flew back into London City, he couldn't get St Trinian's out of his mind. He wanted that place as he'd wanted no other building. This was the one. His final renovation, the one to keep, the one to settle down in and to enjoy his wealth. He could see its potential. He had to have it.

The next morning he called an agency, one he'd dealt with before. They'd see what they could do, they said. They'd get back to him. Each time the phone went he dived for it, but it was never them. Finally, at twelve minutes past five, the call came.

"Mr Tomkins? The property on the Isle of Man. We've made some enquiries and traced the farmer on whose land the property stands. He was unwilling at first, mentioned problems and difficulties ..."

"Yes, yes, that's what they all say."

"But I told him you didn't care. You wanted to buy it anyway. We've finalised a figure. It's at the top of your price range, I'm afraid, but you did say you had to have it. We'll get the papers sorted and then all you have to do is sign."

Richard Tomkins was jubilant, although he'd known all

along that he'd get what he wanted. He always did. He called his building team immediately and put them on stand-by to start as soon as the property was legally his.

So came the last week of August, which is when our story really starts. Richard Tomkins signed the papers in London that morning and was on the Island in time for a late lunch at the restaurant adjacent to the ruined church. He spent the afternoon driving around the countryside, drinking in the beauty of the place. The sun sparkled on sea and mountainside, the hedgerows hung heavy with blackberries and the fuchsia dripped deep pink along the roadsides. That evening he went down to the Sea Terminal to meet his workmen off the six o'clock boat. It was busier than usual, with bikers coming in for the Grand Prix that week, but it wasn't long before men and machinery were clear of the crowds and heading out on the Peel Road. That night Richard Tomkins slept in one of the three campervans the workmen had brought across with them so they could all stay on site. Richard Tomkins trusted his men and didn't usually hang around to oversee work, but this renovation was different, and he wanted to be there.

The next day dawned cool and misty – the promise of a fine day ahead. The workmen set to with a will, as he'd known they would. Richard Tomkins rarely used local labour, and he certainly wasn't going to for this job. He wanted none of this '*Traa dy liooar* – time enough' Manx nonsense that Charlie Kissack was always going on about. No, he wanted the job done and done quickly. Consequently, though the locals looked on with interest from a distance, they never spoke to him. Indeed, there was much they could have told Richard Tomkins and his men had they but asked, but they never did, and so not a word was said.

With the Peel Road closed for the Grand Prix there was an eerie quiet about the place for much of that first day. Whenever the distant hum of approaching bikes broke the calm, the workmen downed tools and took their tea-break, propped against the churchyard wall, watching the racing. Despite the breaks the men worked hard and by the second week the walls were finished and the roof struts were going up. Richard Tomkins had spent much of the first week flying between London and Ronaldsway so that he could keep up with his clients whilst watching over the progress at St Trinian's. Now he spent his days working in the campervan on his laptop, just for the pleasure of watching his new home take shape, and he was pleased with the progress being made. He missed the buzz and bustle of the capital but he was beginning to appreciate the slower pace of life and the tranquillity that the Island had to offer. He felt sure he could be happy here.

By the third week, ancient panelled doors had been sourced and fitted into the front and back walls. Great piles of stone had been delivered ready for the putting-up of internal walls and the base for the waxed wooden floorboards had been laid. Other men had been working on the roof. Huge glass panels, brought over especially, were carefully lifted into place and fixed alongside sections of conventional tiling. By seven o'clock on Friday evening the last roof tile was fitted into place and the workmen grabbed their bags and caught the last flight back to England to spend the weekend with their families.

Richard Tomkins finished his microwaved lasagne and with wine glass in hand made his way out of the campervan and across the field towards the renovated church. Dusk was closing in fast and mist clung to the hillside that was no longer purple with heather but bronze with bracken. There was a nip in the air that hinted at the onset of autumn but Richard Tomkins couldn't help thinking how lucky they'd been with the weather. He'd heard some tales from Charles about the high winds and substantial rainfall that sometimes besieged the Island, but so far, so good. They'd had nothing but the cool misty mornings and long warm days of an Indian summer and so the building work had progressed fast. Now the outdoor work was complete. Come Monday they'd be making a start on the internal walls for the bedrooms and bathrooms and on constructing the gallery. When all that was complete they would lay the floors. For all he cared, the weather could break now. He took a turn around the old church, then returned to the cosy warmth of the van, where he watched the news before taking himself off for an early night.

He awoke with a start in the wee hours. Rain was lashing against the windows and a howling gale was whipping around the van, rocking it dangerously. Suddenly there was a tremendous gust followed by an almighty crash and the sound of breaking glass. The van juddered. Richard Tomkins leapt out of bed, pulled on a raincoat and boots, grabbed his spotlight and flung open the door.

The beam of his torch lit up a scene of utter devastation. The roof had lifted clean off the church and lay splintered on the sodden ground. The main beams had cracked and the huge glass panels were in smithereens. Richard Tomkins slammed the door of the campervan shut behind him and battled against the gale towards the heavy wooden doors of the church. He let himself in out of the wind and stood gazing up at where the roof had been. He was annoyed and frustrated. The loss of the roof would mean the work would be delayed for several weeks, while they waited for new materials to be shipped across and then put it all back together again. He'd hoped to be moving in well before Christmas but it looked like he might be hard pushed to make that now. He sighed, and behind him he heard an echo of that sigh, and yet, not quite an echo but more a low growl. Richard Tomkins froze. He felt a shiver go down his spine. Very slowly he turned and his eyes widened in terror as his spotlight lit up the most terrible form towering above him.

Its head was huge, and covered with a mane of coarse black hair. Its eyes punctured the darkness like fiery torches and piercing tusks protruded from its sagging jowls. Its ugly red mouth was open in a cruel sneer, displaying a row of razor-sharp yellow fangs. Thick black arms ending in huge fists and dangerous-looking claws hung from broad shoulders and its massive leathery belly sagged with wrinkles. Its loins and legs were covered in the same matted black fur that covered its head and curled about its ankles and hefty cloven feet. The beast glared down at him and spoke in a deep grating voice.

"What be you doing here, O Man?"

"I, I live here," stammered Richard Tomkins.

"No, man, *I* live here," replied the creature. "No man has lived here before and no man shall ever live here, in the shadow of Greeba, and disturb my peace. I shall not allow it. Now be you gone!"

"W – w – what are you?" stuttered Richard Tomkins.

"ME?" roared the creature, "Too long have I been sleeping under Mount Greeba that you know not who I am! I am the Buggane of St Trinian's!"

There was a flash of light and a plume of smoke and now the Buggane was a two-headed ogre, with blackened teeth and foul breath. "I," shouted the monster, and there was another flash of light, and in place of the ogre stood a snarling wolf, saliva dripping from its gaping mouth, "can take any form I wish. *Now be you gone.*"

Richard Tomkins was now backed right against the far wall of the church. He would have given anything to be tucked up warm and snug in his bed rather than suffering this living nightmare. Yet here was a man who always got everything he wanted. Despite his sheer terror, the fact that a mythological creature that he could barely bring himself to believe in but for the fact that it was at that moment drooling in front of him, riled him. He was never one to be easily beaten and he was not going to give in without a fight, even against a Buggane. Quickly he thought back to all the monstrous creatures he had ever known, and all the fairy tales he had heard at his mother's knee, and a sparkling plan flashed into his mind.

"Well, good evening," Richard Tomkins replied, as politely and calmly as he could in the circumstances. "I don't think I've ever had the pleasure of meeting a Buggane before. I'm Richard Tomkins." He held out his hand. "How do you do?"

The Buggane was caught off guard. There was a flash of light and a smaller version of the original monster stood before him, eyeing the outstretched arm suspiciously. It made no move to shake hands and so Richard Tomkins cautiously withdrew his arm and put his hand safely back in his pocket.

"So, have you lived here long?" he enquired of the Buggane.

"I," growled the Buggane, "have lived here since before Mannanan himself walked the Isle, though it's no business o' yourn that I can see."

"I bought this field, you know," continued Richard Tomkins, "so it's mine by rights to do with as I wish. However," he paused. "I'm willing to wager it on a contest, and the winner of the contest keeps the land, fair and square."

"*What!*" roared the Buggane, returning to his full height, "You dare to wager me for what is already mine? I'll ..."

Richard Tomkins shrank back against the wall. Oh dear, he thought, I've made a mistake. I may not live to regret this. And then the Buggane laughed. A terrifying, blood-curdling shriek of a laugh.

"A wager!" he screamed. "Against a man! How could I lose? Four hundred years or so I've been slumbering under my mountain and I could do with some fun! Hmm ... How about a race? I fancy a race! Do you walk or ride, O Man Tomkins?

A race around the Island it's to be, and the Little People to judge us. What say you, Man? Are you willing to wager *your* land on this race?"

"Yes, I'm willing," replied Richard Tomkins. "And I say we ride. Here, tomorrow night, at midnight."

There was a flash of light, a shriek of laughter, and Richard Tomkins found himself standing alone and dripping wet, inside his roofless ruin. He hurried back across the dark field to the light and warmth of the campervan, peeled off his clothes, took a hot shower and helped himself to a stiff drink, then slept like a log until late the next morning.

As soon as he awoke Richard Tomkins busied himself with preparations for the night ahead by taking a drive into Peel. Half of him could not believe what had occurred the previous night and yet the memory was all too real, far too real to be a dream, and there were his sodden clothes in the shower, and the shattered roof in the field outside his window to prove it. He may have doubted his sanity, but for now he had to believe that what had happened was true.

That night, at midnight, he was ready and waiting by the doors of St Trinian's. The wind had dropped during the day, and the rain had finally eased off, giving way to a sunny afternoon. Now a crescent moon illuminated the church doors where Richard Tomkins stood waiting.

Suddenly, appearing as if from nowhere, the Buggane was by his side. He was in his original form and was mounted on a snorting and stamping black stallion. Richard Tomkins retreated a couple of steps. The horse was huge, bigger than any he'd seen before, and he wondered about the Buggane's mention of the Little People the previous night. Certainly this stallion looked as though no human could tame it and Richard Tomkins suspected magic was afoot.

"Good evening to you, Man," growled the Buggane. "Are

you ready? Where is your steed?"

Richard Tomkins said not a word, but pushed open the doors of the church. There stood a shiny black Suzuki motorbike, glinting in the moonlight. The best that money could buy. The Buggane stared. He blinked. "*What*," he shrieked, "*is that?*"

"This," replied Richard Tomkins calmly, "is a motorcycle. We don't use horses much these days, you see. We prefer to ride bikes."

The Buggane, being a creature of some years, had always, even four centuries previously, been keen never to seem out-dated, oldfashioned or obsolete. He gathered his wits together remarkably quickly and replied, "Oh aye, for a moment I quite forgot. Well, if you be ready, then, we'll be off. I say we ride across to Peel, round to Ramsey, across the mountain, down to the Sound and then back here by way of Peel. Start and finish at the gate yonder. And no tricks," growled the Buggane. "The Little People are watching."

The Buggane kicked the black stallion. He reared up onto his hind legs, whinnied shrilly like no earthly creature, then cantered wildly over to the gate by the road. Richard Tomkins followed behind with the Suzuki, pushed it through the gate and into the road and mounted. He sat tense and alert, wait-ing for the signal for the off. Apart from a brief practice this afternoon, it was some years since he'd ridden a bike of this power, and his adrenalin was pumping.

"Ready?" growled the Buggane. "Get set. *Go!*"

Richard Tomkins turned the key and the engine roared into life. The black stallion, caught entirely off-guard, whinnied and reared again. The Suzuki shot forward. The stallion bucked and reared and turned in wild circles whilst the Buggane cracked his whip and screeched at the top of his voice. Finally the horse came to his senses and galloped off down the Peel

Road. He went like the wind, but the Suzuki had the advantage. By Ramsey, although the stallion had gained on him, Richard Tomkins still held a clear lead. The long steep incline of the mountain road took its toll on the horse and rider and they dropped further behind, with the Buggane still roaring and screaming and lashing his whip for all he was worth. As they rode south the Buggane drove the black stallion relentlessly forward. Mile by mile they gained on Richard Tomkins. By the time they reached Peel the Buggane could see him in the distance. He spurred the horse on, faster and faster. Richard Tomkins put his foot down. He glanced at the speedometer – 120 miles per hour! He shot through St John's, straight across the crossroads and he was on the home straight. He could do it! He pulled up alongside the St Trinian's gate just seconds before the Buggane rode up and flung himself down from the saddle. The stallion stood panting and steaming, sweat clinging in beads to his body. There was a flash and the Buggane towered into the air. "You ... you ... you ... man!" screeched the Buggane in a rage. "How dare you beat me? It wasn't fair! I'll ... I'll ..." The Buggane reached down with his sharp claws towards Richard Tomkins throat.

"Now, now," said Richard Tomkins, thinking quickly. Don't get overexcited. Didn't I say? It's the best of two. There's another contest yet to come. If I win that then I win fair and square, but if *you* win it's a draw and we have a final and third test. So, what's it to be?"

The Buggane shrank back down to his usual size and nodded at Richard Tomkins. "I see," he snarled, and sized up the puny man before him. "I challenge you ..." The Buggane grinned maliciously. "... to a test of strength."

Richard Tomkins felt what little strength he'd had in the first place drain out of him. Now this he couldn't win. Maybe he should just concede to this monster, and pack up and go home to London. Look for another perfect property. Start all over again. No. He couldn't face it. He had to at least try.

"Okay," he answered warily, "what do we have to do?"

"See those pebbles yonder," the Buggane jabbed a bony finger in the direction of the two heaps of stone that had been delivered and dumped at either end of the church. "He who can fashion the tallest tower before the moon sets wins the wager," announced the Buggane. "I'll take this pile here mesen, and thou canst have t'other."

Richard Tomkins glanced at the moon. He reckoned that gave them about an hour. Then he looked at the size of the stones and his heart sank. He knew he could barely lift one without help, let alone build a tower.

"Ready?" the Buggane whined. Richard Tomkins nodded reluctantly. "Then *go!*

With a tremendous roar and an almighty flash the Buggane shot up into the air until he was as tall as the beech trees along the roadside. Then, as Richard Tomkins watched, he sprouted two more pairs of arms, with hands like shovels. Enormous muscles bulged through the wrinkles and the Buggane set to work, scooping and shifting stones, then placing them deftly to form a solid base for his tower.

Richard Tomkins sighed. He turned his back on the Buggane and walked around the church to survey his own heap of stones. He stopped dead. Now why had he not thought of that before! Standing just beyond the stones was parked a large yellow JCB. With beating heart Richard Tomkins hopped up and wrenched open the door. He could not believe it! What luck! The driver had left the keys in the ignition. What an amazing place. No one in their right minds would leave doors unlocked and keys in the ignition in London. Cautiously he turned the key and felt the power of the machine as it roared into life. He peered anxiously out of the window. He couldn't see the Buggane or its tower, but the creature was apparently so intent on the task in hand that it had either failed to hear the roar of machinery or it was too busy to investigate.

So now Richard Tomkins set to work. Unsurprisingly he had never worked one of these machines before but it didn't take him long to master the controls. He scooped up some stones and dumped them down on the grass. He quickly realised that he would never have the strength, height or skill to build a tower in the strictest sense of the word, but with a good wide base he could aim to produce something more like a pyramid. Scooping up more stones he deposited them beside the first load and then, using the claw at the back of the vehicle, pushed and pulled them into place. With the first layer complete he began work on the second. Soon the pyramid began to take shape, and Richard Tomkins began to enjoy himself. The layers rose higher until it was just a matter of three or four stones being scooped up by the claw at a time, and then slowly, carefully, being positioned on the top of the pyramid. Once or twice there were landslides and the whole top of the pyramid collapsed, but Richard Tomkins kept calm and with increasing skill put right the damage. Finally, with the moon hovering just above the horizon, he placed his final and topmost stone. He reversed the JCB, killed the engine and leaped down from the cab to see how the Buggane had fared.

As he rounded the church Richard Tomkins' heart sank. The Buggane's tower reached up into the sky and must have been at least sixty feet high. His was barely half that. He watched in silence as the Buggane picked up another stone and put it on top of the tower. Was it Richard Tomkins' imagination, or did the structure shift just a little? The Buggane reached down for another stone, but as he put it into position the tower swayed to the right. The Buggane reached out to steady it, but even as he did so the moon sank below the hills and the tower crashed to the ground, scattering stones all around the field and leaving only the first few feet standing.

The Buggane was livid. He stormed around the church to inspect Richard Tomkin's work.

"By Mannanan himself, how did such a weakling as thee ever shift yon stones?" he roared. "I built my tower, that I did, and it was thrice as big as yourn. Didst thou see it? Didst thou? It reached right up into the heavens. I tell thee, I'm the true winner, that I am, and if thou durst say otherwise then I'll …" He moved menacingly towards Richard Tomkins, his fangs bared and his claws out.

Oh dear, thought Richard Tomkins to himself. Could you ever win against a Buggane? It seemed that if the Buggane didn't win then he'd kill you instead, just to make amends. So a man didn't stand the slightest chance. Unless, that is …

"Now, now," he said aloud. "Don't worry. Let's have that third contest anyway. But you chose the last two times, so it really is my turn to pick the contest this time round."

"Aye," grunted the Buggane, appeased for the moment, and calmer, "I'm listening."

"Well," said Richard Tomkins. " You see this little box here?" He rummaged in his pocket and brought out an empty matchbox he'd stuffed there when he'd used up the last match on the camper stove – was it only that morning? "Well, you told me a Buggane can take any form he wishes, and I've seen some pretty terrifying monsters from you, I have to admit, but what about small creatures? What I really won't believe you can do unless I see it with my own eyes, is turn yourself into a creature that can fit into this box here. So that's the third and final contest. You fit yourself into the box and then I'll do the same. The one who does the best job is the winner. So saying, Richard Tomkins placed the box on the ground at his feet.

"You silly man!" snarled the Buggane. "I can make myself into any creature I like! Watch!"

There was a flash and there at Richard Tomkins's feet stood the tiniest monster you could imagine. Richard Tomkins couldn't help but admire the Buggane's skill, and bent down for a closer look. The Buggane had turned himself into a miniature troll, with teeth and claws as sharp as needles, and fierce-looking horns sprouting out of his diminutive head. He hissed at Richard Tomkins, then turned and leaped nimbly into the open matchbox.

Richard Tomkins moved fast. Quickly but carefully he lifted his foot and brought it down hard upon the box. But at the very same instant there was a sudden blinding light and a huge cloud of smoke and there was the Buggane, twenty feet high and full of rage.

"Think ye'd squash me, did ye? Well think again, Man!" he roared. "I was too quick for thee. Thou wast just a fraction too late. But let me just get my claws in ye! I'll tear ye into so many pieces and squash ye so small I could fit ye into yon box in a twinkling." The Buggane reached down with one enormous hand. Richard Tomkins didn't hang around. He leapt up onto his Suzuki and was off. The Buggane took two strides and then stopped in his tracks. The sky to the east was turning golden as the sunrise drew near. The night was almost over. With the last of his strength he roared after the retreating figure, "Now be ye gone, and don't ever return or I *shall* tear ye limb from limb," and as the sun rose so the Buggane disappeared from sight.

Whether or not Richard Tomkins caught these final words we shall never know, but he certainly heeded their advice. He rode as fast as he could to the airport, caught the next plane to London, and was never seen on the Island again.

As for the church, still it stands to this day, roof open to the skies, nothing more than an old forgotten ruin to those who don't know the story. And there I guess it will continue to stand, perhaps slowly more ramshackle as the years take their toll, until some other arrogant fool chooses to challenge the might and magic of the Buggane of St Trinian's.

september

Colin Fleetney was born in Kent and lived there until the 1980s when he moved to the Island to become Vicar of Lezayre. Before being ordained Colin worked as a seagoing engineer and then as a hospital engineer in a large psychiatric hospital. After ordination he continued to work at the hospital as their chaplain and then became Team Vicar for five parishes outside Canterbury.

Now retired and living in Port Erin with his Manx wife Joan he contributes factual articles to magazines in the UK as well as writing short stories and building working steam engines in his garden shed.

"You are standing into danger!"

Colin J. Fleetney

It started with one of Steve's bright ideas. I should, of course, have known better and not become involved. Anyway, Steve – he's my cousin and in catering equipment servicing – was at the time working for the summer season on the Isle of Man. He phoned to say that he had found the 'ideal' boat. Would I help him bring it home? There would be no worries, he would arrange every last detail. And the boat? The 'ideal' boat? She was, he said, a 1950s petrol-engined motor boat. When I remarked that she was, to say the least, a bit long in the tooth, his voice took on the tone of an evangelical preacher: "She was built for the Customs and Excise! What do you think of that?" I suggested that her current seaworthy condition should be of far more interest to us than her provenance. It transpired that she was a medium-sized launch with a cabin forward, was wooden and strongly built. Not only was she "as sound as a bell", to quote Steve, she had got "everything". "All we need to buy are provisions and fuel. It'll be a holiday. We'll take it in easy stages, have a quiet meander across – she's lying in Derbyhaven – from the Isle of Man to Liverpool, then up the

Mersey to Runcorn. Nothing to it, it'll be the trip of a lifetime." I had annual holidays due, so like a fool I agreed to help him.

I arrived at Douglas aboard the *King Orry* as columns of chill drizzle driven by a south-easterly wind marched across Douglas Bay. After a somewhat lively trip from Liverpool I was thankful to lounge back in Steve's van from the sea terminal to Derbyhaven. Steve had been commissioning the boat, as he optimistically put it, for a week. Standing in the wind and rain, my first impression of the vessel caused words such as 'nondescript, tatty, tired and commonplace' to come to mind. To be fair, however, the rain and the bleak wailing of the wind through the rigging of adjacent boats did little to improve the air of desolation.

Working with boats I naturally had tremendous respect for the sea; not so Steve, who simply liked messing around in them. He assured me that he had charts – he had – I checked. Likewise the compass had been 'swung' and was true. I checked the engine over and it certainly seemed sound enough. There were flares, a signal lamp, a radio, two sturdy, if old, lifejackets and a tender in the form of a quite new glass-fibre dinghy.

As soon as she floated on the tide the next day we sailed, under a slate-grey sky, with intermittent rain and a strong southerly wind. Just off Langness Steve turned the bow towards England and shouted, "Runcorn, here we come!"

About an hour later, with the ever-increasing wind whipping up short nasty seas, the rudder broke away from the hull, fouling and damaging the propeller as it did so and leaving us helpless. Within seconds the boat was rolling violently, beam-on to the seas, while every other wave or so swept clear across her.

There was no question of reinstating the rudder; it was constructed of heavy steel and was now dangling at the end of a tangled mass of steering wires somewhere under the boat. In any case the propeller was useless. I started to haul in the dinghy which was towing astern, suggesting, as I did so, that Steve radioed for help. He made his way to the wheelhouse, slid the door open and then changed his mind and, leaving the door open, he came charging back to me, shouting, "I'll give you a hand with the dinghy first."

I shouted, "No, I can handle this, get cracking on the bloody radio." As I spoke a wave swept across the boat. It filled the wheelhouse, wrecked the radio, thundered down the steps and half-filled the accomodation. Waterlogged, the boat stopped lifting to the seas. It was obviously only a matter of minutes before she foundered. I had the dinghy alongside and shouted to Steve to hurry. He had finally gone into the wheelhouse and he came out clutching the tin of flares.

As we scrambled over the side and down into the dinghy, a voice bellowed, "You in a spot of bother then, yessir?" There, no more than ten feet from us, was a massive open work-boat. A young man stood, with a boat hook poised like a lance, ready to hook on to our dinghy. Aft, at the steering wheel, stood a tall, rangy, thin-faced, elderly man, wearing foul-weather gear and a knitted woolly hat. Having gained our attention he shouted, "Get off her now. Jump about! Jump about!"

We scrambled down into the dinghy and as I cut its painter, Steve started frantically to pull on the oars. The big vessel, however, closed with us and within seconds the boat hook locked on to the dinghy. As we scrambled aboard, the helmsman shouted, "Save the dinghy, Dougie, it's valuable." Then he opened the throttle and a big engine thumped with a steady reassuring sound and we sheared away from the cruiser, now very low in the water. "My boat! What about my boat?" Steve turned to our rescuer.

"You're lucky I came along, yessir. That bit of old rubbish

should never have left Derbyhaven. Someone saw you coming and you must be short on wits to have bought her. You are the owners, I take it?"

"I am, or was," Steve said, as he bleakly watched the seas washing clear across the old launch.

"Well, give her five more minutes and she'll go to bottom, I'm afraid."

And that was how I first met Len Gawne.

★   ★   ★

Soon after the loss of Steve's boat, the small boatyard I worked for went bankrupt. I was now in deep trouble, for due to my twin hobbies of horse- and dog-racing I could not keep up mortgage payments on my house, which was repossesed, nor could I service my quite considerable debts. The Isle of Man! I knew it well from bygone holidays. There, I felt sure, I would get seasonal work. So, with no one to answer to I made for the Island and was soon fixed up with an office cleaner's job and lodgings in Port Erin.

I had spent a long day in those sterile, air-conditioned offices and was determined to breathe some fresh air and enjoy something of the warm, still evening. So I had walked round the bay, past the Raglan Pier and on, towards the remains of the old breakwater and then back to the Falcon's Nest hotel. Now, standing at the window of the saloon bar and savouring the pint of bitter that was ice-cold in my hand, I was watching the sunset. In the distance I could see the gentle, vague humps of the Mourne Mountains, while before me the whole panorama of Port Erin Bay was bathed in a lovely soft, golden light. The sea was calm and almost on the top of the tide.

The bar was quiet, unusual for that time in the evening, and I jumped at the remark, "It must be one of the most beautiful bays in the world – my God, I know you! Off

Langness, what – three months ago? That rotten launch?" He paused, then, "Has your pal drowned himself yet? Or are you both over here for yet another floating coffin?" Len Gawne was smiling and offering his hand.

We shook hands and I said, no, I now worked on the Island and Steve had a boat on the Leeds and Liverpool canal. We got talking – you know how things are – the weather of course, the cost of living, and so on. I missed supper and risked my landlady's anger while we watched dusk fall and drained our glasses several times over. I told Len about my boatyard experience and he told me that he had been at sea "on deck", as he put it.

With the caution of someone who thinks that you may be interested in something that is very special to them, but is worried about making a mistake and your treating their special thing with indifference, he told me about the boat that had possibly saved my life. "She's not smart or fancy, mind you. Well, you'll remember her, I expect. A wooden work-boat, old when I bought her but sound, very sound; strong and extremely seaworthy, but as I say, nothing much to look at. She's got an old single-cylinder Bolinder engine – built when God was a boy – but it's a reliable engine, very reliable. Big green lump of a thing – but it's remarkably quiet."

He paused then added, "*Voirrey*. I call her *Voirrey*."

"The name of a Manx hill?"

"No, it's my sister's name, an army nurse, she was killed in the war. Name's Manx for Mary. You might like a trip? Under happier circumstances than last time! She's here, in Port Erin. If you've got the time we could take her out tomorrow."

The next day was my day off, so I jumped at the invitation and we agreed to meet down at the harbour at around 2 p.m. In good time I parked my car across the road from the Raglan Pier and found the *Voirrey* just afloat on the making tide.

Len was aboard as I climbed down the vertical iron ladder set in the stonework and he greeted me by remarking on the weather, weather which was worthy of remarking on, for like the previous day it was sunny, warm and, unusual for the Isle of Man, flat calm, with not a breath of wind.

"Not a lot to see," he said as I looked round. The big boat had the engine and its controls positioned within easy reach of the steering position. There was also a compressor for re-charging air cylinders for divers. At the stern was the steering wheel and, next to the wheel, a locker, the top of which did duty as a chart table. Fitted into the locker was a radio and an echo-sounder that recorded the depth of water under the boat. Next to the locker was mounted a compass. As with all such vessels she carried ropes of various sizes neatly coiled together, plus all the various items one expects to see in a vessel the function of which is work, rather than pleasure.

Len inserted the crank-handle into the front of the engine, gave it no more than two brisk turns and the engine fired and started to run smoothly. I helped let go the moorings and we were soon heading out, round the green conical buoy that marks the outer end of the old breakwater, toward the base of Bradda Head.

It was a most memorable afternoon. Bradda Head was a mass of subtle colours; tawny rock and blue-black slate, gorse golden in the sun, with malachite green copper deposits glinting on the cliff face down by the old mine workings.

The boat was fast. "Over-engined and a damned good thing she is," Len remarked as I watched the bow wave angling out and away to wash white against the foot of the cliffs.

We kept close in to the shore and Len pointed out the sites of wrecks, "There's a big steamer about eight fathoms down, right under us now,' he said as we skirted the base of Bradda. He nodded toward Fleshwick Bay as it opened out on the starboard side, "There's a plane on the bottom over there, just in the mouth of the bay." He told me where to look for seals. With pride and love he spoke, almost chanted, the lovely names of the mighty hills soaring steeply from narrow or non-existent beaches between Fleshwick Bay and Niarbyl. He pointed to the cairn marking the summit of Cronk ny Irree Laa dominating the skyline, and between the summit and the base of the great hill, on the near-vertical side, the remains of a Celtic hermit's tiny keeil.

As we approached Niarbyl, with the sea misleadingly gentle as it lapped those dangerous rocks, Len took the *Voirrey* round in a tight turn, so tight that we cut through our own wake, which caused the boat to pitch and roll for a few moments. Then, keeping out beyond the ten-fathom line, Len took us back, south. Before we reached Port Erin Bay he asked me to hunt around in his canvas bag and find a flask of coffee and a packet of cheese and onion rolls. "Forgot to bring a mug, sorry." We shared the top of the flask.

He took us on, past Port Erin Bay and across to the Calf. Then, with seagulls spiralling and shrieking as if to warn us of danger, he took the boat in very close to the Stack, that conical rock that rises from the sea at the base of the cliffs just under the two disused lighthouses. As if reading my mind he shouted, "Plenty of water hereabouts." Once past the Stack we could see Chicken Rock lighthouse two miles ahead, but Len hugged the coast of the Calf, holding the boat close to Caigher Point and on, round, past South Harbour and back to the eastern entrance of the Sound. We kept Kitterland on our starboard side and as we stormed past Thousla Rock, surmounted by its little beacon tower, I saw, on the port side, several seals loafing around in the sea that was rolling and surging over rocks that were just below the surface. With child-like triumph I pointed and shouted, "Seals! Over there! In the broken water above those rocks!"

Len nodded at the expanse of water, "That's Blind Sound, looks safe enough but you can't get through it. Plenty of seals live there, though. But they're not on rocks, they're on the engines and boilers of the *Clan MacMaster*, biggest ship wrecked on the Manx coast." A minute or two later, as he swung the *Voirrey* northward towards Port Erin and Thousla rock was fast falling astern, he said that the *Clan MacMaster*'s cargo had included sewing machines and, by a strange coincidence, a good many southside families accquired sewing machines during the weeks following the wreck.

Later we made for the Falcon's Nest. During the evening I learned that Len had been master of several of Rayner-Thomson's ships, large general-purpose coasters that used to trade round the British Isles and the near-continent. He had retired in 1983. "It was all finishing then, anyway," he said as he sipped his beer. "Within a year or two the company was dead – killed off by the container trade coupled to heavy road transport – like most of the British merchant marine." He thought for a moment or two and added, "Anyway, this suits me fine. Cottage down on Shore Road and the boat, she keeps me busy!" Late that night we parted, Len to go down to Shore Road while I went up to my lodgings.

It became something of a routine for me to spend almost every Thursday evening with Len, in the Falcon's Nest, and so far as I was concerned, the Thursday evening of the last week of September 1993 was no exception. The room was unusually crowded and pulsing with conversation and music of a certain kind. Although I could hardly see across the room for blue smoke I knew Len would not be there. It was no place for him, or me, come to that. As I turned away from the door I found that he was just behind me. He took one look and firmly suggested that we went back to his place.

As he closed the front door Len told me to stir the fire up while he made the tea. "Or would you prefer something stronger?" He nodded at the cluster of various bottles on the sideboard.

We decided on tea; tea and chocolate wholemeal biscuits. Once settled, with our plates and mugs, he said, "You might be in the position to help me out." Munching away, I was unable to speak, so I nodded.

"Dougie's had to let me down – can't help it – not his fault."

I should explain here that Dougie Kewley, Len's regular crewman, was, in the very best Manx tradition, both a fisherman and a farmer in that he divided his time between working on an uncle's fishing boat, on his father's farm and crewing for Len. As he was heavily into darts tournaments and playing football, he was pleased to have a deputy in me. So I regularly got involved with taking people out to see basking sharks, seals and seabirds, divers out to various wreck sites and sheep to the Calf.

Prior to taking sheep to the Calf we would pen off the entire middle section of the boat. The flock would then come aboard, by way of a wide gangway, in Port St Mary, supervised by two shepherds and two or three extremely businesslike and self-important sheepdogs. There would be a great deal of running, posing and posturing by the dogs as the sheep, bitterly and fearfully protesting, were driven down the gangway. Once aboard, a net was thrown right over the sheep and secured. The dogs then sat, bolt upright on a bench, intent on enjoying the cruise, enquiring and intelligent, peering everywhere but mainly ahead, as if they believed that Len required assistance with the navigation. The sheep hated the thud of the engine and loathed the motion of the boat, therefore throughout the voyage to South Harbour they maintained a constant, uneasy bleating. Thus our progress past the Chasms, Sugarloaf Rock,

Spanish Head and across the wide eastern mouth of the Sound was heralded by this pitiful bleating, the volume of which rose and fell in proportion to the motion of the boat. If the sheep got too noisy, the dogs got edgy and would take to minutely inspecting the pens before leaping back on to the benches for a clear view ahead. At South Harbour I would rig the gangway and then, with ropes, hold it steady while the shepherds removed the net. As soon as the net was thrown back, the dogs would go into action and the sheep would quickly get the idea and stream off to be driven up the long, straight road that took them to the green pastures around the lighthouses.

All this work, although Len didn't know it, was of course a godsend to me because I was now on short-time. So when Len asked me to crew for him on a trip over to Heysham, a trip worth a great deal of money to him, I let him think that I went to a lot of trouble in order to help him out. I had implied this several times before and he appreciated my perceived loyalty and in the long run it paid off, I can tell you!

Anyway, back to my story: Len came straight to the point. He and Dougie were due to tow the big fishing boat, *Girl Daisy*, round to Douglas on the Saturday – all the arrangements had been made – when Dougie had rung him to say that he was stranded in Whitehaven. His uncle's boat, the *Charlotte May*, had broken down and they would be at the shipyard there for several days. Could I crew for him on Saturday?

Certainly I could.

Just before we were due to sail Len realised that he had left all the paperwork concerning the job in the second drawer of his desk. As I was younger and faster than him, would I nip across for it? His cottage was not locked – like many Manxmen he never bothered. I searched in the second drawer, found no documents appertaining to the towing of the *Girl Daisy*, but I did find a copy of Len's will. I read it – well you would have done the same thing, I'll be bound! In it I learned that, apart from a few small bequests, he was leaving everything to me! What colossal good fortune. The only fly in the ointment was that I would inherit at some point in the distant future. Anyway, I found the documents, in the top drawer, and hurried back to the boat.

The voyage round to Douglas was uneventful apart from the fact that we were late leaving Port Erin. We were fortunate in both the weather; no wind and a flat calm sea, and the fact that the *Girl Daisy*, a modern fishing vessel festooned with masts and winches, had been docile enough and followed obediently like a tame old dog on a lead.

Once the *Girl Daisy* was handed over and signed for, Len took the *Voirrey* round to be fuelled up. She ran on paraffin, and as the trip round had been quite a punch, we took on some fifty gallons, from, although we didn't know it, the dregs of the retailer's tank.

While we were fuelling up we got trapped in the inner harbour. Had we not been late arriving in Douglas we would not have been involved, but there you are, it was a situation that one must expect occasionally in a busy harbour. There was a great deal of activity involving the Steam Packet boat moving berths and other vessels coming and going. Anyway, the long and the short of it was that we were further delayed by some two hours and we spent most of the time in the chip shop on the North Quay. Well filled with hot food and coffee, we left the chippy as it was closing. We stepped out into a cold autumnal night and the fog, that was eventually to surround the Island, was already forming around Douglas Head when we sailed.

We maintained a reasonable speed despite the fog until off Port Soderick, when without any warning, the engine started misfiring and discharging dense white smoke. And then it stopped. There was no drama and I won't bore you with tech-nicalities, enough to say that we dropped the anchor and with the sea gurgling and whispering around the hull and the boat snatching at the anchor chain, we found water in the fuel tank. This was, of course, my sphere of work, for we had to dis-mantle the fuel lines, drain them and the tank, of water, and then reassemble the whole lot. For most of the time Len as-sisted me by holding the torch, one of those big, square, heavy-duty things producing a magnificent light. By the time the job was finished, we and just about everything around the engine, stank of paraffin. All in all it was more than two hours before we were under way again.

Off Santon Head we found that the weather was deteriorat-ing in that the fog was fast thickening as the isolated banks merged. The next stage of our course lay from Santon Head across to Dreswick Point, the southern tip of Langness. Half way between Santon and Langness Len said, "We won't es-cape that little lot." and nodded ahead. "It'll be as thick as a suet pudding from now on." Within a minute or two Langness light turned a yellow-orange, became more diffused and then vanished as the fog engulfed it and the bank of fog, dead ahead, looked like a fluid cliff face, grey against the darkness. Along this cliff face skeins of mist were coiling and writhing like smoke rising from the surface of the sea.

Entering that bank of fog was like entering a freezer. The temperature fell several degrees instantly and the beams of our green and red navigation lamps reflected on the millions of water droplets of the fog which glowed ruby and emerald on either side of the boat. From this point there would be no break in the fog, and as we could no longer see the coast, Len navigated solely by compass.

Once clear of Dreswick, our course would take us straight across to Spanish Head and then into Calf Sound. The sea was calm, simply black water lifting and heaving, and the moisture-laden air was cold, very cold.

I nervously remarked that the Langness fog horn seemed to be bellowing just beyond the starboard side of the boat. Without looking up from the compass Len muttered about fog notoriously distorting noise, paused and added, "Langness's astern now, oh, almost half a mile, no worries. I know exactly where we are. It's my job. It's what I do. It's what I've done all my life. We'll soon be able to hear the sea breaking in the Chasms."

For something to say, I remarked that I supposed we would hear Chicken Rock fog horn before we reached the entrance to the Sound. "We might," he said, "but as I say, fog plays tricks with sound and come to that, with vision too … you see, or think you see all kinds of things in a fog, especially at night."

This remark made the hairs on the back of my neck tingle and aroused in me a surge of the kind of fear that one likes to think was left behind with childhood. You know what I mean; those ancient in-built fears that we like to believe have no place in the modern scheme of things. Yet suddenly they were with me again. Fear of the dark, of shapes lurking in the fog, of the black depths beneath the boat. Suddenly the modern scheme of things counted for nothing and the *Voirrey* seemed tiny and vulnerable with her chugging engine and glowing lights. We were simply two men in an open boat and totally alone; on one side of us was the vastness of the Irish Sea, on the other side, somewhere in the fog, but close, very close, were the Chasms – no beach, simply great cliffs plunging into deep water.

"There, listen! Beyond the noise of the engine! Hear it?"

I disciplined my ears to ignore the steady, rhythmic thud of the engine and I heard the voice of the Chasms, a hollow, echoing and, to me, terribly sinister sigh, repeated again and again as the sea broke gently at the foot of the cliffs and inside the caves. I shivered not so much with cold as with fear. Len, on the other hand, was delighted. It proved to him that his navigation was spot on. He knew exactly where he was.

A few minutes later he said, "Chicken Rock, hear it?"

I heard it. A faint, distant, musical, bell-like fluting whistle that seemed to come from all around us. "Where are we?"

"We're off Spanish Head and just about to enter the Sound. We'll be passing Kitterland soon, to starboard, and then Thousla light very close on the port side." Then he muttered about the tide through the Sound, "Running like a drain".

He increased the engine's speed to compensate for the power of the tide, and our bow-wave grew in size, giving the impression that the boat was going faster through the water. It was an illusion of course; the tide was simply flowing faster past the boat. Now the surface of the sea was no longer smooth, the black water was flecked with foam and currents tugged and pulled at the boat, causing her to shudder and fight against Len's grip of the steering wheel.

Through the swirl of the fog I caught a glimpse, just a glimpse, of humped rocks close, so close to the starboard side that they were illuminated in the green glow of the navigation light. Kitterland. It must be Kitterland.

A flashing light – Thousla beacon – and I used its light to glance at my watch. It was just on 1.30 am. We drew abeam of the stumpy white tower, bathing it with the ruby glow from our port light, and we were past, our wash slapping and hissing as it surged along Thousla rock.

A minute or so later we heard a ship's whistle. It was a deep, rumbling double bass note, the voice of a big ship cautiously groping her way through the fog and she was close, very close, for the sound reverberated off the cliffs.

"What's he doing in here! His radar must be on the blink, but can't he hear his whistle echoing off the cliffs? What the hell's he about? Here, take the wheel and keep sounding the klaxon." I grabbed the wheel with one hand, pressed the hooter button with the other and the air was filled with the harsh raucous sound of our hooter. The ship, still hidden, but very close, sounded another long booming note.

As he snatched the torch, hanging on the side of the locker, Len said, "Keep sounding the hooter for God's sake." At my bidding *Voirrey* cackled again.

Then we saw the ship and she was indeed close! From our position, low down near the surface, she seemed huge, a great black wall sliding cautiously through the fog. She was moving slowly in the opposite direction to us, just a few feet off our port side. Yard after yard of black hull slipped past and then as the fog gusted and coiled I caught sight, high above us, of her white bridge front and on the port wing of the bridge I could see a group of a men. I sounded our klaxon horn again and again. Above us the rich red glow of the ship's port light gleamed through a pink nimbus of fog. Now I could see her white lifeboats and, near them, men standing at the guard-rails. Beyond the boat deck, its top lost in the fog and dark-ness, was a tall funnel. A jet of steam, pure white against the grey fog and the darkness erupted from in front of the funnel and we were treated to another long, deep, organ-like note from her whistle. I replied on our puny little hooter, trying to attract their attention, for their safety not ours, for the ship was no longer a danger to us.

Len was waving the torch, flashing it on and off and its beam was lancing through the fog and playing on the ship's bridge structure and catching the faces of the men on the boat deck. "You are standing into danger!' he shouted, followed by a muttered, "Oh, bloody hell." He cupped his hands again and bellowed a second time, "*You are standing into danger!*' Then he half turned to me and shouted, "A ladder! The sloppy bastards have left their pilot's ladder down! Take us alongside him! Quickly now, come on. *Come on!*"

"Fenders!" I shouted. "I'll put fenders over."

"No time! Just put us alongside her. Come on, Jump about yessir!"

I took the boat close to the ship's side and above the noise of our engine and the hiss and slap of the sea trapped in the space between the two hulls, I heard the grinding and splintering of woodwork as the boat's gunwale juddered along the rivetted steel plates. Then I saw the ladder, a rope ladder with flat wooden rungs pierced with hand-holes. I threw the boat's engine out of gear and she continued to crunch and scrape along the ship's hull plates as the ladder came closer. Just as the ship's whistle sounded again Len, balancing on our gunwale, grabbed the ladder and gracefully stepped across. He climbed nimbly and his torch, hanging by its nylon cord on his wrist, was still on, its beam twisting and flashing as he climbed. I watched him reach the top and climb over the guardrail and, waving his torch, run, still shouting, towards the bridge.

As soon as I saw that Len had reached the safely of the deck I slammed the engine into gear and bore away and round, in a tight circle in order to catch up with the ship and keep pace with it, at the foot of the ladder.

It was not as easy as that. Although I gunned the engine and put the rudder hard over, the *Voirrey*, at thirty feet long, required a large turning circle and in turning I lost the ship in the fog. Oh, I heard her whistle and made for the sound, but could not see her, and with mounting fear I remembered Len's words, "Fog plays tricks with sound." I swung the boat round and tried in another direction, or thought I did, but in the fog, direction, unless you are carefully working to the compass, is meaningless. I heard the whistle again, but further away. God, was I scared! I put the engine on tick-over and in the relative silence thought I could hear, a good way off, men calling, but it could have been seagulls crying.

I sat there alone and cold, so very cold, not knowing what to do. Later, how much later I don't know, I realised that I had not heard the ship's whistle again. With the wind increasing all I could hear was the slap of the waves against the boat. I motored around aimlessly for a considerable time then decided that I had better report to the coastguards the fact that Len had boarded a ship in an attempt to warn her of her danger.

The events of the rest of that night will always remain rather confused in my mind. Using the compass I slowly eased my way northwards. After some time I heard the Port Erin fog horn, but fearful of wrecking the boat on the old breakwater, I took her too far north and almost wrecked her on Bradda Head before turning east and entering the bay. Once ashore I phoned the police and from then on everything was out of my hands.

In my statement I reported, in detail, the incident with the ship, explaining that Len had boarded her by way of a ladder in an attempt to tell them that they were dangerously close to the Calf. The police and the coastguards looked at me oddly, were extremely polite, helpful and, yes, well, gentle with me. There were, they said, no ships, large or small close to the south-west corner of the Isle of Man at that time on the night of September 30th. Fog, yes, and it was dense, but no ships, none at all.

I was given a thorough medical check-up and they found traces of carbon monoxide in my blood. Exhaust fumes, they said; yes, it must have been exhaust fumes from the engine that drugged me causing me to hallucinate and Len to fall overboard. I was very lucky, they said, recovering sufficiently to get into Port Erin. Yes, I did well, they said, very well, getting into Port Erin on a thick night like that. A nasty experience, they said, very nasty. Len's body, they said, would no doubt come ashore within a day or two. They were wrong. Len was never found.

In so far as the damage in the form of splintering and scouring along the port side gunwale of the *Voirrey* was concerned, that was easily explained, they said. While I was unconscious the boat must have scraped along a rock. They repeated the fact that I was very lucky.

I was indeed lucky for I had always envied Len his little house and his boat and now they were mine! I mastered local navigation and took on any work available, indeed some jobs I did, meeting ships far out to sea and picking up packages – no questions asked, paid incredibly well – but would have horrified Len. Life was good, very good indeed.

While examining my newly acquired possessions, I found, pasted inside the cover of an old sewing machine, a piece of paper on which was written:

This sewing machine was part of the cargo
of the S/S Clan MacMaster which was wrecked
in the Blind Sound
at the moment my dear son was born.
1.30 am Sun. 30th. Sept., 1923

Mona Alice Gawne

Due to the events I have recorded, together with this note, I attempted to find out all I could about the wreck of the *Clan MacMaster*.

Word got around – you know how it is – and I was put in contact with an elderly lady who had some bits and pieces from the wreck. She agreed to let me see her treasures and I arranged to call one afternoon.

While we had tea, drop scones and bonnag, she showed me her "museum' as she called it. As she did so she said that work was hard come by in the early 1920s and her father had been delighted to be employed by the company that was going to attempt to remove the cargo before the ship broke up. Hence she said, "Mother's sewing machine." She nodded to a machine identical to Len's.

She went over to a glass-fronted cabinet and opened the door. On the top shelf were displayed a few pieces of cutlery, a tablecloth, table napkins and crockery all bearing the Clan Line crest. Standing up, behind these items, was a yellowing book of music, a selection from the musical "Enter Kiki' that was playing in the West End during the summer of 1923. "My parents loved music. Dad took that music actually off the piano in the ship's saloon. A lovely instrument, he said, finally destroyed by the sea." On another shelf stood a copy of Reeds Nautical Almanac for 1923, a copy of the Admiralty Sailing Directions for the Irrawaddy Delta, dated 1920, a broad-based, cut-glass inkwell, the inside stained with dried ink, sets of navigational and azimuth tables and a heavy-duty torch. The torch seemed old, but smelled faintly of paraffin and I swear to God that when I last saw it it was swinging from Len's wrist as he climbed up the side of that damn ship!

Then one afternoon in early autumn when a rain-laden gale was booming in from the west the nightmare started when the police called, and they were neither understanding or sympathetic as they accused me of the murder of Len Gawne.

I need not go into the details of the following six months. Although it was a decade ago I'm sure you read about my trial in the papers or saw the reports of the trial on TV.

I was found guilty and sentenced to life for murdering Len during the early hours of September 30th and then disposing of his body at sea.

I am now on parole and live in a Salvation Army hostel in Liverpool. By delivering newspapers I managed to scrape enough money together to get me over here, to the Isle of Man. This evening, luck, for once, was with me and fog came down early. Thus it was easy to take a rowboat from the moorings at the Raglan Pier. I have been sitting here, finishing my story, just off the western entrance to the Sound, in this dense fog for an hour or more listening to the slap of the sea against the the boat, the distant crash of the breakers against the cliffs and the occasional haunting bark of a seal. It is nearly 1.30 am on September 30th and my fingers are chilled and stiff with writing, for it is cold, so cold, but there's not much longer to wait, for I heard a steam whistle blow in the distance, just now. Soon, I know, there will be a break in the fog and I'll see again the ship's high, black side and the ladder. The ladder! I've waited so long for the moment that I leap onto that ladder and then climb up to the deck where I am sure this whole damned mess will be explained and all will once again be well.

Note: The above story was found in a box in a dinghy drifting off the Calf of Man.

october

Peter Carlé was born in London and worked in various parts of the world before moving to the Island to train as a Manx Advocate. Prior to taking and passing his Manx Bar exams Peter worked as a police officer in England and abroad and later qualified as an English barrister.

Peter is married with two children and since his recent retirement now finds time to pursue his many interests of fishing, travelling, writing and hunting down pubs that sell real ale.

The ghost walk

Peter Carlé

It was a cold damp October night and James sat alone at a
large table in the Creek Inn, Peel. He had been hoping to meet
up with friends for a drink but he had just discovered that the
usual crowd were away playing golf. He put his mobile phone
away despondently. He desperately wanted company; he felt
lonely and miserable. His fiancée had dumped him earlier that
evening. She had thrust the engagement ring and a Victorian
necklace into his jacket pocket, with the words, "Take your
ring and your present. I don't want to see you or them ever
again!" Then she had walked out of his life. He remembered
so well the smile on her face the day she had picked out the
old Victorian engagement ring from the jeweller's window and
he had added the matching necklace as an engagement present
to her. Now, the two items of jewellery were just unwanted
trash in his pocket.

He supped his pint slowly. There were two alternatives open
to him: to remain in the pub all night by himself or to go
home and watch television on his own. His face, normally
happy and smiling, was downcast. Then, he spotted a leaflet

on the bar, *The Peel Ghost Walk*. All the time he had lived in Peel he had never been on the walk. It sounded like fun. The barmaid nodded towards the leaflet, "Watch out, they dress up and play a trick on you – really frightening! Kippers and spuds to eat afterwards."

Half an hour later James walked along Peel Promenade, one of about thirty people in the group. Their guide pointed out the haunted houses – spoke of people who had died in dreadful circumstances – how furniture moved around, electrical items switched themselves on and off, temperatures of haunted rooms dropped dramatically for no reason, and the young woman who had died in terrible circumstances 150 years ago, after she was parted from her lover. Some of the party moved closer together, the young girls giggled loudly and nervously but there was an air of tension and expectation. It was dark, misty and cold, ideal for a ghost walk. James was enjoying the tour – better than a night in front of the television.

The guide was taking them close to the castle, "Terrible tortures occurred in the dungeons. Men stretched by the rack, screaming for mercy. And just here is where the public executions took place – there were beheadings and later there were hangings. On dark nights there have been plenty of sightings of a hooded figure with a rope noose dangling from his hand walking just here."

James was interested – the guide was very convincing and people were listening spellbound. Unfortunately, James was beginning to suffer a serious distraction. The beer he had drunk earlier was having its effect on him. His bladder was getting painful. As they made their way through the tangle of back streets in the gloom, he looked for somewhere to relieve himself. He was desperate. He dropped back from the main party and ran through several alleyways to a public convenience he had remembered. The relief was wonderful.

James ran back through the alleyways, then down the lane, hurrying to catch up with the others. It was now very dark. The air was bad; sea mist had rolled in and was thick with the smell of smoke. He walked quickly but he could not see anyone. It seemed that the street lights had gone off. He turned a corner and sighed with relief. There was a busy narrow street, full of women and children, with the odd man lounging around. A beggar dressed in rags was crouched in a doorway holding out his hat for money, another lay sprawled in the gutter beside him, with open sores showing on his face. Two young men leaned against the wall in an alcove, their heads sunk low, with an air of mischief about them. They were wearing caps pulled down low over their faces just like some of the youngsters would wear hoodies to obscure their faces.

Then he realised that the clothing worn by the women was odd. They had long skirts, big blouses, shawls and large hats. The men wore big cloth caps, mufflers, heavy boots, and smoked long thin clay pipes. The children skipped around James as he stood in the street, and they were pointing and yelling at him. Their language was Manx, their clothes were like something out of *Oliver Twist*. His chest felt tight and he could hardly breathe. Sweat was forming on his face and under his armpits. Panic gripped his stomach but he told himself it was all part of the ghost walk – of course, these were locals who were dressed up to play their part in the drama. His heart was pounding – these people were so authentic, so convincing. He tried to speak to those around him but got nowhere with them. They had switched to Manx and he only knew a few words of the language.

One man was holding a strange musical instrument that made an unusual whirring and tinkling noise as he turned a handle on the side of it and produced a rough old tune. James guessed it was an old hurdy-gurdy or something similar.

A woman with pockmarks on her face and who smelt strongly of fish grabbed James's arm and yelled something he could not understand in his ear. He could only shrug and smile nervously. Another woman grabbed him from the other side. They were trying to pull him towards a dark alleyway. He shook his head vigorously and managed to slip out of their grasp. The second woman smelt strongly of drink, had bad-looking teeth, and wore clothes that smelt rancid with sweat. He shuddered – the make-up people had certainly done a good job on those two.

He stopped at an open doorway. Inside was a large room with long wooden tables, rough wooden chairs, and a low ceiling. There were six or seven men sitting at tables drinking. Two women were serving drinks and leaning over the men, joking with them. He looked up and saw an old sign 'The Crown' above the door.

A woman stepped out of the room and came towards him. Her voice was soft, gentle and pleasant. She gave the impression of being warm, caring, and helpful as she asked him. "Are you just off a ship, with your strange fine clothes?" She had a smooth, unlined face, a strong nose and jaw, long blonde hair loose round her shoulders, and a good, well-rounded figure. She wore no make-up and no rings or any kind of jewellery. Her English was quaint with a strong Manx accent. "What drink is it for you?"

He gasped. The atmosphere of the old pub was so real. She was completely authentic in her costume and manner. He asked for a pint and said he would buy her whatever she wanted to drink. She smiled, her whole face lit up and her grey eyes sparkled.

"How much money have you got?" She nodded towards his wallet as he pulled it out to pay. He put a Manx twenty pound note on the table. She stared and called out something in Manx he did not understand. People gathered round to look at and examine the note. There was a lot of shaking of heads, of throatclearing and laughter. The other banknotes, tens, fives and ones were also handled and tossed around with derision. Awkwardly, he produced some pound coins and fifty pence pieces, but the crowd greeted these with similar behaviour. James felt confused and annoyed by their behaviour – they had gone over the top with their playacting – it had all become rather tiresome.

The barmaid appeared to sense his feelings. She spoke apologetically, "Very sorry sir." She gestured towards the table. "That paper money and those coins are no good here. Have you got anything else to pay with? Or something you can sell?" She said something in Manx to the others and they dropped his wallet and banknotes back on the table. He picked up the wallet and replaced the banknotes, then tried to stuff the wallet into his pocket quickly, but something was already in the pocket. He pulled it out to examine it – it was the Victorian necklace. He had forgotten all about it. The flickering light reflected yellow and red flashes off the necklace.

The woman gasped and leant forward to see it. She was entranced by it. He held it up so she could admire the dark red garnet stones and the fine gold settings. She reached out to touch it, he nodded to her and then told her to hold her hands out, gently dropping the necklace into her cupped hands. After oohing and aahing over the necklace she held it up against her throat. One of the women ran off and came back after about thirty seconds clutching a small rough and dirty mirror. There was a frenzy of activity and the room seemed to fill with females admiring the jewellery round the neck of the attractive blonde. One woman held the mirror, another worked the clasp of the necklace, two others were adjusting the way the necklace sat round her shoulders and above the swell of her breasts.

She admired herself in the mirror for a long time, moving this way and that. Finally she sighed, "You'll get a fair price for this." She called over to a man in the corner and he scuttled through the door, out into the street, and was gone. In a short time he was back. Behind him came an elderly wizened man who held a large magnifying glass. James guessed he was supposed to be a pawnbroker or a jeweller. Taking the necklace from James, he examined it carefully for a long time.

"It is all right, but might be difficult to sell, stones are not good quality", mused the elderly man. His English was strained and heavily accented. "Never," said James, "just look at the faces of the women." Half a dozen women were gathered round, staring with fascination at the piece of jewellery and making loud, appreciative noises. The man snorted and pretended to look at it again.

There was some haggling between the man and the blonde woman, and finally the man pulled out a greasy leather purse – to count out a pile of gold, silver and copper coins into James's hand. James was impressed; the coins looked and felt real. The gold coins were heavy and he felt a desire to make a theatrical gesture of biting one to see if it would have the softness of real gold. He was still confused about this playacting but was sure that no one was going to steal the necklace. It would be given back to him later. He dropped a few gold coins on to the table and nodded to the woman. She picked them up with what seemed to be genuine excitement. The elderly man was just about to leave when James remembered the engagement ring. He decided to play along with the charade that was going on around him. He pulled the old Victorian ring from his pocket. "Could you take a look at this – tell me how much it is worth?"

The women had loved the necklace but they were quietly

mesmerised by the matching garnet ring. The elderly man took a long time and named a price in guineas. James shook his head. "No, this is not for sale. This is for the special person in my life." He took it back and carefully placed it in a zip-up pocket of his wallet.

The girl grabbed his hand, asking "Are you hungry, would you like some food?" He suddenly felt famished and he agreed eagerly to her suggestion. She called out to the serving women who quickly disappeared. She took his hand. "Come this way, sir." She led him to a small back room. A table was laid before him and bread, fish and potatoes were put on rough bowls.

He sat down and ate. She stood watching him. He invited her to sit down and join him. She sat down opposite him but did not touch any food. He was very hungry, and the food was rough but good. The bread was unusual. He asked the woman about it. "It's just barley bread," she shrugged. "And that is Hollantine Fairings, good to warm you up on a cold October night." She was pointing to a dark brown flat piece of warm bread. He broke a piece off and tried it. "Wow, this is good. It's gingerbread."

Her eyes were large, warm and soft. He felt as if he could float in them. She asked about his ship and his sea voyages. He played along with her little game. "Six months voyage coming back from the Far East. We were low on food and down to half rations but we survived." She asked him about China, Japan, and what Oriental women looked like. His stories got wilder and she got more excited. "We had to fight off pirates, there was nearly a mutiny on board when the water ration was halved, we almost drowned when the ship was in the middle of a typhoon. In the East Indies a volcano erupted on an island near us, showering the ship with hot ash, we were lucky to escape with our lives."

While he spoke of his great adventures he watched her

carefully. She sat upright and alert. She seemed to have a good way of listening and asking intelligent questions. He was captivated by her. There was a chemistry between them he had never experienced before. Their heads were close. The back of her hand brushed against the hairs on the outside of his arm and it felt to him like an electric shock. It was clear to him that when the playacting was finished he must find out her real name and ask her out. Strange that he had never seen her around before. A stunning woman like her would be very noticeable in a small place like Peel. Perhaps she had recently returned to the island after working away. Certainly her accent was Manx. She was an excellent actress, she played her part perfectly. About twenty-six or twenty-seven years old, so she was a couple of years younger than him.

Suddenly he realised that the inn was almost empty. The two serving girls were cleaning up, all the men had gone and the front door was shut. He asked the woman her name, "Victoria Quirke," she replied softly. He hesitated. Maybe that was the name of her character or maybe it was her real name. Should he break the spell and ask her where she really lived and what her true name was or should he play along with the farce? He decided to say nothing. She carried on, "My father used to be landlord here but he died last year. My mother is very ill, I do what I can to look after her and the inn. It has been hard for us recently but now you are here and maybe more wealthy sailors will come. You can stay here for the night, we have a good room."

James had never felt so happy. This beautiful actress was playing the part of a woman who really liked him, and she was sending all the right signals to him. They chatted for another hour or so. Suddenly he saw the candles were flickering and the fire was dying. In the dark room he held out his hands to her and she grasped them tightly. "You are a very beautiful woman," he said softly, and she smiled back, her white teeth shining with pleasure.

Still firmly holding his hands she led him up the small wooden staircase, all the while chatting excitedly to him. He was in heaven. He took the engagement ring out of his wallet and held it out. "I want you to have this. It is meant for you." She smiled radiantly and kissed him. It was the best kiss he had ever experienced – long, warm and sensual.

He woke cold and stiff. His body ached. He was in the open air. He struggled to open his eyes and sit up. Through the morning mist he could see stone tablets around him. He looked around him. For a few moments he was completely disorientated. Ah, he was in the old ruins of St Peter's church in Peel. Lying amongst the gravestones. He could hear the sound of cars nearby. So what on earth was he doing in the middle of Peel in the open air, lying on cold stone and surrounded by memorials to the dead? He felt inside his pockets. He still had his mobile phone, his wallet, his keys – he sighed with relief – at least he had not been robbed – but then he realised that the necklace and the engagement ring were gone. he pulled out all the contents of his pockets to check: a pen, some ten pence coins, a couple of five pence coins, a couple of pound coins … and a heavy, shiny golden guinea.

He looked around. He had been sleeping on a grave. The gravestone was marked

VICTORIA QUIRKE 1830–1857
MAY SHE FIND HER LONG LOST SWEETHEART

november

Aidan Alemson lived in Australia and Italy before settling in the Isle of Man, where he currently works as a property manager. Aidan achieved a B.A. from the University of Queensland, Brisbane and then studied the history of art and painting in Florence, Italy. He also completed courses in screenwriting and has contributed to various short films and documentaries.

Aidan has also written a novel entitled *The Point However Is To Change It*, a double-novella *Wolfhound the Troubleshooter* and a stage play *The Mesopotamian Legacy*, all published by Artisan Productions, Brisbane, Australia.

Hommy-Beg

Aidan Alemson

The darkly dressed stranger rose up from out of the ship's hold, as though he had stowed away down there since leaving port. Slowly creaking the thick metal door open on its faintly rusting hinges, he entered the area on Deck 7 reserved for passengers travelling with pets. There were several people arranged on the fourteen or so rows of strawberry vinyl twin seats, positioned alongside large rectangular windows to enable weary passengers to admire the choppy, grey-green view of the Irish Sea as it waved past.

At this time, however, there was nothing much to see. They were travelling on the 2.15 a.m. scheduled sailing from Heysham to Douglas, on the *Ben-My-Chree* ferry. It was so dark outside that the main view was the mirror-like reflection of themselves in the halogen-lit cabin interior. Only a few objects could be discerned a few feet away on the blue-and-white painted metal deck outside; including an inflatable orange life raft with an explosive ejection device. The operating instructions were barely visible. Hopefully it wouldn't be needed on this night.

As the stranger approached an available space on the divided seat, a black dog emerged from the floor under the seat in front. It growled at him in an agitated manner; baring its yellowish, saliva-drenched fangs as it narrowed its angry brown eyes.

Everyone seated nearby looked up to see what the commotion was. A couple of passengers who had nodded off, even woke up momentarily to drowsily survey the scene. None of them had noticed the stranger before.

The black dog's eruption into full-throttle barking also drew the unwelcome attention of several other assorted canines guarding their unfamiliar territories fore and aft on the Designated Pet Area of Deck 7. All their owners, as well as their travelling companions, were driven to distraction. Most upset of all was the owner of the black dog who had started the fuss. He slapped his pet on the snout.

It had the desired effect, apart from the vestiges of resentful growling.

"Shut your trap, boy," snapped the owner. He was a balding, stocky man in his late forties, wearing a Manx Tweed jacket which gave him the air of a country gentleman. His blue-grey eyes blinked up at the sudden arrival to make an apology for his Labrador's bad manners.

What he saw made him shudder. His mouth was agog, and his speech faltered.

"Oh ... I ... I'm sorry, Mister. His bark is worse than ..."

The stranger still stood over him, as if considering the sincerity of the dog owner's remarks.

He was dressed entirely in black: a double-breasted black suit, black silk waistcoat, black woollen overcoat, black shirt, string tie, black shoes and socks, black Homburg hat, black gloves and black-framed sunglasses. The only contrast was the exposed skin of his neck and head which was so milky white that it lent his physiognomy the appearance of an archival newspaper photograph. Even his eyebrows and visible strands of hair creeping out from under his hat were as blanched as those of an Arctic fox.

The stranger said nothing though he kept staring. The dog owner had to evade his unnerving gaze. He felt as though he was being assessed for some future purpose. Even the black dog backed away under the seat, still growling in retreat.

The other passengers, some of them pet owners themselves, kept watching the odd bod from the rows behind until he eventually lowered himself onto the available seat. Some of their creatures on leashes expressed their displeasure as well. Despite not even being able to see the sudden intruder they could still sense his presence.

The collective canine grumblings gradually subsided as the novelty faded. The prevailing din was consumed once more by the general chatter of hardy diners in the cafeteria area encircled by whirring and clanging electronic fruit machines nearby. Others over there, a few yards fore, were engrossed in a DVD film being shown on a large TV monitor suspended from the ceiling; its volume was almost full blast. Mercifully, at this time of night, most if not all of the children on this nocturnal crossing were fast asleep at awkward angles; incapable of delving into the playpen not far from the gift shop. Somewhere beneath it all, the massive propeller shafts throbbed monotonously as the *Ben-My-Chree* turned away from timidly hugging the Lancastrian coastline and set a course for the Isle of Man some 60 nautical miles west by north.

Outside in the darkness of the wintry night, the red warning light which capped Blackpool Tower receded from view from the ferry's bridge. It was replaced in kind by other similar beacons: those of gas-drilling platforms clustered like a herd of grazing metal giraffes rusting relentlessly in the middle of the Irish Sea.

It wasn't until two and a half hours later that the illuminated Tower of Refuge, a maritime sentry standing guard at the entrance to Douglas Harbour, appeared in front of the *Ben-My-Chree's* bow, surrounded by the glimmering promenade of the still-sleeping town.

"*Moghrey mie*, ladies and gentlemen. This is the First Officer speaking," came a booming male voice over the ship's public address system. "We've just arrived at our destination. Would all passengers please remain seated while docking procedures are under way. I'll be giving you further instructions shortly. *Gura mie eu.*"

Many of the passengers were woken by the disembodied voice from on high. The owner of the black Labrador was startled out of his slumber. For a brief drowsy instant it sounded like a running commentary on Judgement Day. His dog stirred too. Its growling resumed; similar in attitude to that endured earlier.

"Shoosh boy. It's only the crew. We'll be back home in Cronk-y-Voddy soon. I'll give you your breakfast then."

The dog owner glanced to the left out the cabin window – not simply at the welcoming view of his homeland but also to take a furtive peek askance at the peculiar stranger sitting behind him, reflected in the glass pane.

"Good God!" he exclaimed under his breath, fearing he might be heard. He couldn't shift his eyes away from the form reflected from behind his back. It was a dark shape, but it wasn't human at all.

As the ship turned on its axis like a pirouetting whale, to permit the unloading of the motorcycles, cars and produce-laden lorries from its stern, the tweedy gentleman plucked up enough courage to look directly over his seat at what sat behind.

It was his own dog, now whimpering in conscious disobedience. The black and white stranger had vanished.

* * *

Ignoring the safety procedures as though his life were irrelevant, the strangely dressed individual was the first passenger off the ship; even beating the vehicles spilling out of the bowels of the *Ben-My-Chree*.

He had no items to carry. No bags to collect off the cargo carousel. He ignored the sleepless taxi drivers queuing up in their cars outside the sea terminal's main entrance. The top floors of the building, officially opened by the Queen's sister in 1965, resembled an oversized spinning-top come to rest in perfect symmetry.

However, this recent arrival took no interest in the local sights as he first set foot ashore. He kept walking briskly, almost comically, in the manner of a misplaced Olympic athlete in a walking event. And like such an athlete, he knew just where to go; along a set course he'd never set foot on before. The course led directly from the sea terminal along the broad, splendid sweep of the promenade around the edge of Douglas Bay.

He didn't have far to go – which was just as well. Cold northeasterly winds were lashing high waves against the sea walls, blowing spray over into the sunken gardens beyond. Their flowerbeds were empty, salt-sodden soil – yet still hardy weeds clung to life in their botanical cradles.

There was hardly any traffic. It was just 6 a.m., but sunrise wouldn't be for several hours yet. After all, this was the last day of November, less than a month away from the winter solstice – the shortest day of the entire calendar.

He stopped a hundred yards or so along, surveying the stylish facades of late nineteenth-century terraced guesthouses. Many of them were modest hotels, Bed and Breakfast establishments and restaurants. Although most were of a similar late-Victorian architectural style they were not all of the same colour. Even under the sulphurous amber hue of the fog-defying streetlights, the subtle differences in the painting of each property were discernible. Bright, cheerful colours too – more rainbow-like than what the stranger had seen during his travels across the north of England.

However, he wasn't simply admiring the architecture. He was scanning the names and numbers of the individual hotels. Some of them were unadventurous traditional British names: 'The Wellington', 'Millrith', 'Ashleigh' and 'Sunnybrae'. Others were in the local Manx Gaelic which looked exotic to the unfamiliar eyes of 'come-overs' – especially to those who had just literally stepped off the boat. One of these caught the shaded attention of this particular 'come-over'.

He strolled across the main road of the promenade without even watching for traffic coming in either direction. Fortunately for him there was none at that moment. He even paused briefly halfway across the road; not to look sideways but directly downward at the two parallel sets of steel tram tracks embedded in the bitumen. He was puzzled for an instant by the narrowness of the gauge. He wasn't aware that they were built for horse-drawn trams which plied their route in the warmer months.

Continuing on quizzically but unscathed, the stranger approached the steps of one of the central guesthouses on Loch Promenade. It was four storeys high with an extra basement visible beneath, its facade painted in a light caramel colour with white borders around its bay windows. Golden lettering across the glass pane above the crimson front door announced its genuine Manx moniker: *Traa Dy Liooar* (Time Enough).

The stranger knocked on the door several times; faintly at first, then, after a lack of reaction, more determinedly.

There was still no reply. He tried the doorbell, despite not hearing any sonorous response deep within the building. After thirty seconds or so he took a few steps back onto the chequered front path to survey the windows above. In a short while a light went on in the front room of the first-floor bay window area. Floral-printed rose drapes glowed through the sea salt-encrusted glass, signalling signs of life. The caller grunted to himself, well satisfied. His astrakhan-collared woollen overcoat shielded him from the biting north-easterly wind.

Another light went on inside *Traa Dy Liooar* in the ground floor lobby. A figure approached the traveller, seen through the large, dimpled glass pane of the front door. It was hurriedly putting on some sort of outer garment; most likely a dressing gown. This was confirmed when the front door was opened by a late middle-aged woman in a baby-blue terry towelling dressing gown, not completely enfolding her. Her short chestnut hair, visibly returning to its greying roots, was dishevelled. Her face was careworn, emphasised by a lack of time to apply any make-up. The awareness of all this contributed to her irritated disposition. Her bleary hazel eyes squinted as she addressed the untimely caller.

"This'd better be the real deal. I don't start making breakfast till seven thirty ... Oh!"

She clasped her chest with both hands, wrapping the dressing gown more tightly around her sagging bosom.

"What is it? Who ... who are you?"

The caller replied in a hoarse whisper, thickly accented with Eastern European vowels, "Please, Madame, I am wanting in to be with you."

* * *

Mrs Kissack didn't bother turning to face her husband as she sorted out the washed crockery from that morning's breakfast.

"I've got my worries about this new one, Reg."

Reginald Kissack didn't look up at his spouse either. He sat at the large, laminate-topped kitchen table, studying the newspaper with last night's lottery tickets propped up against a jar of rindless marmalade.

"Who's that?"

His fatigued wife Iris gritted her false teeth in mild annoyance. She knew without looking that he wasn't looking either. Still, it was a mixed blessing that he wasn't going to make any derogatory remarks about her not being able to adequately tie the frayed apron strings around her waist any more.

"The new guest of course. The one who woke us up this morning, just off the night boat."

Reg grunted in recollected disapproval, "Humphf ... Oh, him. What's his name again?"

Iris put the plates down carefully on the worktop to think clearly without distraction. Reg kept searching through each page of the paper, looking for the Lotto results. He used his left finger, while munching on a marmalade-encrusted diagonally cut slice of cold toast to go with his tepid Tetley's – the tea, not the beer.

"Nastase, I think it was," recalled Iris.

"How's that?"

"Nastase – like the old tennis player."

"Yeah," blurted Reg with a mouthful of congealed breadcrumbs, "that's just what I was about to say. We used to watch him on the telly playing at Wimbledon. Oooh, he was a nasty type – that's what they called him: Ilie Nasty."

"Don't talk with your mouth full, Reg."

"Why not? It's my own home, isn't it?"

Mr Kissack's voice grew louder. Mrs Kissack recognised it immediately as his 'I'm-the-King-of-this-Castle' tone. She was just about to change the subject when her husband began to choke on his own words; or at least on the remnants of his toast. His round shaggy head turned crimson like a blocked leather bellows sucking in a red-hot piece of coal. Letting go of the newspaper to clutch his throat, he tore a strip off the top half of page 3; accidentally self-censoring the second most important subject matter he was interested in perusing.

Mrs Kissack knew better than to comment on her husband's hardships. She kept her back turned to disguise her grin, while continuing with her original train of thought.

"Yes. He's a Romanian as well. I'm not sure whether they pronounce it 'Romanian' or 'Roumanian' or 'Rumanian'? I suppose it might even be said differently in their own tongue. I asked to see some form of identification. It was an unusual document; he claimed it was a passport, but it was different to ours. Vlad, his name is – Vlad Nastase. He'd booked on the Internet to stay for four days with us. I checked the records. It's all been paid for in advance – even for last night when he was on the boat. He gave me his credit card details. Says he's in his fifties but he looks much older ... It's difficult to tell really ... He wears those pitch-dark sunglasses. I can't even make out the outline of his eyes. And that old-fashioned hat he refused to take off once inside. Maybe he's going bald and doesn't want to show it. I took him up to his room on the third floor. I was completely out of breath but he hardly raised a sweat. Carrying no luggage either – all the way from Eastern Europe. I ask you! Is that normal to go on holiday? He didn't even have an overnight bag, unless he was hiding it under his hat. He just wanted to rush into his room. I tried to open the curtains to show him the lovely view of the sun rising over the sea but he hurriedly shut them; tugging the edges instead of using the draw-strings, before ushering me out into the corridor. In my own house! I ask you! These foreigners can be terribly abrupt. He claimed he couldn't sleep on the ferry; been travelling since yesterday from Whitby. He needed some shuteye or he'd collapse. Fair enough, I guess. He hasn't been down for breakfast and it's over now. I wonder should I take him up a bite to eat?"

Reg Kissack didn't respond to his wife's rhetorical question. Instead he muttered to himself, "We got used to the Poles. I suppose we'll get used to this latest lot from the EU as well."

★   ★   ★

Iris Kissack climbed the staircase in the manner of a sherpa heading for the summit to retrieve a foreign mountaineer who'd been foolhardy enough to attempt it on his own. She paused beside a fire extinguisher on the third-floor landing.

Her attention was drawn to the third step above the landing; more precisely the edge of that particular step. The brown and orange interlocking patterned carpet was fraying badly.

"Arghh. I'll need to get Reg to brush some shoe polish on that tomorrow. Just a dab of brown Kiwi. He mustn't overdo it like some old army boot. Funny how the guests make a point of stepping on the frayed sections to make it worse. You'd think they'd know better ... but then it isn't their home so they couldn't care less."

As though on cue, a black leather Cuban-heeled boot came to rest smack dab on the frayed-edged step before her, instantly joined by its right-footed companion.

Mrs Kissack was taken aback; so far aback that she backed into the fire extinguisher and detached the hose nozzle from its side holder. Fortunately the release trigger wasn't activated as well, or Reg would have had to have done a great deal more shining.

The recent arrival was looming over her on the stairs. The overall effect of the third step gave the impression of his being nearly eight foot tall. He was still dressed in the same attire

– black on black.

"Oh! Mr Nasty ... Nastase. You gave me a start! I ... I was just coming up to see you; to see if you were all right."

She waited for some sort of response but there was none. His eyes were still hidden behind 1950s-style sunglasses, despite the low indoor light of the energy-saving light bulbs. Reg reckoned they were saving energy simply because they weren't as bright as the old ones. Nastase's long bony fingers were swathed in black kidskin gloves; curled up as though holding imaginary objects. They were reminiscent to Mrs Kissack of a bird of prey anticipating clutching a wriggling mammal. She felt the desperate urge to force the creepy guest to talk in order to take his mind off whatever it was he was thinking of.

"You ... You haven't had any breakfast. Nothing all day. The other guests are down in the dining room having their supper. Shall I show you where?"

She glanced at the gilded sun/moon watch her daughter Claire had given her for her sixtieth birthday. The Punchinello-style crescent moon had already risen into the window of the mock night sky, herding a flock of golden stars across the top of the dial.

"It's seven forty now and we finish serving at eight. The staff have to get home to have their own meals. If you come now they can whip up something for sure. I'll give you priority, seeing as I overlooked mentioning it to you this morning. Huh. You were in such a hurry to fly up to your bedroom."

Mrs Kissack detected a brief twitch behind the Ray-Ban sunglasses. Mr Nastase's right eyebrow lifted slightly above the black nylon frame. As eyebrows go it was barely perceptible: a few dozen short blanched strands which were camouflaged into his white skin as efficiently as a polar bear's. His thin lips finally split apart. Globules of saliva stretched across his mouth, in the manner of unset glue. His canine teeth protruded with a particularly sharp overbite. He hadn't spoken since this morning. His mouth was parched. A wheezing rasping noise resonated from deep within his frame. The inarticulate sound gradually took a coherent form as his command of the English tongue reasserted itself; though still cloaked in those heavy Eastern European vowels.

"I have no need of your food. My taste are different. Perhaps I grab a bite to drink once I am outside."

Mrs Kissack was relieved to hear the man speak again, or at least not to be stared at silently. However, she shielded her throat with her wrinkled hand almost defensively.

"A bite to drink – quite. Ha. Well, I can't force you to have your supper in my establishment, but you're always welcome to."

Nastase nodded slowly. It was the only gesture of human warmth he had displayed all day. The lady of the house was equally chuffed.

"Well, I'll leave you to it then. We're well situated here on the prom to explore Douglas by night. Er … if you don't mind me warning you, it's preferable that you stay away from the pub and club entrances after midnight. Things could turn nasty if you're on your own. It's the drink that does it, you know. Young people don't know when to stop. Of course, I hardly ever touch the stuff myself. My husband Reg enjoys a tipple; mostly when he thinks I'm not looking."

"Ah, but I am not wanting to drink alcohol in Douglas," replied the Romanian, "I desire visiting a place on island named Maughold."

Like most 'come-overs', including those from the rest of the British Isles, the foreigner pronounced the place name as 'more gold' instead of the indigenous form which sounded like a portmanteau combination of 'mackerel' and 'tackled'.

But the local lady didn't have the disposition to react with a knowing smile on this occasion. She was genuinely astonished.

"Maughold?! At this time of night?! Oh you won't want to be going away there at this hour, Mr Nastase. That's a wild and windy spot – Maughold Head. It's a huge headland along the coast to Ramsey, exposed to the elements without much shelter. Better to see it in the daytime when the weather is clear."

Nastase shook his head slowly; not nearly as pleasantly as before.

"It is not the Head that I am wanting visiting. It is the cemetery. Good night."

With that the eerie guest continued on down the stairs, past the bemused proprietor, and descended several flights to the entry lobby. Mrs Kissack could hear the front door slam shut. She rushed across to the nearest window to watch which way he would go. The salt-sprayed panes were in need of washing. The particles were eating into the glass. Outside it was already dark.

She could see numerous cars, both parked and commuting. Even the odd pedestrian, though not the oddest of them all. He had instantly vanished. Either she was too slow to catch sight of him or her eyes were playing tricks on her – maybe even his black ensemble camouflaged him into the nocturnal mist.

What Mrs Kissack did see, however, was a large winged creature swooping across the promenade. Its dark shape was illuminated in ghostly fashion by the sulphurous rays of streetlighting bouncing off the buildings. She gasped as the unidentifiable creature flew off across Douglas Bay in the direction of Maughold.

* * *

"I'm telling you, Reg, there's something not right about that 'un."

Iris Kissack stood over her husband in the television lounge. He was reclining on the communal sofa which had the visual texture of a Mississippi Mud Cake – chocolate on chocolate – watching a highlights package of the Icelandic round of the World Rally Driving Championships. So as not to disturb their paying guests, Iris had insisted that Reg should order a special device to go with his latest NHS hearing aids, allowing him to listen to the goggle box without anyone else hearing it. It proved to be a mixed blessing. Now Reg couldn't hear anything else whenever he felt like it – especially not his wife. He occasionally nodded to induce the semblance of comprehension, though his gaze was firmly transfixed by the volcanic Icelandic landscape. He grunted now and then as well; mostly in approval of the driving skills on display.

"I was just talking to Rosie after she'd finished changing the bed linen and making the beds. That Mr Nastase wouldn't let her into his room. She told him she was the maid but he wouldn't budge. He held the doorknob firmly with those creepy hands of his – Have you seen 'em? They're like talons, they are! For such a scrawny man too. My sister used to have a thing about thin men – a thin thing, I suppose you'd call it. I could never quite understand it. Preferred the athletic type myself …"

She looked down at her husband ensconced upon several sofa cushions. He was going to leave a lasting impression on them long after he'd upped sticks to head for the kitchen.

"… But then, most athletes do retire in their thirties."

At the instant the landlady was set to continue her commentary, a figure appeared in the doorway a few feet away. She didn't really see him walk into view as such – he just manifested himself into her peripheral vision in the preferred manner of a spectre. Without touching or commanding, he made her jump.

"Oh! Mr Nastase! You're up!"

The foreign guest stood still, watching them both. Mr Kissack barely acknowledged the presence of his wife, let alone the interloper.

"Did you enjoy your sightseeing trip last night to – where was it now? Oh yes, Maughold Cemetery?" enquired Mrs Kissack, determined to force some utterance out of the newcomer. She felt that his taciturn tendency was bordering on rudeness.

Mr Nastase took a while to respond. In keeping with his continental bluntness, however, he didn't bother to answer the actual question.

"I am wanting visiting museum of history. Where is it where I go?"

"Ah, well there is a nice big museum in Peel," replied the landlady, somewhat mischievously, "but that's on the western coast of the island. You wouldn't be able to make it there in time – what is it now?"

She glanced again at the ascendant lunar dial on her sun/moon watch. It was becoming a regular occurrence; like clockwork one might say. Strangely, the traveller wasn't wearing a watch at all.

"Nearly four o'clock. Hmm. No, you'll never make it to Peel in time. Their last admissions are usually an hour before closing time."

"Please do tell me, is there other museums here in Douglas who are open still?"

"Any particular type of museum? Motorcycles, for instance?" enquired Mrs Kissack, with a teasing smile that betrayed her intent.

Nastase registered her attitude. He was slower to respond,

his tone sterner.

"Museum of history, as I say. Why do I come to Isle of Man to visit motorcycles?"

"Why indeed? That's just as well because the Motorcycle Museum on Snaefell Mountain has closed its doors. The TT races don't begin until the late spring and they tend not to race in the dark."

"Excuse me?"

"So, Mr Nastase, your best bet is to go up Crellins Hill to the Manx History Museum. It's located behind the prom, above the multi-storey car park, across the footbridge. You should just make it if you hurry."

The landlady gesticulated in the general direction of the museum, without feeling the need to repeat the place names to the ignorant 'come-over'.

The 'come-over' didn't oblige her by asking for further instruction. He turned tail without thanking his host, turned up his astrakhan collar with his gloved hands to shield his neck and pushed down his Homburg hat to anchor it against the wintry wind before gliding silently out of the front door.

Mrs Kissack didn't even bother to check if her visitor was heading in the right direction. Mr Kissack didn't even know that he'd been in the lounge.

★ ★ ★

Christmas was making its presents felt throughout the island. This was especially so in central Douglas, where the seasonal shoppers gathered in material tribute in the manner of Christian pilgrims along the Via Dolorosa of Strand Street. It wasn't as grandiose a thoroughfare as its namesake The Strand in London, but the concentrated variety and friendly mingling more than made up in communal charm what it lacked in metropolitan chic.

The surrounding canyons of assorted commercial buildings sheltered the material pilgrims from incoming gales. Fairy lights and animated multi-coloured Yuletide imagery rendered the illusion of warmth – in the heart if not on the skin.

Similarly on the promenade not far away, though here the setting was more exposed and the Christmas decorations danced wildly on their electrical marionette strings. The Tower of Refuge in particular lent a magical illusion to the vibrant spectacle; its shape was outlined with dots of glowing bulbs. Apart from the rest, set in the midst of the maritime darkness, the tower for marooned sailors appeared from the shore like a radioactive rook chesspiece expertly positioned by the giant Finn McCooil.

★   ★   ★

Iris Kissack glanced momentarily at the illuminated tower as she passed the Victorian sash window on the third-floor landing of the *Traa Dy Liooar* guesthouse. It appeared strangely enticing yet at the same time otherworldly: a nineteenth-century whimsy reminiscent of a medieval bastion. A functional folly intended to save lives. Ironically, once some foolhardy youth had drowned trying to swim to it for fun. Iris had no intention of following his example. Besides, she had other objectives in mind at the moment. One more flight of steps and she would reach the third floor where the enigmatic houseguest hibernated during the diminished daylight hours. Nastase had returned just half an hour after the 5 o'clock closing time of the Manx museum. He had scurried up this very staircase to his room as if possessed by the Devil.

Whatever he had encountered in the museum had fired him up. The landlady had watched him return and go back out again eagerly into the night several hours later. Judging by his past behaviour, he wouldn't be back till after midnight.

The inquisitive landlady continued determinedly onward and upward until she could go no further. She had reached her objective: the third floor.

The foreigner's bedroom was at the end of the corridor. She wouldn't have been surprised if he had materialised before her eyes. Iris Kissack fumbled for the large batch of keys attached to her extendable key ring. She tapped lightly on the door of Room 12.

There was no reply.

"Thank God," Iris whispered to herself. It emboldened her to slide the key into the old-fashioned lock. After several clinking attempts she got it in. One turn was all it would take, then she might learn the secret of the true nature of the most disturbing occupant. Iris turned the handle and creaked the door open a few inches. Of course it was pitch dark. There was no sound. She knew instinctively where the bedroom light switch was located on the wall and turned it on, with distinct trepidation at what she might see.

There was nothing.

Or rather, there was nothing unusual. Except for one thing.

The bed was made; there was no sign of it having been slept on. All the furniture was in place. There was no luggage or clothes or accoutrements belonging to anyone. Room 12 appeared to be in the state it had been in immediately prior to the arrival of Mr Nastase, despite the maid not having been allowed in to tidy it since. The only thing out of the ordinary was the mirror hanging on the wall beside the drawn pink window curtains: it had been completely covered with a fluffy white bath towel.

"That's odd, covering the mirror like that. I suppose he's so ugly that he can't stand the sight of himself. Ha. I can't blame him. Or maybe ... he can't see himself. Maybe he's a ... Oh God, no!"

Mrs Kissack backed out of Room 12 so quickly that she neglected to switch off the light. She closed the door too hard and pulled out the batch of keys without actually locking the door. The banging and rattling was sufficiently loud to stir some guests from Belfast sleeping next door. But on this occasion Mrs Kissack didn't care. She just wanted to get away from the area as rapidly as possible. It was as if a fire alarm had been activated in her mind, frightening her into evacuating herself from the building.

Iris didn't stop running down until she reached the entry lobby.

There, to her shocked amazement, stood the Romanian guest.

She wanted to scream but it came out as a gasping gurgle. Her terror was tempered by the realisation that Mr Nastase was accompanied by two Manx police constables: a male and a female, both in their late twenties, dressed in caps and uniforms with walkie-talkies attached to their shoulders, squawking like piratic parrot epaulettes.

Almost as an afterthought, she noticed her husband Reg who had just let the trio in.

"Oh, there you are, love. I was wondering where you'd got to. The police have escorted Mr Nastase here. Apparently he was wandering around the Peel Road like a lost soul in the dead of night."

"I can see that, Reg. And I'm glad you're both here, officers, I can tell you."

The blonde policewoman replied in a pleasant but no-nonsense tone.

"Fine, Mrs Kennaugh."

"That's Kissack," Reg corrected her politely.

"Pardon me," said the WPC, "Mr and Mrs Kissack. This gentleman who calls himself Mr ... Nastase claims he's staying here at the *Traa Dy Liooar* Guesthouse. Your husband has just confirmed this. You're both the proprietors?"

"Yes, that's right. I do most of the work here, but we're both legally the co-proprietors."

The two constables glanced at one another. Reg didn't get the dig; he simply grinned.

The male policeman continued more forcefully, "Your hotel guest wasn't actually wandering aimlessly on the Peel Road – he was loitering outside the main gates of Greeba Castle. The owner spotted him staring at his house for nearly half an hour and called us in. Mr Nastase claims that he's a tourist from Romania and that he was only doing some sightseeing."

"A rather strange time to be seeing the sights, in the middle of the night," remarked the policewoman in a mildly sarcastic way.

"Especially wearing sunglasses," added Mr Kissack, "you hardly need those around here even in broad daylight."

In reaction the mysterious Mr Nastase, who had remained silent since entering the building, raised his left glove up to his face to remove his dark sunglasses. What he uncovered was a pair of hideous eyes; both blood red. The skin around them was as black as bruises from lack of sleep – the only area of his face that wasn't as pale as a cadaver's.

This time Iris Kissack let out a full-blooded scream which woke up most of the household.

"He's a vampire! I knew it! He really is a vampire!"

The group in the lobby was stunned; apart from Nastase who laughed with a devilish intensity – the first time since his arrival that he had displayed any depth of emotion.

"Madame," chortled the Romanian, "simply because I am coming from Transylvania region there no need to stereotype me in this negative way."

"But I saw his mirror, or rather I didn't see it – he's covered it up because vampires have no reflection! Everyone knows that."

Nastase's grin hung wearily on his lips like a snarl.

"If true, Madame, then no reason to cover mirror. I block sunlight reflecting on bed. Curtains too thin."

"You're like a vampire: afraid of the sun," retorted Mrs Kissack, unwilling to be dissuaded from her discovery.

"Love – aren't you getting a little carried away? I'm sure Mr Nastase has his reasons."

The policeman, who was becoming equally confused, added to Reg's plea, "Yes, I think the gentleman had better explain himself more clearly."

Mr Nastase replaced his sunglasses. He had already begun blinking in the artificial light which was affecting his severely bloodshot weak eyes. He continued, "I am no vampire. I am writer. To some, no difference. Both living alone in shadows, outside society. Yet we feeding off you all. We sucking out your life's blood – your souls. We existing by taking your existences: your physical appearances, names, natures – your petty little lives. Your energy attracting us to every walk of life, every town or city or country, every race or religion; man, woman or child."

The policeman and policewoman stared worriedly at each other. The WPC touched her communication device attached to her shoulder, preparing to call HQ for back-up.

"What writer desiring most is new characters. We remove it from you painlessly, then you, our fresh victims, will become like us – immortal. Un-dead."

"Oh. So you mean to say you're a novelist who's come to the Isle of Man for inspiration?" enquired Reg Kissack. Iris shook her head in disbelief.

Nastase nodded. "Both novelist and historian. I am writer now of literary historical connections of Romania and British

Isles. In particular how the novel *Dracula* by Bram Stoker influencing English-speaking peoples' views of Romanian peoples and culture. I travelling here to research for my new book."

"But *Dracula* wasn't set here. That was in Whitby in Yorkshire, wasn't it?" queried the ginger-haired policeman.

Mrs Kissack answered for her unpopular guest, "He came here directly from Whitby. He told me earlier."

"This is correct. The reason I coming here is to see for myself the homeland of the man Bram Stoker dedicated his novel *Dracula* to. His dear friend, his fellow writer, 'Hommy-Beg'."

"Hommy who?"

"Hommy-Beg: that means 'Little Tommy' in Manx Gaelic. I studied it at school," explained the policewoman. "That was the nickname of the nineteenth-century writer Sir Hall Caine; or Sir Thomas Henry Hall Caine. You know, the one who wrote *The Manxman*."

Reg Kissack nodded. "Aye, that old Hall Caine was a cunning critter. Hardly read now. He was a popular novelist in his day but not very popular as a person with the local Manx folk. He told too many of their secrets after befriending them. Many felt he made a mint from betraying their lives – in a literary sense, mind."

"Oh yeah," added the policeman, "he used to live at Greeba Castle, didn't he?"

"And he die there too. That is why I visiting there tonight to see it for myself with my own eyes. Better be able to write about it when I return home. This is also why I visiting Caine's impressive grave at Maughold the other night."

Iris couldn't contain herself. "Yes. I saw you flying up there myself."

Nastase looked puzzled. "You are mistaken, Madame. I take

taxi."

Determined not to be fobbed off, the landlady got her false teeth stuck into the perceived 'Prince of Darkness'.

"Then why the hell are you creeping around at night like a bloody ghoul, giving us all the creeps?"

"I am thinking I have showed to you why, Madame. I am albino person. Photophobic. My eyes, my skin, it cannot accept strong sunlight. My body reacting badly, even in daytime here. But I determined to visiting to research my book. So I come in winter when day is shortest and night is longest. I am sleeping in daytime with curtain closed and mirror covered with towel to block glowing light reflect into bed. I not allowed lady to disturb my room. I make bed nice and cleaning room myself."

"But you have no bags, no luggage for such a long trip. It's not normal. Even folks from Ramsey bring a toothbrush!"

"My baggage? It is disappeared on train to Lancaster; maybe even stolen from wagon. Stationmaster take my name and this address. He say if baggage found, he send it here on boat from Heysham."

Mrs Kissack's eyes narrowed in anger. Her foolishness had been made complete; in front of her husband, the Isle of Man Constabulary and, most likely now the word would get out, in the Isle of Man itself. Already several guests had descended the staircase in their dressing gowns, anxiously alerted by her screams.

"Oh no, Mr Nastase, your missing bags won't be entering these premises – and neither will you again. I realise you booked to stay for another two days, but I want you out by noon tomorrow. I'll refund the difference. I don't care whether you shrivel up like a desiccated prune, you won't be welcome here again!"

The writer glowered intensely at his hostile landlady. Somehow he had expected as much. He was used to it. He replied with polite contempt:

"Madame, I will immortalise you."

✻ December ✻

Alan Lawton was born in the village of Micklehurst in the midst of the Pennines and moved to the Isle of Man in 1962. Alan worked for many years in the farming and construction industries and also served for a time in the armed forces. He has a degree with the Open University and has undertaken research work for the University of Liverpool on the structure of the Manx construction industry.

Alan is a keen historian and writer and achieved first place in the Olive Lamming short story competition in 1979.

Now retired, Alan lives quietly in Onchan with his long-time partner and concentrates on writing, light gardening and culinary challenges.

A Walk Along the North Quay of Douglas

Alan Lawton

The sniffing of a dog and the feel of its soft nose against his cheek woke the old man from his slumbers. He opened his eyes and tentatively moved his arm and the nervous creature backed away as if fearing for its life. He had been asleep, the man reasoned, and not in some comfortable bed for a thin layer of winter frost lay upon the raincoat that he was wearing. He noticed a stout walking stick lying by his side and he used it to steady himself as he clambered to his feet. But where was he? Somewhere near a busy road, he concluded, for he could hear the noise of car engines and the occasional screech of brakes. He took a few difficult steps, then a few more, and he almost collided with a big green Land Rover that stood in his path. A white Volkswagen was parked alongside it – then his eyes began to come into focus and he could see many other cars drawn up in orderly rows. He recognised this place. It was the car park that was adjacent to the big supermarket that stood on the site of the former Quiggins timber yard. He tried to recall the name of the supermarket chain, but he was quite unable to do so.

The old man took a firmer grip upon his stick and began to make his way between the vehicles, but his progress was slow, for his joints were still stiff and sore from hours of exposure to the cold night air. His grasp upon the stick weakened momentarily and he blundered against the side of a silver Mercedes saloon and the shriek of its anti-theft device beat upon his ears. The face of a young woman, distorted by anger, appeared before him.

"Get away from my car – you dirty old tramp!" she screamed.

"My husband spent long hours at his desk to buy me this vehicle as a Christmas present and I won't have you putting your filthy hands upon it!"

The old man tried to frame a reply, but his brain didn't seem to work properly and nothing came out of his mouth.

"Why – the likes of you should be locked up in Ballamona Hospital!" she continued, "and then we would not–"

At that moment a young trolley attendant arrived upon the scene and he took the veteran gently by the arm. "I'll deal with this matter, madam," he said quietly. "I'm sure the old gentleman meant no harm – best you cancel the alarm signal and allow me to take care of this unfortunate situation."

"You meet plenty of decent folk on this job," the attendant remarked as he led the old man past the front entrance of the supermarket, "but you come across a few nasty folk with no respect for anyone. Tell you what – why not lean against that wall near Banks Circus and I'll bring you a nice cup of tea or a couple of mince pies?"

But the old man shook his head and pointed his stick towards the opposite side of the roundabout.

"Walk ... me ... over," he uttered with difficulty and the attendant simply shook his head and did as he was bidden.

"I'd better get back to work before the boss notices that

I've gone, for we are always as busy as hell during the run-up to Christmas," the attendant said as the pair reached the sanctuary of the far pavement. "Now take care of yourself and watch out for the traffic."

The old man had hardly taken a couple of steps before the shriek of a steam whistle split the air. He turned his head and he was just in time to see a small locomotive and four carriages, filled with children wearing Santa hats, pulling out of a nearby railway station. Once again, the whistle sounded and he recalled a sunny morning, long ago, when he had boarded that little train in the company of a young woman who wore a light summer skirt that moved in the breeze. The garment was made of white cotton and was printed with a pattern of yellow marigolds, that much he remembered, and he also recalled lifting a heavy wicker picnic basket onto a vacant seat, whilst the woman comforted a child that had been frightened by the train whistle. Yet he couldn't remember the woman's name, or the identity of the child.

He turned again and moved determinedly towards the thicket of masts that marked the head of Douglas Harbour, paying little attention to a group of grey-suited men and smartly dressed women who strode past him clutching leather briefcases. One of the women accidentally dropped her briefcase at his feet. He tried to pick up the case and return it to her, but his back refused to bend far enough. The woman gave him a warm smile as she retrieved it. She then slipped two cigarettes into the pocket of his coat and she wished him a Merry Christmas before hurrying off to join her colleagues.

The veteran shuffled along until he came to the intersection at the bottom of Railway Hill. He paused and wondered if anyone would help him to cross the busy road, but nobody volunteered and he finally lost patience and stepped off the kerb.

The driver of a red single-decker bus spotted him at the last moment and swerved to avoid the old man, skilfully applying the brakes to bring the ponderous vehicle to a halt. He opened his side window and yelled angrily at the aged jaywalker.

"You stupid old git – you could have got yer'self killed yessir! How the hell would I look after me wife and kids if I lost me job through the likes of you?"

The driver's tirade hardly registered upon the old man's consciousness and he kept moving at his best pace until he disappeared around the corner of the former Clinch's Brewery. He almost collided with a rough plywood hoarding that temporarily blocked off a shop front and he was drawn like a moth towards a doorway giving access to the chaotic scene of industry which lay within. The front of the shop had been completely torn away and the upper storey was supported by a solider-like rank of steel props that were firmly grounded upon the hard-packed gravel of the quayside. Bales of bricks, lengths of rough sawn timber and bags of cement seemed to claim every metre of spare ground space and it seemed almost impossible for men to find room enough to carry out the necessary task of reconstruction. The old man stepped over the threshold and halted before a half-finished brick wall that was obviously intended to support a new shop front. He stretched out his hand and picked up a mortar-grimed trowel that rested upon the wet brickwork.

"Come to lay a thousand brick before finishin' time?" said a voice from the far corner of the building. "That would be just like the old days when they used to call you the 'Flashing Blade'!"

The man who appeared from the shadows was well into his middle years and he wore a pair of old-fashioned bib and brace overalls that were stained with splashes of wet cement. He gently took the newcomer by the arm and led him to a spot where an upturned packing case was acting as a table, with a scattering of smaller boxes serving as impromptu seats. He ran his gaze over the veteran and shook his head.

"Thaa's in a fair pickle!" he remarked in a distinctly northern accent.

"Thaa's nowt' like the chap who took me under his wing, when I fell off the ferryboat those many years ago! Now take a seat and I'll get thee some breakfast for thaa looks famished."

He raised his head and his voice echoed up into the far reaches of the gutted-out building.

"Ho there Fieldmouse! Get thyself down here – I've got an important job for thee to do!"

The youth who descended a flight of ladders to ground level was slightly built and his narrow rodent-like features had obviously given rise to his apt but unfortunate nickname. He brushed a layer of dried plaster dust from his jacket and halted before the two older men.

The tradesman handed him a five-pound note.

"Get thyself to the sandwich bar around the corner and bring this gentleman a mug of hot tea and a bacon roll – and make sure that the tea's fresh brewed and that there's no stintin' with the bacon!"

The youth glanced at the old man and made no effort to hide his distaste.

"Don't know why you waste your money on old scavengers like him, Mister Higgins," he remarked. "I've seen better offal in the dog-pound."

"What I do with my cash is no business of thine," the tradesman exploded. "And you'd best keep a civil tongue in your head when you're speakin' about my old friend, or you'll land up back in the dole queue where I found you!"

The youth disappeared without speaking another word.

"Take no heed on yon lad," the craftsman said. "He's no oil painting and the girls have been givin' him a hard time lately and it's no fun to be loveless at Christmas."

The box on which the veteran was sitting swayed a little and Mister Higgins stretched out his hand to stop him toppling over.

"Aye, it's many a long year since we drove your broken-down old Ford van all over the Island and did odd bits of repair work on old farm buildings," he reminisced. "Hard days – but good days, then we parted company and went our own separate ways. But I never thought that I'd see you in such a poor state, I never did!"

The youth returned with the tea and the bacon sandwich and the tradesman steadied his old friend's hand as the elderly man refreshed himself. Afterwards, the veteran indicated his wish to leave by pointing his stick in the direction of the exit. He was immediately helped through the doorway and allowed to continue his journey along the North Quay.

But where was the pavement? And what had happened to the roadway?

Each swing of his walking stick was landing upon an unfamiliar surface of interlocking brickwork and pedestrians moved in either direction instead of noisy diesel wagons and speeding cars. He almost tripped and collided with a Christmas tree which stood outside a brightly lit restaurant, but he instinctively regained his balance and moved on.

The old man's arthritic neck creaked painfully as he turned his head to the right. He had expected to see a line of fishing boats moored against the quayside. Instead, his gaze fell upon a gaggle of yachts and cabin cruisers. His eyes did indeed focus on a single fishing boat but it appeared to be crewless and abandoned.

Fred paused and stared towards the far end of the quay.

Was that a collier discharging its cargo of coal into waiting trucks? Or was it a surviving fragment of memory that had surfaced like a scrap of driftwood?

Even so, the old man remembered he had somewhere to go and there was something very important that he must do.

He recognised a back lane that passed behind the premises of the Manx Electricity Board, and he followed it until it intersected the busy thoroughfare of Lord Street, and across the tarmac stood his immediate goal, the Douglas Citadel of the Salvation Army.

He was about to step out into the traffic when a young woman emerged from the doorway of the Citadel and sped across the road at a full run.

"Thank the Lord!" she gasped, as she took him by the arm. "I happened to glance out of the window and I was fortunate enough to see you arriving."

She led him to the Citadel by way of a nearby pedestrian crossing and the pair were joined in the communal sitting room by a tall gentleman whose jersey bore the emblem of his organisation.

"Ah, Susan, I see that you have Fred with you," he remarked. "Please find him a comfortable chair, for I'm quite sure that he would like to take the weight off his legs for a while – and perhaps a cup of tea, for he might be in need of a drink."

The young woman guided him towards an armchair, but the veteran realised that comfort was not the prime reason for his visit and he impatiently shook off her arm. He turned back towards the officer and drew a crumpled five-pound note and an assortment of coins from his pocket of his trousers. He released his shaking grasp and allowed the donation to fall into the man's hand.

"You were ever a good man, Fred," the Salvationist remarked. "You've had troubles enough in your own declining years, yet you still offer help to others in need."

Susan assisted the old man into the waiting armchair and helped him to take a few sips of tea before moving along to offer aid and comfort to the other elderly and infirm occupants of the room.

The veteran stared across the room and his gaze fell upon a middle-aged woman who was perched precariously upon a high stool. She played a guitar with no small skill, and sang to the audience seated around her. Most of her songs failed to trigger a response in the old man's mind, yet one song had him tapping his stick upon the floor. It was an old fifties love song that ended in a chorus with the lines 'Lay down your arms and surrender to mine'. He recalled a dancehall filled with young men in khaki uniforms and girls whose skirts whirled in time to the music. The memory was extremely vivid, but faded abruptly with the ending of the tune. Other songs followed, but they were only background noise to the veteran and he eventually struggled to his feet and began making his way towards the exit. The young carer noticed his imminent departure and she was impelled to consult the officer in charge.

"Should we try to detain him?" she asked. "He could easily fall over and break a leg, never mind the danger from speeding traffic!"

The man smiled sadly. "We are often faced with quandaries that would make 'The Judgment of Solomon' seem like a simple exercise in logic," he answered. "Fred is hardly fit to journey down a garden path and we are probably failing in our duty of care if we don't restrain him. Yet he is still a human being with the legal and moral right to act in accordance with his own free will – to deny him that right would be to rob him of his humanity!"

The man paused. "Best that you follow him discreetly until he regains the quayside, then return here to take care of your other duties."

The young woman did as she was bidden – but she was far from convinced by the words of her superior.

The old man regained the quay and he advanced as steadily as possible until he reached the area where the Clarendon Hotel had once rubbed shoulders with the main bus station. Both were now gone, and in their place stood a huge monolithic structure that was obscured by deck upon deck of steel and timber scaffolding. The veteran stood mystified, as a giant tower-crane added yet another precast concrete section to the growing structure that was destined to become the Island's newest and largest hotel. The noise of industry was deafening and the old man was unable to decide whether to advance or retreat. Suddenly, a worker wearing a red safety helmet hung out from his workstation high amidst the tangle of concrete and steel and pointed his bricklaying trowel towards a silver limousine parked about a hundred metres from where the veteran was standing.

"Make for the car, Mister Fred – your daughter is waiting to take you home!"

The old man shuffled towards the vehicle, but he was now moving at a snail's pace, for exhaustion was finally gripping his body.

"Keep moving Fred – not far to go now!" shouted the bricklayer, and his words of encouragement were reinforced by Christmas greetings and loud cheers from a score of building operatives who were now lining the safety rails.

Old Fred was almost asleep when a white uniformed nurse helped him into the back of the limousine and began stripping off his urine-soaked trousers. He was certainly unaware of his daughter's tearful words as she leaned over from the driving seat.

"Oh Heavens, father!" she wept. "Dementia is such a terrible affliction – it strips down a person's mind like a cook stripping down an onion. We shouldn't let you go on these dangerous wanderings – yet how could we rob you of the only small pleasure that remains to you – how could we?"

The woman started the engine of the limousine and steered away from Douglas Harbour and the site of the half-finished hotel. In her rear view mirror, she momentarily caught a glimpse of a temporary billboard that was attached to the front of the hoarding. It read,

A MERRY CHRISTMAS TO EVERYONE
FROM
FREDERICK QUIRK AND SONS LTD
BUILDERS AND CIVIL ENGINEERS
We remember the past – but build for the future.